Second Helpings

An Anthology

Copyright © Women Who Write With Elves, 2015

Women Who Write With Elves have asserted their rights under the Copyright, Designs and Patents Act, 1988, to be identified as the authors of this anthology. All rights reserved. No part of this publication may be reproduced, stored or transmitted in any form, or by any means electronic, mechanical or photocopying, recording or otherwise, without the express written permission of the author.

All trademarks are acknowledged.

Cover Art by RJ Ashby
Photography Credit: Pixabay

Women Who Write With Elves are Annis Farnell, Elves, Enza Vynn-Cara, Julia Chalkley, Mairibeth MacMillan, Palo Stickland, R Cohen, RJ Ashby and Sue Cook.

Women Who Write With Elves is a group of nine writers who met through the Open University. Scattered from Scotland to Switzerland, we keep in touch via an online forum.

Once a year we meet for a creative writing break which is stimulating, educational and far from the relaxing holiday some of us hope for! Our inaugural meeting was on the Isle of Tiree in the Inner Hebrides. It was a perfect writers' retreat — isolated, beautiful, windswept and, best of all, free.

Members include published novelists, poets and short story writers who have gained success in competitions and national magazines. Our name reflects that we are all women except for one lone gentleman — the eponymous Mr Elves. His claim to be the descendant of a Portuguese pirate has earned him the role of volunteer galley slave.

Contents

THE STORIES 9

Love Lessons	11
An Atlantic Alliance	19
The Well	25
Chapattis with Everything	32
Missing	42
Money, their only Vice	50
The Last Supper with Jill	57
The Last Week of Autumn	62
Pitching a Fit	69
Grief Knots	88
Favourite Soup	97
My Summer Holiday	101
Tyler Loves Parathas	108
Darkness	114
The Cleaning Programme	122
Walking Wounded	125
Snowbound	144
Murder Most Foul	157
Moments in Time	173
Searching for Grandma	189
Hamster	200
Witches and Whales	209
A New Life	219
The Shop at St George's Cross	225
Star Party	236

THE RECIPES 245

Metric and Imperial Measures	247

Baccala (cod) Roman style	249
Beef stew with dumplings	250
Black Forest Gateau	252
Brown and Black Urid Dal	254
Chapattis	256
Cheese scones	257
Chicken Caesar Sandwich	259
Chilli Oil	261
Cider	262
Courgette (Zucchini) and Onion Frittata	266
Cranachan	267
Cup Cakes	268
Favourite Soup	269
Fish and chips	270
Filled Parathas	271
French Onion Soup	273
Grandpa's Special Toast	274
Iced Coffee	275
Janet's Vegan Pie	276
Lamb Stew with Parsley Dumplings	278
Melting Moments	280
Obatzda	281
October Casserole (Sailing Stew)	282
Pasta with Roasted Peppers	284
Special Lamb Curry	286
Spicy Eggs	288
Vegetarian Spaghetti Bolognese	290

BIOGRAPHIES   **292**

The Stories

Love Lessons

RJ Ashby

June 1992

I sit at my dressing table. I lift my long hair, pull it this way, hold it back, and scrape it tight to my head. I like the slim rise of my neck, regal. I can imagine the gentle caress of a man. I close my eyes. I'm seventeen, well nearly, and I want it all. I want freedom. I want love. I want respect. My parents keep me caged by childhood and school doesn't help.

I don't call out to my mother as I pull the door shut. She will be standing at the kitchen window, mug of tea in hand, looking out over the back garden seeing sparrows, blackbirds and maybe even a grey squirrel and listening to the radio. She talks to the radio as we, the family, come and go. None of us has time to talk. Father's morning run leaves little time, even for breakfast, and I and my younger sister move in different time frames – I live with order while Kiera creates chaos. She grabs for everything: bathroom, toast, even my clean tights, and is still last out of the house, with a garment trailing or unkempt hair – looking fantastic. Her gang meets at the corner of our street. It's her gang. She is the popular crowd.

Today, I hurry. I am avoiding Mum, avoiding my lie. I have my Walkman secreted in my bag, totally against house orders. Sometimes I want to be just a bit cool! The exams are over. The pressure is off. It is months till the results come. Maybe I'll leave and get a real job!

In school the corridors are heaving. Boys constrained are amplified: barging with bags shoulder high, bragging with bad manners. I follow, ducking past the group when they stop to check the notice board.

I'm early. The sixth-year common room is empty. I sit by the window with my bag on my knee. I plug in headphones and listen. Charlene sits down and lifts an earpiece from my ear to her own. Smiles complete the connection.

'I hear you won,' I say. She is the tennis star of the county. She trains with my Dad.

'Yeah. It was a good game.' She grins. 'The big one's on Saturday.'

'I know, Dad said. Are you playing tonight?'

'Mmm. Are you coming to watch?'

That was the lie. I had told my mother I would be late. I had told her I was going to help at the tennis courts till seven, but I had given up tennis. Not that I told anyone. My Dad is a total embarrassment. I answer, 'Sure — like I have nothing better to do! I don't think so!'

'I knew you would say that, Jen. Just checking.' She grins again.

The bell rings and the group from the common room shows indications of movement. I thrust the headphones back into my bag, zip it and follow the crocodile of pupils that meanders out of one room and into another. Higher English promises a dreary start to the day. It is Shakespeare, *A Midsummer's Night Dream*. I try to listen but the beat of the June sun through the window carries my mind to a different place.

My casual presence continues. Even some teachers can't see the point of today's lessons and we are allowed to work outside where the boys wrestle and the girls sunbathe. The day slips by until games. I have no kit. Excuses are my talent and mine are outstanding. The teachers joke as I offer today's justification but there's no argument. I get permission to retreat to the library.

From the library I can see into the art rooms. Mr Shian has a class. I watch him move from pupil to pupil. Sometimes he stands at the front and speaks or sketches. I know his routines. I know his style. I know his words and his passion, his care and his gentle encouragement. I especially love that about him. He's a great teacher. I study his lips.

He is wearing that shirt I like: thin stripes of white, pink, green and yellow. It hangs open at the neck. I try to imagine what he would smell like: like flowers, or musk or mint. I don't know his smell. I close my eyes. His hand had rested on my neck. I could feel it still. A light special touch as he put his hand on my skin, bare skin. Hairs trembled. My skin trembled at his caress. Now I should explore his bare skin, his neck. The buttons on his shirt would open. I would smell his... his intimate warmth, his... his breath.

My eyes open, embarrassed. I am in love. Will he get close to me again? I had asked if I could do some work on my piece after school. My lie... Sometimes he stayed, other times he went off and I was left on my own – painting. I hope he will stay today.

'Why don't you study art? There's room in the higher group,' Mr Shian had asked.

'I'm not allowed. It would just be a distraction. I'll never make an artist, never make a living...'

'Who says that?' he had asked.

'Well, I won't. I'm not that good. I just like it. It's a hobby.'

I am working on a piece that will take ages to finish, it is like a mosaic. I have drawn the outline and then divided the sketch into tiny sections and now I am building it up with graded colours. It is painstaking, but I am determined to let it – emerge – an experiment. Mr Shian is intrigued.

I can't wait for the bell to ring – but not for the painting.

I imagine how it would be... 'Come and have a coffee before you start.' I would sit on the paint stained stool in the cluttered art room cupboard. He would squeeze past me – ever so close. I would pretend it was normal and just breathe...

My classmates are ambling back across the playground from the sports field. Some boys are charging, jumping, pushing — elbows digging and arms entwine as they stumble and tumble towards the gym. Others sidle in, tight to the girls, chatting, flirting, laughing. I am glad to miss that, that closeness. The immaturity of the boys irritates. I can almost smell their sweat.

When the bell rings I close my jotter. I have added some sentences to my essay. The corridors empty. The warmth of the day draws the screeching throng out from every exit. I can see Kiera in a crowd at the school gates. I feel a thrill as I hurry to meet the most important man in my life.

'Hi. You remembered.' Mr Shian looks up. He smiles.

'Yes. I've got loads of time today.' I drop my eyes in case he sees too much, my cheeks flush pink.

'You happy to work in here? I've got some setting up to do for tomorrow. I'm just going for a drink.'

'I've got this.' I wave my bottle of water.

'Ice cold beer by any chance?'

'Vodka – it's got no smell.' I giggle.

'I'm going to get a bottle of something cold.' He picks up his jacket and saunters out.

The room is warm, but cool air from the corridors makes it pleasant. I don't notice the silence as I collect paints, brushes and paper towels. I pause from time to time to look back at my piece that is now propped against the back wall. I settle at the back table. Music whispers from my Walkman. I hunch over the table. A steady stroke from my right hand is the only movement. I don't hear the teacher approach.

'That's good!'

I am startled. My bottle of water flies to the floor and the jerk pulls my Walkman over the edge of the desk. Mr Shian is quick, he catches it while his other hand rests on my shoulder and he brushes his cheek onto mine. I can smell him.

'Sorry Jen. I didn't mean to give you a fright.' He lays the Walkman safely back in its place and picks up the bottle of water. 'Just as well you had the top on this.'

I am embarrassed. Already the encounter has become something more – the firm hand on my shoulder, the brush of his stubble, the smell of his breath – all to be remembered.

He sits down and we talk quietly. He asks about my music and amuses me with stories of his favourite bands.

We laugh, comfortable together. He forgets about setting up for tomorrow and I forget about painting.

Time slips by.

Then the cleaner raps on the door. 'You going to be much longer, sir?'

And the spell is broken.

Mr Shian hurries off to cut paper. The cleaner wipes round the sinks and sweeps the floor. It is after six when I step out of the building into the warm evening air. I know Charlene will still be at tennis but I am going home.

I cross the acre of tarmac that surrounds the school, walking towards the railings that guard the deserted road. 'Dad!' My voice screams in my head and a bolt of guilt makes me duck down.

There is nowhere to hide. The car creeps on by at a steady pace towards the sports ground and the tennis courts. Is he looking for me? Have I been found out? I hide in the shrubs and watch.

He parks by the gate to the tennis court. I hear his voice, cheery, laughing. Someone gets into the car. I hear their voices. He drives off.

I freeze. 'That was Charlene. That was definitely Charlene's voice. What the hell?' My thoughts are confused. Maybe I am in trouble. 'Why would he pick her up? Why? It doesn't make any sense...' The scene replays in my head. My thoughts circle round truth and lies, guilt and innocence, and men.

I brace myself as I open the front door. Mother shouts. 'Jen, is that you? You got Charlene with you?'

'No. Why?'

'Her mother's on the phone. Have you seen her?'

'She's at the tennis court.' That was another lie.

'That's what I said. She can't get hold of the coach. What time is she finishing?'

'After seven, I think...'

Everything looks normal, the hall: pale carpet matching the walls; crisp lacquered oak framed everything. A breeze from the garden steals through unnoticed carrying the scent of cut grass as a neighbour works: the distant hum of summer. The kitchen table's hygienic gleam mirrors the lonely mug. A lidded pan on the cooker simmers. The dinner plates wait on the empty black granite work-surface. Mum grins and waves me towards the pan while she talks and laughs on the phone. Dinner is our family time. She has made beef stew, *'the family glue'*, with dumplings. One of the many family rules – she tries to make sure that we always eat together, our normality.

Mother's conversation continues. I try to drown out the questions in my head. Today I am alone. It is just me eating, just me thinking. My family...

Later, I hear Dad come in. He clatters upstairs. I hear the shower punctuate his carefree singing.

'Jay!' Mother shouts.

'Down in a sec. I'm starved.'

Then he is there and as usual he fills the room: wet hair – slicked back, tight jeans, distressed T-shirt, a hum, a skip. His grin caresses us all. He messes up my hair. At the cooker, mum grumbles. That too is normal. Her hair is loose, her leggings sag, her shapeless top hangs, but I love her. There are no questions. Nothing is wrong.

And then Father is behind me. His hand, cool, sits round the base of my neck, slips down my pony tail, and I breathe in. There is no prickling skin, no thrill, no skip of my heartbeat but an ugly thought: an *old* man, a touch, a kiss on young skin, easy. It would be easy... It would be wrong.

I brush him off. My mind whirls. Mr Shian? Charlene? Dad? Confusion crowds in on me.

The following morning I meet Charlene at the school gates.

'Thanks for covering for me.'

'What?'

'Last night. You told mum I was at the tennis.'

'I thought you were?'

'Well I was, sort of. But thanks.'

'Sort of, what does that mean? You've got a boyfriend...'

She looks away. Her free hand touches her neck, her cheeks glow.

'Married is he? Got kids?' I try to keep it light.

'I don't want to talk about it.' Charlene jogs across the playground to the PE Department.

'Charlene,' I scream. 'Real love is what my Mum has. You need to grow up. Act your age. Get drunk. Sleep around. Just don't think you can be part of my family anymore.'

Jen started work in the local factory, making circuit boards for phones, at the end of that school term.

An Atlantic Alliance

RJ Ashby

Althea Saltzman stood watching the lights of New York, which seemed beyond bright against the dark of the sky. The lights flickered. At first the blue ones, isolated and chilling, caught her eye, then urgent flashes of red reflected to the left. Every colour of the rainbow pulsed, a mirror to her excitement. This was the world that she had come to find, come to explore, come to enjoy. She pulled the curtains closed. It was wrong to shut them out but she needed to sleep.

'I should have abandoned them years ago.' She spoke out loud as she relaxed into the huge bed and the luxurious mattress. Six years of caution, vigilance and selflessness had kept her at home – hovering round those she loved, clutching to memories that were keeping her under the burden of parenthood. She had broken that spell. Three stunned faces had waved her off. Not that any of them had come to the airport. Not one of her three children had been free to do that.

Lois, her elder, had a husband and her own three children. Jefferson was married and Fizz, the younger, hadn't emerged from adolescence yet. She lay in bed sleeping while her mother called for a taxi to take her to the airport. She didn't even get up to wave her mother off.

Lois was thirty-one. Planning had never been her strong point, which was why her children would suddenly be foisted on their grandmother. It was one of those unplanned weekend trips that Althea remembered.

The day when she began to see that her children didn't deserve her.

'Just take them to the park, Mum.' Lois asserted, as if her mother was stupid. 'What could be easier?'

Althea stuck to that plan. 'Come on, we're going to the park.'

'What, now?' Mags had an edge to her voice and a scowl on her face. She played *'it's not fair,'* almost as well as her mother did, even at eight years old.

'Yippee!' Tristan, the baby of the family, circled the room in jet mode. He had filled the house with noise and commotion since his birth, now four years later he was never still or silent.

'I'm going on my roller blades.' Fran kicked her shoes off and hurtled into the hall.

'If she's going on those I'm not coming.' Mags moved to the corner seat, putting the table between herself and her grandmother.

The day was a disaster. From those fraught beginnings the day had spiralled till bed time. She tucked little Mags into her bed at nine thirty wondering if she would survive another day, at the same pace. Mags smiled a sleepy goodnight and said, 'You weren't bored today.'

'No, Mags, I was not bored.'

'Mum says you're bored when you're at your house. It's nice to not be boring.'

The comment played and replayed in her head. Each time it meant something different: was being bored her problem or being boring? Did Jeff call her a bore too? Althea laughed as she whispered to herself. 'Jeff has to live with his own bore!' She stopped short of criticism. She didn't want to fall out with Jeff, but she had little time for her daughter-in-law. The same phone call had come once too often. 'Could you bring some of your wonderful home-baking over, Mum?' And she knew they had houseguests. She also knew that she would not be invited to stay.

'You are wonderful, Althea. How could I compete with you? You are the baking queen.' The sycophantic excuse made the hairs on her neck rise. Boredom had no time to settle with perpetual servitude.

Fizz was pretentious and sophisticated beyond her means, but she still played the little girl at home. Boredom was impossible in her emotional whirlwind. Her mother never knew what disaster was pending, or when it had passed.

'Is that white blouse washed?' Fizz had asked.

'You were wearing it yesterday.'

'Yes, but you could have washed it this morning. I need it.'

Althea obliged with an immediate hand wash, tumble dry and iron.

Six years of being mother and father and no one saw a person anymore. No one phoned to ask, 'Mum, come to the theatre?' 'Mum, come for the weekend.'

In her head she challenged each of her children. In reality nothing changed. She practised saying, 'I'm busy. I can't manage today. Bye.' She tried to escape. Then, one day, as she dashed from the hairdressers to pick up Fizz's dry cleaning, (it cost her fifty pounds) before collecting Tristan from nursery, she noticed the travel agent had a poster in the window. Long Weekend in New York –

shop, explore and relax – only three hundred and seventy five pounds. That was it!

She told them. No big deal, no fanfare. The date was etched on her forehead. The brochure lay on top of her bed. Every day she tidied her room and laid it neatly on the bedside table but each morning, once again, it had filled her dreams.

She fingered the plastic collars that remained on all the suitcases that stood together in the attic. One was labelled for a flight to Dublin, when Shaun had flown home for a funeral. Another had the tag from a romantic, childfree, trip to Rome. It was the only holiday they had ever had without their children. There were two small matching suitcases that they had bought for short breaks together. Sean's sudden illness meant they had never been used.

It was one of the small suitcases that stood, full of promise, in her bedroom. She unearthed her passport and placed it safely inside, along with the tickets. Chills of fear and excitement played with her as the time came close.

Then the predictable phone call, 'Mum can you babysit at the end of the month?'

Her answer was polite, but firm. She hung up as she laughed out loud. She clapped her hands. She turned the radio up. She danced. Steve Wright was singing along. She joined in.

Then Jeff called. He wanted a recipe for a black forest gateau, but they both knew what he actually wanted was it to be prepared, cooked and finished for Saturday evening. 'It's in two weeks, Mum...'

It was such a pity that she had left all her packing to the last minute. There was no time for her to bake. She carefully wrote the recipe with additional hints. 'It's easy.' She insisted. Jefferson looked unsure. It was his responsibility now.

Fizz had her own trip planned. She was flying to Stockholm to meet the parents of her latest boyfriend. They took a late spring holiday in Sweden each year, skiing, a family tradition. And Fizz had been invited. She agitated endlessly.

Althea packed. She considered blouses, skirts, jackets and trousers. Some were thrown on the bed. Some were folded and placed in a pile for the charity shop and others were hung back in place. She knew what to wear: the boots, the cardigan, the pleated skirt.

That one task took a whole afternoon, but her organisation was seamless. By Thursday night her case sat complete and her travelling outfit hung ready. The documents were zipped into her hand luggage. She even remembered to slip spare underwear into her handbag (advice from Fizz). Her expectations simmered.

That night, she slept fitfully. Her nerves strained. She told herself off, 'Don't ever be called boring again. Get a life… LOL.'

She sat in the departure lounge, endless people-watching before her flight. Others were travelling alone. She talked to them.

The hotel was just as she had imagined, all glass and marble and the view from her window was breath-taking. She sat on the bed and checked her phone. The bed wrapped her in comfort, just what she expected from America, sheer luxury.

Her phone buzzed. It was a text from Fizz.

Phone Me NOW!!!

Two hours in New York and her world ground to a halt. It was not the weekend she had planned. She was too tired to care. There was no point in even opening the case, she knew whatever was inside wouldn't fit her. Six hours later she was back at the airport, JFK International Airport, and she was flying back to Heathrow. Her bubbling excitement had vanished. She noticed no one. She was tired and edgy. She fidgeted as she watched the screen for her flight. She needed to get home.

Fizz had blamed her. Why had she decided to use the matching suitcase and not her own? Fizz had packed her passport safely beside her knickers, packed in the very suitcase that had flown with Althea across the Atlantic. Althea's eyes narrowed as she remembered the way her daughter had howled into the phone.

'Never, never again!' she muttered to herself.

'Something important in London?' A handsome American gentleman was looking at her.

'How did you know?' she asked abruptly.

'You look as if you can't wait.'

'I can't. My daughter... I was just wondering if I could strangle her...'

'Do you need a counsellor? I could introduce myself as a lawyer or perhaps you just need someone to listen.' His smile showed concern.

Althea beamed, and she offered her hand. 'Perhaps you can help plan my escape...'

The Well

Palo Stickland

Punjab, 1960

I remember when the men came to cover up the old well. I watched with Ma at our door, thinking how I would miss running round its perimeter wall, dropping stones into it to hear that satisfying click, but most of all I'd miss the clear echo of my voice when I leaned over and called into that huge round space. Sometimes it seemed as if another child called back to me.

First, they took down the wall letting it fall in, then they carried rubble and soil, on their heads in metal bowls, and threw them into the well. There was a sliding noise as the rubble left the bowl, then no noise at all, and finally, a dull thud. It took them five days to fill, smooth and then cover the top with bricks. I was pleased because now there was a large open space, a square, in the middle of our seven houses. I ran around the edge of it, touching the door of each house, then I ran to the middle of the new space and lay on the bricks, but when I closed my eyes I felt as if I might fall into the well. And if I pressed my ear to the ground, I imagined I could still hear the echo.

That night, when I woke up to take a pee in the corner of our courtyard, I thought a saw a light; I peered through a crack in the door. There was a pale girl, about my age, in a thin white nightgown, running across the square in a straight line from our house to the house opposite. I stepped back, my heart racing in my chest, and ran to my bed.

The next day I knew that the grown-ups had other ideas about how to use the new square. Instead of perching on the wall, as they used to do, they brought out their string beds to lie in front of their doors in the cool breeze of the summer evenings. I sat near Ma, who usually had sewing or embroidery to do for people who paid her. On the other beds the families had loud discussions about things I didn't understand.

In the house right across from ours there lived an old woman with her son and daughter-in-law. He went to work early every morning, his wife was always cleaning and cooking, while the old mother lay on her bed.

'She's ill,' Ma said. 'You mustn't stare, Latu.'

At that moment, the old woman waved an arm to everyone. 'We must have a blessing for the new square. Send for the priest. We'll all contribute what we can. You make the dal, as you usually do, Shanti.'

My mother cooked dal for everyone whenever there was a festival. She made some for the two of us every week, and it was our food for three days. I liked to help her. First, she put together the black and brown dal in a tray to pick out the little stones and tiny bits of wood. I would sit close, cross-legged like her, peering over the little pulses, but she was always too quick. She found lots more than me. Then she would place water to boil on her fire in her clay pot. It was the biggest pot she had. Ma would wash the dal and put it into the boiling water with white salt and yellow turmeric. The oven would be ready by now. It was a hole in the ground with a lid. The cow dung patties would be hot by the time my mother lowered the clay pot into the oven. Then we'd cover it and leave it for all of the day. I always kept an eye on it but the oven quietly kept the dal cooking without Ma having to look at it.

'The secret is to put the right amount of patties into it,' she told me.

Later, she'd fry up the turka telling me to keep away because the oil, the onions and spices made me cough. She said it was too strong for a young throat.

'When will the blessing happen, Ma?' I asked that night.

'It will be in five days because the priest has to collect the sweet spices that we burn in the fire and we all must buy the food for the visitors to eat,' she said as she rolled my roti. I sat near her fire watching her as my stomach rumbled and my mouth watered at the sight of food. She heated some butter in a pan and spooned some dal into it. It sizzled deliciously.

That night, the girl in the white dress came from the square into our house. Ma slept in her own bed, the one my father slept in before he died, and I had a little bed beside hers. She was fast asleep. The girl stood over my bed with her hand stretched out.

She said, 'Come into the square.'

I was afraid but I sat up, swung my legs off the bed and followed her out. The moon was full; stars sparkled above us. She ran to the door of the house opposite and I ran after her. When I turned to go round in a circle, she wouldn't follow me.

'Why do you run to that door?' I asked.

'It's my house,' she said.

'No. They have no children.'

When it was becoming light, I went home because I was tired. Ma woke me but I was still half asleep when she brought my tea. We always drank milky tea in the morning.

'Ma, I have a friend. She says her house is the old woman's house.'

'There's no girl there. Where did you meet her?'

'In the square.'

'Did you have a dream, last night? I think I need to send you to school to make friends of your own age. All the boys in the square are older.'

'I don't think it was a dream.'

'Drink your tea. I'll ask your cousin about the school. You're old enough now. Five is the right age for boys to start school.'

'What about girls?'

'They don't have to. It's not important for them.'

I took out my spinning top and went into the square. The girl was crouched in the middle with her ear to the ground. She got up and came towards me. One of our neighbours, walking back from the fields, nearly bumped into her. He said hello to me, ruffled my hair but he didn't seem to see her.

The girl spoke, 'The old woman is ill. Let's go into the house.'

'You said it was your house. Go in by yourself,' I argued.

She became really angry then, her eyes turned red, her face dark. I took a step back, she came towards me, I walked across the square; we entered the house together. The old woman was lying on the bed in the veranda.

There was a candle on a little table beside her. The girl snarled at her, like a dog. I would have run but she had my arm.

'Throw the candle on the bed,' the girl urged.

'No, I can't. The cover will burn.' I was nearly crying and I didn't want to hurt anyone.

Then the old woman turned over to look at me, at the girl; she'd heard my voice and she could see the girl.

'No! Go away!' The old woman screamed, pulling the cover over her face.

I tore myself from the scene and ran back to my house, to Ma. I grabbed her as she was sweeping the floor.

'What is it, Latu?'

'The old woman... she knows the girl, Ma. You said they didn't have a girl! I'm afraid of them.' I cried into Ma's shoulder when she picked me up.

Later, Ma took my hand and walked me over to the opposite house. I didn't want to go but she pulled me along.

'What's this about a girl the same age as Latu?' Ma was not afraid of anyone. I cowered behind her salwar, thinking it was all my fault.

The old woman sat up in her bed, pulling the cover around her shoulders. The daughter-in-law, a thin, pale woman who never smiled, came and sat at the end of the bed.

'Mother was upset this morning, it must have been a bad dream.' The daughter-in-law spoke in a voice as dull as her eyes.

'Since the well was filled there's been a girl playing in the square. You saw her this morning.' Ma spoke to the old woman, at the same time settling herself down on the floor and pulling me on to her lap.

We all stared at the old woman when she spoke in a low voice. 'We'll have to tell the priest. The girl came out of the well because... that's... where...' she paused, looked at her daughter-in-law and let out a huge sigh. 'Because that's where I put her. I'm sorry.'

'You threw a child into the well?' Ma's voice shook.

'I was thinking of my son. He doesn't earn much. A daughter is such an expense. She didn't cry when she was born. I wrapped her in a cloth and threw her away. It was wrong. I've regretted it every day.'

The daughter-in-law had covered her face with her hands; now she let out such an awful sound, like cats fighting in the night, and she leapt, with her arms stretched out, towards the old woman. Ma rose quickly and grabbed her, hugging her tightly.

'It's done now, and can't be taken back. What should we do now?' Everyone was weeping, I think for different reasons. I was sad. When I looked towards the door, the girl was standing outside, watching.

'What's her name?' I said, then I shouted, repeating my question. 'I don't know her name!'

Ma held the daughter-in-law's shoulders and repeated, 'What's her name? Your daughter's name?'

'I wanted to call her Piari... loved one. I wanted her so,' the daughter-in-law sobbed.

'She's at the door,' I said. I went to hold the girl's, Piari's, hand to bring her in. When she set foot over the threshold of the house her mother could see her and bent down with her arms held out wide. The girl ran to her mother who lifted her, kissed her and carried her into the back room.

The old woman said, 'Shanti, tell the priest everything. He must lead the prayers to bless the well and to help little Piari's spirit.'

The whole town came to the blessing, which took place over three days. Ma made six pots of dal. The priest threw sweet spices on the fire and we all sat with him to call on the gods, and our ancestors, to witness our good deeds, and to forgive our mistakes. Piari was mentioned many times. On the last day I looked up over the flames and thought I saw her, she waved and then disappeared. I never saw her again.

The day after the blessing her grandmother died.

Chapattis with Everything

Sue Cook

Mr Kumar was pitifully thin when he was admitted to the home, so thin that the staff worried his arms would snap whenever they helped him out of his chair.

Tabitha couldn't help but compare him with Derek, partly because they were the same age and partly because she thought it was only a matter of time before Derek had a stroke, too. Apart from that there was no similarity. Certainly there was no danger of Derek's limbs snapping – Derek ate everything Tabitha put in front of him, albeit with suggestions for improvement. Mr Kumar ate nothing except sweets: sponge and custard, spotted dick, Mr Kumar liked those, but as for actual nourishment…

Every time his portion of fish pie or sausage and mash came back to the kitchens untouched, Tabitha puckered her lips and wondered what else she could try to tempt him. She longed for suggestions for improvement from him, but his English was poor and her knowledge of Asian cuisine largely limited to curry houses. If she knew anything it was that home-style 'curry' was not chicken tikka masala or anything with the word 'Balti' tacked on the end.

Fortunately, his family brought in home-cooked titbits, so little by little his skull began to shrink beneath his skin and the girls complained less that his arms would snap and more that he was getting hard to shift.

When Mrs Akhtar was admitted to the home and she would only eat sweets as well, Tabitha felt increasingly inadequate.

'How would you like it when you retire to Spain and you get ill and have to go into a home and they feed you nothing but paella and things with suckers on a skewer?' Tabitha asked the manager, hands on hips. 'With garlic,' she added as an afterthought.

The manager wrinkled her nose. 'I'm still not sending you on a "learn to cook Asian food" course. Not for two residents. Can't you use cook-in sauce or something?'

Tabitha glared, her lips clamped into a thin line. She shook her head and wheeled round. 'You have no idea,' she said, and strode out of the office. As she crossed the resident's lounge back toward the kitchens, she saw one of the waiters from the curry house where she often ate with Derek. Tabitha enjoyed curry evenings very much – an excellent meal at a reasonable price and she didn't have to wash up afterward. There was also the candied spectacle of the waiter, the one now standing in front of her in jeans and hoodie and holding a small Tupperware box.

Tabitha knew he was about twenty because he had been at school with her son. Not that they had been friends, heaven forbid; no, fancying someone like that would be far too close to home.

Ever since her son had left home, Tabitha watched the waiter week by week maturing from a scrawny teenager into a broad-shouldered man who filled his white shirt, with its tiny black buttons, very nicely indeed. She found it satisfying to surreptitiously watch his long dark lashes, his almond eyes and chunky biceps while dunking her poppadums and slicing her tikka in the long silences that she and Derek enjoyed these days. And then there was that very short and magnificently trimmed designer beard which led the eye upwards to his lovely full lips as though to say 'kiss here.'

Derek's beard looked more like a used Brillo pad.

She raised her eyebrows. 'What are you doing here?'

'Visiting my dad,' he said. 'Mr Kumar.'

'I never knew...'

He shrugged. 'No reason why you should.'

That was true. Apart from his age she knew nothing about the waiter. She didn't even know his name.

'I worry about your dad.' She pointed to the Tupperware box. 'I feel bad that you have to bring food in, but I don't know how to cook what he likes.'

After a brief exchange, Mr Kumar junior, who said his name was Amit, looked at Tabitha a little shyly and offered to teach her. He said his days were quite boring anyhow as he had to stay home and look after his mum who had also had a stroke but wasn't as bad as his dad.

'I do the cooking now, before I go to work in the evening. You'll be doing me a favour,' he explained.

'Don't your sisters do that?' Tabitha asked, wondering if that was being sexist, or possibly racist.

'I have only one. She married and went to America.'

'Sister-in-laws?'

'Ay-ay-ay!' he said and rolled his eyes. 'Sisters-in-law!' and he explained how one had left his older brother because of unreasonable behaviour and the other was still trying to get a visa from the government so that she could come here and live with them.

'They have got very strict,' he said. 'She's been waiting over a year. My brother isn't happy. Not happy at all. One year married and still sleeping alone.'

So, one afternoon Tabitha drove to the other side of town, to the red brick terraces which now housed immigrants from South Asia where once they had housed migrants from the countryside, and Mr Kumar's youngest son taught her to cook family meals in the family kitchen while Mrs Kumar shouted questions and instructions in some foreign tongue from the living room where she was confined to a high, winged chair, the same functional mid-brown as those in the home.

At about three o'clock Mrs Kumar always fell asleep. The first time it happened, Amit smiled and shook his head and said, 'Mothers! Not you, Mrs Wilkes.' And Tabitha said that he should call her Tabi, like everyone else did.

Did he blush? It was difficult to tell with his milk chocolate skin, but he looked as though he had done and was trying to hide it. Tabitha blushed too. It was probably a terrible faux pas asking someone the same age as her son to use her first name, her familiar name, someone from a different culture, where the gulf between the generations and the sexes was as wide as the Indian Ocean. She fanned herself with a small chopping board and muttered about hot flushes.

That first week Amit taught her how to make basic chicken in fried onion sauce, and his mother's rice. She made it for Mr Kumar and Mrs Akhtar and the plates came back empty. He taught her a simple dal, and jeera chicken which, being made with drumsticks and thighs, was good for the rest home's budget, as she explained to the manager who called her in to find out why they were running dual menus now.

And Mr Kumar and Mrs Akhtar ate every morsel, and some of the white British residents (who Tabitha had started to think of as 'The Joneses') did too, especially Colonel Jones who claimed he had been stationed in India in the sixties, though Colonel Jones said a lot of things that few people believed. But he cleared a full plate of jeera chicken and rice and asked for more.

The third week, or possibly the fourth, Amit said it was time to learn how to make chapattis. 'It's a staple. We eat them with everything,' he explained.

'You make your own bread?' Tabitha asked.

'Of course. It's easy. You don't have to let it rise like English bread. And you can add fillings for variety. Dad likes it with jeera.'

'That's cumin seed, right?'

Amit grinned. 'You're learning, Tabi.' And Tabitha turned away before he could see her red cheeks.

The kitchen was small and Tabitha became used to their touching now and then because it was almost impossible not to. But how those touches made her flesh glow. They grew more and more frequent, turning her skin to a seething mass of hot spots so that Tabitha felt increasingly like a pot of boiling toffee approaching hard ball stage. It was only because they were getting used to each other and feeling less awkward, she knew that, but when she went home, in the evening, when she was lying awake in bed with Derek snoring beside her like an elephant swinging its trunk through a vat of crisps, she liked to read more into it. A deliberateness. A course being followed to an inevitable conclusion.

When Amit had shown her how to mix the atta flour, which was just the same as whole-wheat flour really, with enough water and the salt to make a smooth dough before oiling it and leaving it in a covered bowl for a bit, their hands touched often and it seemed that brief brushes became lingering ones, that Amit increasingly left his hand next to hers longer than was necessary.

It was the menopause, obviously. Yet it still created heat, a heat so great that Tabitha doubted very much that Derek would be able, or willing, to douse it when she got home.

Mrs Kumar was already asleep when they stepped into the back yard with a drink to wait for the dough to do whatever it had to do for fifteen minutes. They chatted about what Tabitha's son was doing now and about Amit's life plan (his own restaurant, a good marriage—not like his oldest brother who didn't know how to treat women —and lots of children to look out for him as he got older). Amit explained that his older brother did not command respect in the bedroom and from there he struggled to get respect from his wife anywhere.

His picnic chair was closer to Tabitha's than it needed to be and sometimes their knees touched and he didn't appear to mind, which seemed odd for a good Muslim boy. Or was he Hindu? Really, she should ask. And if she wasn't an overweight, menopausal mother with grey hair and a chin that she had to pluck else she too would have a beard within a month, and if she wasn't at the stage of life where she wondered at each act of sexual intercourse whether it would be her last, she would think that he was interested.

Which was ridiculous.

When they returned to the kitchen Amit showed her how to divide the dough into five balls and turn the balls into patties, which were dipped in flour. And in showing her how to roll them into thin rounds his hands pressed over hers on the rolling pin and stopped her breath as sure as if they had been round her neck. He stood close, too close, as she did the rest by herself and he praised her effusively.

Her heart effervesced deep inside her ample bosom as they put a hot fire under the skillet. Individual pulses blurred into one as Amit showed her how to tell when the chapatti was ready to flip the first time and the all important second time (brown spots underneath and bubbles on top) and, covering her hand with his, he demonstrated how to gently press on the side of the chapatti with a balled tea towel to encourage it to puff up when done.

Tabitha praised Amit for being both a skilled and patient teacher. And, when the last chapatti was lifted out of the pan and placed with the others on a plate and wrapped in a tea towel to keep soft and warm, he slipped his arm around her waist and whispered that now perhaps she could teach him something in return?

Tabitha, almost not daring to ask, whispered, 'What?'

'Teach me about love,' he said. Eyes as dark as raisins locked onto hers, and his neat, firm torso pressed into her expansive softness.

He felt young and hard and very, very real.

'When you say love, you mean... you mean...?'

This time he definitely blushed and his eyes dropped, just for a moment, before fusing again with hers again. 'I don't want to be like my brother. When I get married I want my wife to respect me.'

'Why me?' she asked.

'Why not?'

'But I'm...' too old, she had been going to say.

'You are caring and sensual. You have supple, soft, cook's hands,' he said, holding up one of them and kissing the finger tips. 'You have lovely eyes—hungry eyes—I have seen them. And I want to be taught by someone who has lots to teach.'

So while the chapattis kept warm in a very low oven, Amit led her quietly past the sleeping Mrs Kumar to his bedroom where he said they would be undisturbed because he had slipped his mother an extra tablet and she would sleep until evening, and his brothers were all at work until six. And then the impossibly young waiter finally touched his generous lips to hers.

It was the tentative kiss of the unsure, the sort of kiss that reminded Tabitha of aged aunts at railway stations. The sort of kiss, in fact, that Tabitha was almost too old to remember. Certainly the aunts were long dead.

With bodies edging toward each other, memories stirred and she showed him how to grow those kisses and how to let hands explore where she had always wanted them to explore but had never even hoped that they would. And because she was not quite sure where his would explore next, unlike Derek's that had a set, if neglected, routine, soon her whole body burnt for him as hot as any tandoor.

All too soon it was over. Lying beneath the deep maroon and gold throw, which she clutched tight around her chest in case he glimpsed things he didn't like in the afterglow, he said that it was lovely and asked if she had, you know…

She shook her head and he looked disappointed.

Tabitha smiled. 'That can be a good thing.'

'It can? How?'

'Because,' she said, wondering how best to explain it without going completely puce, 'because the oven is still hot. It's like making bread, really. English bread. It has proved once and been knocked back. Now it needs to slowly rise again and then we can cook it, good and proper.'

A slow smile spread across his youthful features, and she felt the second rise get underway.

'I hadn't thought of that. Your English breads are cool.'

'It needs a very hot oven for about half an hour,' Tabitha said. 'Or ten to fifteen minutes for buns.'

Amit's mouth found hers, and his hand found her breast, and her hand stroked his swelling finger roll and his tense, plump tomatoes. She led his fingers to her thermostat and showed him how to adjust the temperature and test the moisture content and when it was just right she told him it was time to put the bread in the oven. And this time, under careful instruction and supervision, as well as the occasional metaphorical slap on the back of the hand from the bread knife, he left it in long enough to produce the most satisfying sticky bun that Tabitha had had in years.

As she was leaving with her plate of still warm chapattis, Amit suggested something more challenging the following week. 'Lamb with chickpeas. My dad likes lamb with chickpeas. It needs to be simmered for an hour,' he said.

For an hour? Gosh, what would they do? But because they were standing on the doorstep she said, 'Well, if it will encourage your father to eat… Would chapattis go with that?'

'Of course. Chapattis go with everything and we'll have to do something while the pot bubbles.'

Amit was right. The chapattis went surprisingly well with a pork casserole that Tabitha had left in the slow cooker, although Derek thought they had been kept warm for too long and were overly moist.

Missing

Elves

The woods looked forbidding. Sam stood at the top of a slope that led down towards the stream, deep inside the darkest part of the wood. The trees grew sparsely where she was, and there was grass and wild flowers growing in abundance, but not far ahead, she could see where the grass and flowers petered out. The trees were thicker, and she could see any number of large, thorny bushes. Down there, down in the valley, the sunlight penetrated only dimly.

She swallowed hard and stood, stock-still, staring at the darkness, her eyes swivelling from side to side. Try as she might, they could make out no sign of another path. There was only the one that stretched before her.

She had to press on. She knew that. Her friends would be waiting on the far side of the valley, in the picnic area, as arranged. She would never live it down if she didn't show up. Okay, the wood was said to be haunted, but believing in ghosts was just for children, wasn't it? And she was fourteen now, wasn't she? Still, she wished she hadn't accepted the dare.

She swallowed again, felt her heart beating hard inside her chest, and took the first step towards the stile that marked the entry into the wood. There was no going back. Sam had to go through with this. She would go through with it.

'Sam, you need to get the bowl out of the cupboard. No, not that one, it's too big. Get the next size down. And bring the kitchen

scales too. Just put them there on the bench. Do you know how to use them? Have you used them before, at school?'

'We've never done anything like this at school, mum,' came the reply.

'I don't know what they teach you at that school,' said mum. 'Now, when I was your age ...'

'Do I press this button, mum?'

'That's right dear, the one that says "Start". Now, what does the reading say?'

'It says "0", mum.'

'That's right, dear. So now, when you put the flour in, you can see exactly how much it weighs. The scale ignores the weight of the bowl.'

'That's clever, mum.'

'It's handy, dear.'

The wood was quiet. Even the birds were silent and the breeze didn't penetrate down there, although there was a sort of whistling sound high above Sam's head, high in the canopy, as though the wind were shaking the trees about up there. She could also hear the occasional sound of rustling in the thorny bushes coming from all around her, evidence of the small creatures that made the haunted forest their home. And something, or someone, had made the narrow track through the trees that she was following — and was maintaining it.

'What does the recipe say next, Sam?'

'It says to measure out a hundred and fifty grams of self-raising flour.'

'Well, put that into the bowl, then. No, don't pour it from the bag. You'll get flour everywhere. Use a tablespoon. That'll make it easier to be accurate too.'

It was just about then that Sam heard — or should that be "felt" — something else. As if there was someone, or something, near her, not on the path but moving with stealth.

She disentangled herself from the thorny grasp of some plant that had sprawled across the path, the way Dad sprawled across the sofa when he came home from the pub at night, and stood perfectly still, her ears straining to hear any further sound from within the trees. There it was again, then silence.

'I think you need to get the cheese ready next, Sam. Have you got the grater ready?'

'I've watched you do this before,' said Sam. *'I know I cut the cheese into small pieces before I put them into the grater.'*

'But first you have to weigh the cheese, dear. How much do you need?'

'Seventy-five grams.'

Sam took another few tentative steps. How far could it be to the stream? Had she become lost? No, she was still on the path, still going downhill. Wherever it led, that's where she was going. And there was that sound again. There was someone out there. Very close.

'I've cut off eighty-five grams, mum.'

'That's all right dear, it'll just make the scones a bit more cheesy. Just the way you and Dad like them. You can grate it straight onto a plate.'

She couldn't stand there for ever. She knew she had to make a dash for it. If she could just reach the stream, the woods might be thinner on the other side. She steeled herself. Took a deep breath.

'What do you want to do next?'
　'I have to add mustard, salt and cayenne pepper.'
　'Well, measure them out and add them straight to the bowl.'

Sam couldn't make out the sounds of pursuit, since she was making so much noise herself in her attempt to escape. But it seemed she was in luck — until a tree stretched out a root to trip her and she went head first down the path, fear drowning out any pain.

Slowly she got back to her feet. Her dress was marked with the dirt from the path and she tried to brush it off, successfully smearing it a little further as she did so. Then she remembered the pursuit and again stood still as she forced her ears to listen. The sound was still there, but now further off, as if whoever it was had passed her by and was still going down the hill.

That was when she made the curious decision to carry on, rather than to turn around and escape back the way she had come. She rubbed the graze on her left knee and proceeded, as quietly as she could, hardly daring even to breathe.

'I've got the butter ready, mum.'

'Good girl, just chop it up into small pieces and drop it into the mixture, then get your hands in after it and break the butter up so that the whole lot starts to look like bread crumbs.'

'Ooh, this is fun, mum.'

'Baking is fun, dear,' said her mum.

On the other side of the stream, Sam paused for thought. Her heart was still beating hard, from the running as much as from the fear, but she needed to think about what had happened. She had panicked. No doubt about that. She had allowed the stories about the wood to play on her mind. No doubt about that either. Did that mean that the wood was safe? That there was nothing in there to be afraid of? Well, no, it didn't quite mean that, though the sight of two deer taking a drink from the stream convinced her that she wasn't being followed and that she had allowed her imagination too much play.

'I think they look ready now, don't you, Sam?'

'I think so, mum. Do I add the cheese now?'

'Is that what the recipe says?'

'Oh. No. It says to add in most of the cheese, and then to mix it in.'

The path was no less steep on the far side, and no lighter either, and Sam soon found herself gasping for breath as she hurried uphill. And hurry she did. She had no wish to extend her time in the wood. She found herself wondering if Linda had ever been down there, and if Linda had been just as scared. No, of course not. Linda wasn't scared of anything.

'I've got to mix an egg in with some milk next, mum.'

'You'll need a small bowl for that, dear. And the measuring spoons. Yes, that's right, just break the egg on the side of the bowl then let it go into the bowl.'

'Yeuk, mum, I've got some of the egg white on my fingers. Stop laughing. It's not funny.'

'The egg won't hurt you, Sam, and anyway you've got to put the egg and milk mixture into the flour and mix it with your fingers. Put the milk in now, and give it a good whisk with a fork.'

The slope eased off without warning and Sam could see the light of day through the trees. She'd made it. She was almost at the top.

'Just pour it into the bowl and stir it around with the fork for a few seconds. That's it. Then get your hands in again and start to make it into a nice, soft dough.'

There was no one there. The picnic area was deserted. She'd been duped. That Linda had set her up and never had any intention of meeting her. Just wait. She'd get her own back. And now she was going to have to walk home the long way, around the road. She hadn't the smallest intention of going through the wood again.

'That looks good enough now, Sam. If you just tip it out of the bowl and onto the bench. Then you need the rolling pin.'

Thoughts of harsh words went around and around in her head. She'd never speak to that Linda again. That'd teach her. And in that frame of mind, Sam reached home, unharmed apart from the graze on her knee and a dress that was decidedly dirty, something which attracted the wrath of her mother from the moment she went into the kitchen.

'You need to make the dough about an inch thick, Sam.'
   'An inch, mum. Don't you mean two centimetres.'
   'Oh Sam, you know I don't use those new-fangled measurements. Feet and inches were good enough for your grandmother and they're good enough for me.'
   'Is that about right, mum?'
   'That looks perfect, dear. All you need now is to get out the cutters and choose the one you want to use.'

Sam was in her room later that evening. The sun had gone down ages before and the darkness of night streamed through the window. She could hear an owl hoot, somewhere out near the wood, and she shivered, inexplicably. Downstairs, she heard the doorbell chime, and she ignored it. Whoever it might be calling at that time, it certainly wouldn't be anyone for her.

'Anything spare just gets squashed up and rolled out again, until you've only got enough left to form a last scone by hand.'
   'I think that's the best one of all, mum.'
   'I know you do, pet.'
   'Why can't I make them all like that?'

'Because then it wouldn't be special, now would it?'

Sam's confidence in that conclusion was shattered when she heard her mother call to her up the stairs. 'Sam, Sam? Come on down here. Quickly?'

There was mum, standing in the hall, and dad was with her, and someone else. It was Linda's mum. What did she want?

'Is the oven on, dear?'
'I've set it to 220C, mum.'
'Well, just brush the scones with milk and sprinkle the rest of the cheese on to the top of each one. Then they can go in the oven. Do you know how long for?'
'About quarter of an hour.'
'Good girl.'

Sam held onto the bannister. She could hardly believe her ears.

"And that was the third instalment of Ainsley Owen's exciting new murder mystery, The Missing, produced by Radio 4…"
'Have you put the timer on, Sam?'
'Yes mum.'
'Good girl. Now turn the radio off and put the kettle on, would you? We can have a nice cup of tea while we wait for the scones to bake.'

Money, their only Vice

Enza Vynn-Cara

The summer of his fortieth birthday, he takes the boys trekking in the Dales, mountain climbing in the French Alps and, in the week before their return to school, teaches them how to water ski in Porto Cervo. At the end of their journey, in a renowned local restaurant of his choosing, he sits the boys facing west to watch the last trickle of sunset, what he calls a neither-here-nor-there moment of profitable trade between the rusty red day and the indigo night. 'Money,' he tells them, 'gets you noticed when dusk falls and sets you up for the climb at sunrise. It's your safety net and also the rope that pulls you up.'

Instead of the chocolate sponge cake the boys ask for, he gives each of them a wallet: red leather bi-fold Valentino to his elder, cobalt suede tri-fold Hugo Boss to his younger. 'They are for paper money, not coins. Do you know why?'

The boys shake their head. With fidgeting fingers, they draw geometric shapes on the wallets' smooth surfaces. They're worriers, he thinks, just like their mother; but they're also mine. Patiently, he holds the boys' gazes, shifting his eyes rhythmically from brooding brown-streaked shades of jade to anxious gold-rimmed amber. He waits, silently, to find out how much of them belongs to him.

'Paper money is lighter. You can hold more of it inside,' the elder son observes.

'But coins count too,' the younger chirps in. 'Mum always says the more weight we pull the more we get, that's why when I throw out the heaviest rubbish bags she pays me with coins, each coin one pound.'

'Dad gave us paper money when we made good time trekking, five of them, and each note is a five pound, so paper is more.'

You're both right, in a way.' He can't help but twitch up a lop-sided smile. His boys were skilled thinkers and fast learners, but not yet doers. 'It's true,' he tells them, 'paper money is lighter and you can hold more of it in your wallets. And it's also true that the more weight you pull with your efforts the greater your return. In the end, though, what counts, is not the amount of money you carry or its weight, but what you buy with it, the profit you make once you sell or trade whatever you have bought.'

A wave of his hand, and a waiter appears from nowhere with a serving dish of chocolate sponge cake and ice cream sprinkled with ruby cherries and chocolate chips.

'I'll trade this for your wallets,' he tells them. 'It's what you asked for, isn't it?'

A wanting hunger glazes the boys' jade and amber gazes.

'Don't you think it's a good trade?'

'No.' The elder boy stops his younger brother from reaching for the gold-rimmed tray. 'We can buy more with the money we get if we sell the wallets. Double that, I'll bet.'

'Well done, you have already made your first profit. Go ahead, open your wallets. Inside each of them there is a hundred pounds. That's worth a whole lot more than a slice of sponge cake. Now, do you think you can double that value? Triple it? I tell you what, if you can make a profit, I'll give you a new wallet full of money every year and keep on doing it as long as you make a profit. I'll bet you can do much better than your mother.' He pauses, recalling another rusty-red sunset on the Sardinian coast, the clink of champagne glasses, the lapping of emerald water against nearby rocks and the sad-clown stare she had given him. An amused twinkle peeks out of his narrowed eyes. 'So far, she has never made a profit. But she gets to keep her wallets, you won't.'

The morning after their return, the usual routine kicks in. She walks the boys to the school bus stop, a quarter of a mile to the corner, sometimes in silence; sometimes in chaotic shrills, but always with their hands safely in hers. When the bus stops, criss-crossing her arms in front of her, she joins the boys hands together and lets them go free, waving one last goodbye at the fuzzy faces behind the moving windows. Only after the bus trudges out of sight, does she retrace her steps back to his BMW where he is already waiting. His light kisses on her cheek and lips are interrupted by the newest addition to their routine: a 'good morning' chime echoing across the lawn; their neighbour's wife number three, Marilyn-blonde and deceivingly young, wearing her white silk robe like it's a wedding dress, the rolled-up morning paper a bouquet clasped to her bosom.

Marilyn waves.

They wave back.

She thinks of her replaced friend. 'I miss her', she says, 'I miss both of them.'

'Money can buy new brides every few years. We probably haven't seen the last of them, but don't you fret, my dear.' The touch of his lips on hers is lighter than the breeze of her breath on his face. 'We boys need you.'

To celebrate her thirtieth birthday, she takes the boys across the city to the old home she keeps, not for profit, but as a reminder of the memories she sometimes wants to forget. Torn lace covers the windows and the paint on the door is a faded memory of autumn leaves, but in the rear garden a shaggy dog peers excitedly from between the rails.

'I used to have a dog,' she tells them. 'Would you like one? It's my birthday, Dad will not say no to it.'

The shelter where she chose her first dog still houses an abundant selection of unwanted mutts, some strong, proud, and totally dismissive of their unwanted genes; others, shy and fearful, crouching in a corner of their cage.

'He is going to be your best friend forever,' she tells them, 'choose the one who will love you the most and you can trust the most.'

With a thoughtful scowl, the boys pass by the proud medium-sized Basset Hound, the playful, floppy-eared cross between a basset and maybe a Beagle, and point at the golden brown fluff that offers them his bone.

In the winter months, he comes home past suppertime, when the boys are already asleep and she has given up looking pretty. She tells him she has sliced his roasted chicken dinner into Caesar chicken salad sandwiches and egg-drowned and fried his portion of zucchini au gratin into a green-speckled frittata. 'Nothing is going to waste as per: *How to Make Tonight's Dinner into Tomorrow's Lunch: six, one to one, private lessons with chef Alfredo.* It's bit pricey.'

'What's pricey?'

She stands by the kitchen table and hands him the bill of her new culinary course. 'You won't taste its money's worth tonight.' Her arms make a wide sweep, as if wanting to embrace the wrapped containers still on the table. 'But the boys will love their funky school lunches and there is enough left for tomorrow's dinner.'

'Cost-effective and undoubtedly delicious, I'm impressed.' He smiles to himself, thinking that, for all her efforts, she, his prized possession, will never trade for profit, will never see it his way, and will never leave him. 'Tomorrow, perhaps, I'll get to have a taste.'

'Perhaps.'

The down-turned corners of her mouth flatten but never reach his desired smile. He leans forward letting his lips breathe into hers.

'Are the boys sleeping?'

'Perhaps.'

The king-size bed, with the high headboard glaring down at her, feels as cold on her skin as his touch, the warmth only in his breath, heavy yet unrushed like their lovemaking. When it's over, he rolls to one side, his back to her. She rolls the other way. In the grey drizzle of moonlight peering from the window, her left hand reaches for her nightly bliss: two white capsules and a glass of semi-skimmed milk, sitting, each night, side by side, on her night table.

'Money', she says to herself, 'can even buy sleep.'

'What?' He asks between puffs of snore. 'Boys not sleeping?'

'They're sleeping'.

In the clouded November afternoon of his parting, his mahogany coffin has gold-plated handles and hand-carved miniature Pietà on all four sides. The grass upon which it rests is wet, the priest is tired, the mourners are few. As he is lowered below ground, his sons clench their jaws at the nagging drizzle and in their Jimmy Choo ankle boots steer toward dry ground.

Staying behind, she lingers by his coffin for one last moment, watching her boys walk away side by side, shoulder touching shoulder. 'Look at them. They're men, now. And they're mine,' she whispers, lowering her sad-clown gaze onto the mahogany gleaming with silver raindrops. 'I can still remember their first baby word: Dada; their first baby steps towards you, their first scowl of disappointment at your disapproval, and their first trade-for-profit success. They showed them to me when they came home that first year you left me behind. I have kept the mementos, all eighteen leather wallets, reds, cobalt blues, sunshine yellows, military greens, pale browns, dirty browns, midnight blacks. They're on a shelf in the boys' old bedroom, inside a cardboard box with the label *Pocket Money for Profit*. I've kept mine too, a whole wardrobe of purses and wallets I should have donated to charity a long time ago. No matter, there is time for that, now that you've gone.'

A handful of wet soil sieving through her fingers cakes dark brown the diamond ring from their first Valentine, the emerald band from their fifth anniversary, and the ruby oval from their tenth. With a slap of her leather glove, she dusts the dirt off her hand, letting her gaze slide across clumps of wet grass and Italian cypresses in search of her boys. They are waiting for her by the car, her younger son tapping the crystal of his Rolex to let her know she's upsetting their schedule, his moving lips silently calling her away from him, while her elder, clicking open his Burberry check-lined umbrella and threading carefully on the scarce patches of dry grass, begins to trace his steps back to her.

'You got your wish, though,' she tells him. 'Money is their only vice.'

The Last Supper with Jill

Enza Vynn-Cara

'Let's enjoy dinner first, Jill, here at our restaurant, tucked away from indiscreet eyes. I had our table moved behind the lemon tree. Would you believe how it has grown since we were last here and how unnatural it is to grow lemon trees indoors? Maybe George keeps them in only in the winter. And you know what else he does? You would never think of it considering how he runs the place so efficiently and caters to a specific clientele, but, every month, he offers a free buffet of leftovers from the day before to migrants and refugees, right here in his best dining room. There're so many of them now, kind of makes you think. No, we'd better not, not while eating. Who wants to hear that they might have been shipwrecked right at our holiday shore?

'I can see you've been there. Great tan. It's a nice juxtaposition with the short and sassy cut. A newly rediscovered you? Hope your taste preferences haven't changed, because I've ordered two dry martinis and wine to go with the meal and, thinking of you, it had to be Beringer Private Reserve Cabernet. I do like this new short-crop look. Even with that wayward long strand playing hide and seek with your left eye, you can't hide anymore. Strange, you never liked short hair or short skirts or spiked heels, quite a diverging tangent from the white T-shirt, grey jeans and black trainers you insisted on wearing even at fine restaurants like Da Giorgio. Don't get me wrong, you've refined yourself. Casual chiaroscuro isn't you at all. I can see that now. It cast a sad glow on your face, sadder than Anna Magnani in *Rome, Open City*, sadder even than the refugees.

'Oops, there I go again talking about something no one wants to hear. You should see the man at the next table to your right, the one looking like our local councilman but without the perennial grin. He's glaring at me as if I have cursed against God, but hasn't stopped gorging on the spaghetti. Isn't spaghetti *al ragu* a European Union migrant import? Oh dear, I should have said it *sottovoce*; he's looking meaner, all puffed up with spaghetti in his mouth and still glaring our way instead of keeping tabs on those tomato-soaked strings dangling down his chin. They're murder on white shirts, as if someone has just shot you in the chest. I know, I have a stack of them. It's not the same without you, Jill. Even the shirts know it, and the white, linen covered sofa, where we made love joined like Siamese twins practicing the Kama Sutra, feel cold, empty, too clean even.

'How refreshing: you've become one with the coral red of your crew-neck satin blouse, red all the way to your pointy ears. Blushing, another divergence from the old, the familiar. I don't recall seeing you this flushed without the exercise sweat of our... workout. But you know? This virgin flush and the sassy cut brings out... your best... It's always in the eyes with you, so tuck that wayward strand behind the ear. Like that, yes, with you it's all about those accusing, brooding, laughing black pools that keep changing on me. Why didn't you cut your hair before? I know, I know, I said I was into Stevie Nicks' long shaggy cut, she was my puppy love, that's true; but, honestly, it was more because you were so self-conscious of your elf ears, and with a shake of the head the shaggy haircut fell perfectly over them, like a curtain at the end of the final act.

'Actually, I've always liked that laborious little elf in you, and you know what? The combination of the pointy ears and the rhomboid emerald pendants kind of brings out a geometrical precision hardly ever found naturally. I remember now, I bought them with this very thought in mind and gave them to you on our fourth anniversary, right here too. You cried. Too much of Giorgio's chilli oil made you sneeze and tear. Don't worry, this time, I've ordered deliciously under-spiced dishes for you: spaghetti and roasted peppers, tasty eggplant meatballs, radicchio and fennel salad. You can skip the chilli oil this time around. And here it comes.

'How is the spaghetti without the chilli oil? I can see you are enjoying gobbling it up so go ahead, revert back to old times; though, I think that flashbacks like any good representation of the past are best savoured on the slow, like our home-made Italian dinners, eaten while slouched on the sofa watching *Bitter Rice, Paisan, Shoeshine*, before the Kama Sutra workout. You remember, De Sica, Rossellini, my dissertation, you helped me type it... Yes, yes, you've helped me research and write it too. There, I've said it. I owe it all to Rossellini and you. Go on, finish your spaghetti, and the salad, you always leave it for last, like Rossellini would have. I suggest a drop of balsamic vinaigrette to go with it and, for dessert, you can have your pick.

'Did you say tiramisu, Jill? I thought you would, so I've asked Giorgio to prepare it for you especially. Five hours refrigerated, just the way you like it, and it's brandy not vermouth. You see, I know what you like, what you want, how you want it. I even got Giorgio to reveal all the recipes of this dinner because I know you want to try them and then we eat slouched on the sofa watching Rossellini. Like old times, better than old times, you cook, I'll clean. No, we'll do it together, the cleaning I mean. See, I've changed too. I even leave the kitchen rubbish for the next day and the stained shirts are piled up, well, folded, in the living room. The living room, Jill. I have changed!

'The balsamic, Jill, try the balsamic. Don't nuke the spaghetti, and the salad too. It's too hot this chilli oil, you're powering up like a Virgin diesel engine. Why do you keep losing yourself in the spaghetti? Fork it and twist, like so. No, dear, no, you still can't do it can you? The hell with etiquette, then; best if you tuck the napkin into your collar. No, not yours. It's already stained. Take mine. You've got chilli oil on the chin, on the nose and on that wayward strand that should be kept behind the ear. That's it. Keep it away from those black pools of yours and the chilli. Watch it. Now you've got it on your elbow. Not that one, the other. It's even on the blouse and the table.

'Stay put... or else...

'There goes the salad — and the eggplants — and the chilli oil.

'We're inundated.

'No, I don't want your napkin! My shoes are soaked with oil, the eggplant meatballs are on my lap, and the waiter is sliding over the fennel on the floor. For Christ's sake, don't make any more sudden movements. Just hand over the papers, carefully. You win. I'll sign on the freaking dotted line.'

The Last Week of Autumn

Julia Chalkley

Steve closed the top gate after us and leaned on it, wheezing a little. When I turned back to smile at him my boot slid on the path, and I turned away to concentrate on the wet grass and cow pats. Steve did say that we were rescuing the apples from the cows.

Still, it was good of him to let us scrump his orchard.

'Is it scrumping if the landowner gives you permission?' I called to Mark.

His hearing aids don't really work well enough. He claims that they're calibrated to bring his hearing up to normal, but there are times when he just doesn't hear me. I restrain my sarcasm. His hearing was damaged as a teenage apprentice in a machine shop in the 1960's, working lathes and cutters without earmuffs, but for years he refused to admit it. To him, deafness only happened to old people. When he finally gave in to my nagging and got a pair of hearing aids it was such a relief to have him hear me even part of the time that I don't criticise. I can't risk him throwing the hearing aids into a drawer and slamming it shut on any future communication, so I waited until he paused at the end of the path before I repeated the comment.

'What?' he said.

'I told my guys at work I was going scrumping today,' I said. 'I don't know what the Head of Finance thinks of a chief accountant who steals apples, so maybe I should have said I had the landowner's permission — is that scrumping, though?'

'We're not stealing,' he snapped, nodding back towards the top gate. Steve had gone, probably wandering slowly back to his warm kitchen. 'Steve said we could take the apples.'

It wasn't worth explaining the joke. I clicked the foldable plastic crates into shape and set them down. We looked around, considering the choices.

'They're whoppers,' Mark said, pointing at the nearest tree. The branches were bent low with huge striped apples. One of the smaller branches had snapped under the weight, its cargo resting on the muddy ground. 'We could fill up with those and go straight back.'

'Best to get at least six different kinds of apple,' I said. Again. I tugged one of the stripy giants and it fell easily into my palm with a cool solid weight. 'I reckon these are Newton Wonders. Not a pure cider apple, though they'll make a fair brew. See if we can find some true cider apples as well.'

'How do you know they're Newton Wonders?'

I pointed to the lump of apple curling over the stalk. 'That nose – and the size – and the red and yellow stripes.'

He didn't look convinced, but he began to pull the giant fleshy apples off the branches. We filled a crate within five minutes and I pointed to the next row of trees.

'No more of these?' he asked.

'We've six crates to fill,' I said. 'Six types of apple – '

'What if there aren't six types?'

'There are,' I said, hoping there were. I needed him to move on or we'd have six crates full of huge hybrid dessert/cider/eater apples. We wouldn't know whether the apple would make a decent cider until the first racking, six weeks along, and by then the apples we'd discarded would be rotting in the cowpats below the trees, or eaten by the cows. Safer to take six different types now and hedge our bets.

'Why six types?'

'Just blending it, so you don't get loads of sweet ones or loads of sour ones in a batch. Remember that course I went on at the start of all this?'

Mark rolled his eyes. He put up with my fondness for the local college's rural skills courses. He'd had some ripe opinions on the goat-keeping course, and didn't believe that dowsing found anything other than gullible students. The cider course had won his approval after the batch of fermenting apple juice I'd brought home had matured into something we'd enjoyed to the bottom of the demijohn a few months after.

'Well, the tutor said there's a few types of apple like Katy and Stoke Red that can be used alone and still make a decent cider. But he said that it was safer to get a mixture of at least six different varieties, so the sweetness of one type was balanced by the sharp or sour in another. I did tell you that at the time.'

'Is this one sweet or sour?'

I bit into one of the Newton Wonders. 'Fairly sweet,' I said.

'Don't eat them all.'

I swept an arm dramatically at the laden trees around us – how could I eat all these? Wasted on Mark. He was concentrating on the trees in the next row.

We filled the next crate with long, squarish, pale green apples that looked like Golden Spires – proper cider apples – great news for this batch if I was right, but they're pretty rare. I bit into one just as Mark turned around.

'Are you going to eat every apple in this orchard?' he asked, half joking and half disgusted.

My mouth squared off as the hard hit of tannin dried it out. 'Just testing,' I said, and spat the mouthful out. 'I think these are real cider apples.'

He grinned. I would check the Pomona, the definitive apple reference work, before I claimed these were Golden Spires, but it looked – and tasted – likely.

The row by the fence had tiny round apples. 'No crab apples,' Mark said. 'Those crabs spoiled the whole batch last year. You could taste them.'

I fished in my pocket for my penknife and cut one of the apples in half. The flesh was pale brown like rot. 'These might be Slack-Ma-Girdles,' I guessed.

'You made that up!'

'If I'm right, they're good cider apples. They smell like dead beetles, though.'

'Well, I think they're crab apples, and I don't want to risk the batch by putting any of those jokers in,' he said, and set off towards the next block of trees. I put a couple of the apples into my pocket, along with a few leaves. I'd check them in my 'Pomona' tonight.

I didn't need to check the apples on the next tree. We both knew those apples.

'Oh – no,' Mark said.

We both knew better than to include Bramleys in a batch of cider. We remembered the acidic taste of the only batch of cider we'd put Bramleys into. We left them weighting their branches down to short cow level and moved on.

Within the hour we were ferrying full crates of apples back to the Land Rover. Steve's dog barked from the safety of its pen, and Steve came out to see us off.

'You've a good load there,' he said.

'Yes,' Mark said. I'd have had to yell or write it down, but he heard men's voices first time. 'There's loads in that orchard. You should make a batch of cider yourself.'

Steve shook his head and pulled a grim face. 'Too old, now.'

'Well, thank you,' I said. 'You've got some rare trees there, I think? Golden Spires?'

Steve obviously had the same range of deafness as Mark. He didn't hear me at all. 'I couldn't do all that messing around, not at my age,' he said to Mark. 'I miss it at times, but it's a right palaver. My grandfather planted that orchard in the days when Weston's was taking local apples from the little farmers. Used to come down here with me pals and help out with the harvest. Got paid up in cider after I turned fourteen.'

Steve looked out at the overgrown remnants of his grandfather's orchard, scowling. 'Close to dead, those trees are now. Not been worth planting replacements since Weston's stopped taking the fruit. Same for all of us. Dead trade, is apple farming.'

As we turned the Land Rover towards home and wound down the windows to say goodbye, Steve had the last word. 'Only thing left to do is to sell those fields for housing. That'll pay for me funeral all right.'

I read in the Pomona that evening that the little round 'apples' were probably perry pears, and were most likely Dead Boys, but it agreed with me that we had a crateful each of Golden Spires and Newton Wonders. I hoped we'd have some good cider to offer back to gloomy Steve for his generosity. As we tipped the crate loads of apples into the scratting machine and watched them explode into mush on its whirling blades, I said to Mark; "He had a nice orchard there. His grandfather had a good grasp of what makes decent cider when he planted that lot. It's a shame, letting it all go to waste.'

'It won't go to waste. We can go back next year,' Mark said, concentrating on the mash being puked out of the scratter's chute into the bucket below. He shifted the full bucket away and shoved a replacement bucket under the chute just in time to catch the next barf of finely mashed apple. That used to be my job, before he realised that I would stand dreaming while a bucket overflowed with apple mush.

I thought of Steve walking slowly and painfully, of the cankered trees in his orchard and his destructive funeral plan. 'We might not get the chance, next year,' I said.

'We will. I'm intending to still be here and making cider next year,' Mark said. 'Steve seemed happy to let us take the apples. He won't be using them.'

Steve wasn't happy. He was a man with a seven acre orchard full of rare cider apple trees, but without the strength to walk as far as the first laden tree in the row. The cider he'd offered us had been dated six years ago and had tasted of mould and soap.

We watched the creamy mash pour out of the chute and splatter into the bucket. Within a minute of landing, it was brown. By tomorrow the mash would look like a bucket full of pale cowpat, a porridge of apple mash the same colour and texture as diarrhoea. We'd spent our autumn weekends over the last eight years talking to friendly craft cider makers in Gloucestershire and Herefordshire, and we knew enough to let the tannins leach out of the mash before we pressed it. Vile as it looked, we knew that the juice we could press from it the following day would be a clear pale gold, tasting sharp and sweet and purely of apple. It's a taste we have never found in any apple juice we've bought or any we've coaxed from our kitchen juicer. Every time we pressed a batch of apple mash, we took a glass to catch the first juice to fall from the lip of the press and drank to the health of the batch. I was infamous at work for my alcoholic hobbies, but I kept the secret of this drinking tradition to myself.

Mark didn't hear the next thing I said to him, and I gave up trying to get through. I watched him concentrating on the mash bucket, deaf to the world outside the scratter's grinding roar and blind to the ways in which his future might tear him to shreds.

Pitching a Fit

Mairibeth MacMillan

Why was the holiday turning out to be so miserable? Surely Sarah's first holiday alone with Ryan in twenty-five years should be more fun than this. A lot more fun. They didn't even have any kids with them to curtail their activities.

Of course, basing their holiday choice on Sarah's fond memories of her childhood family holidays in a VW Camper might have been the mistake. Ryan had wanted to go on a cruise – he wasn't fussy where – so long as it was relaxing and the food was good.

Given that he was the one who hadn't got his way with the choice of holiday what was currently annoying Sarah the most was that he was the one who seemed to be enjoying every minute of the current nightmare.

Well, of course he was – he wasn't the one who was doing contortions round the interior while trying to draw all the curtains along their precariously hung wires and then stud them in place. Why had she remembered this sort of thing as being fun?

'Just leave it,' Ryan muttered as she leaned on his neck in an effort to reach the final stud which lay, not only behind him, but also across the expanse of cupboard on which he had rested his large mug of coffee, yesterday's paper and his dirty lunch plate. Evidently he was expecting the dish fairies to move it into the basin for him. She certainly wasn't doing it.

Sarah had made his lunch for him and had also spent the last hour trying to cook dinner on the miniature twin burner and grill. She'd carefully followed the recipe book – written specifically for VW Campers – before discovering at the final hurdle that it also required something called a Dutch Oven. Whatever that was.

'Should have read the whole recipe through before you started cooking,' Ryan advised her from behind his paper. It was probably just as well he missed the gesture she made towards him. Or maybe he hadn't because he chose that moment to announce that he was going out for a walk. 'It'll give you some space so that you can cook,' he said as he dumped his paper on the table and pulled on a jacket.

So that she could cook? She could scream.

Admittedly, it probably wouldn't make her feel all that much better and it would probably scare the neighbours and judging by the size of the RV next door it most likely had a built in Dutch Oven – and a cook.

'I'll buy a Dutch Oven at the shop tomorrow,' she said dumping the half-made meal into a plastic tub and putting it on the last free shelf space in the fridge. 'Pick up a couple of fish suppers while you're out.'

Ryan borrowed twenty quid from her purse and left. Sarah groaned out loud in the empty van. She'd reminisced for years about her childhood holidays in a camper van but her own kids had never really warmed to the idea. Probably just as well. There was no way a family of four could ever fit in this thing for a holiday. Absolutely none. What must her parents have been thinking? She pulled out her mobile and stubbed her finger on the screen as she hit her dad's number.

'How on earth did we have family holidays in one of these without killing each other?' she yelled at him when he answered.

He just chuckled.

'Different era, love,' he said. 'Expectations were totally different in the seventies. No one expected to be able to afford a luxurious holiday. The eighties – now that was a different time. That was all planes and Spain and beaches and–'

'Surely even in the nineteen-seventies people must have expected that there would be enough oxygen in their accommodation to get them through the night?' Sarah interrupted.

'It's not that bad,' Dad said.

'That's only because you're not here. Ryan's gone out for a fish supper and it still feels cramped and we haven't even set the bed up yet.'

'Have you put the roof up? That always makes a difference,' her dad said calmly. 'Put the roof up.'

'I don't think the roof being up is going to make enough of a difference.'

'For goodness' sake, there are only two of you,' her dad exclaimed. 'Somehow we all survived when you lot were wee. Two weeks in Yorkshire or wherever every summer. Always enough air. Open a window.'

She hung up, mumbling under her breath about rose-tinted spectacles. And not necessarily just her dad's – her own were clearly as pink. But she did put the roof up and there was a little more air. Sort of.

How times must have changed. It wasn't even as if this thing had exactly been cheap. And it was going to end up bloody expensive if she ended up trudging across the campsite and staying in the hotel next door for the rest of the week – which was exactly what might happen.

It was only the end of their second afternoon and Sarah had no idea how she was going to survive another thirteen days of possibly the worst holiday ever. It wasn't just the fact that she and Ryan were living on top of each other in the cramped camper van. It was just, well, everything.

Why had other holidays always seemed like it was so difficult to fit everything in? Now that it was just the two of them and they could make their own choices rather than pander to their children there seemed to be nothing to do. The thought that it had just been their kids holding them together all these years had been occurring to her more and more often as the months passed since their youngest had headed off to uni. This holiday seemed to be proving her right. Maybe it wasn't really the holiday that sucked – maybe it was her life.

She poured herself a glass of Prosecco and wandered outside. The midges were starting to gather in their hordes and she knew her time outside would be limited, but there was no way she was sitting any longer in the cramped van. She noticed the blinds on the RV next door fluttering closed. Talk about nosy – or maybe they'd just been closing the blinds.

She took a deep breath then a long draught of Prosecco, finishing it before it became a midgey swimming pool. She was letting her anger at the whole situation get out of hand. She couldn't even really work out why she was so angry. Just that she was. And that Ryan was making it worse. Wasn't he? Actually, it wasn't so much anything he'd done that was annoying her – more that... No, she had no idea. She was just annoyed. She frowned at the empty glass and headed back inside with one last glance at the RV.

Who knew that there would be a social status competition on a caravan site in Argyll? She couldn't decide if the girl at reception had found it amusing to park the forty year old VW van next to the brand new RV complete with satellite dish on the roof. What was the point of camping if you brought a bloody satellite telly with you? Ryan would just sit and watch the football on it and they might as well be at home if that was all he was going to do. Maybe they'd both be happier.

She settled into the spot he'd vacated and poured herself another glass. She wriggled in the seat and leant back against the cushions. This was better. Much more comfortable than the single seat she'd been relegated to earlier. At least now that she had the curtains closed the woman next door couldn't stare in horror at the orange camper van. Well, she could. But Sarah didn't have to know about it, so it was all good.

She sighed and picked up the book that she'd not managed to read any of so far just as Ryan opened the sliding door. The smell of the fish and chips actually managed to make her smile. Almost enough for her to forgive him. Until he spoke.

'Stick the kettle on for me will you?' She slid the book down from its place in front of her face as a choking sense of frustration filled her again.

'Pardon?'

'Stick the kettle on, love.' Ryan spoke louder and slower.

'You're closer,' she said, just as slowly.

'The knobs are too small for me to work them,' Ryan said smiling at her. 'Please, love.'

She edged round the table, pushing past Ryan on the way, and muttered in her head the words 'small' and 'knob' an amazing number of times as she filled the kettle and settled it onto the burner.

Ryan reached across the van for his paper and stole her seat while he was at it. Was that really why he'd asked her to put the kettle on? Nothing to do with small knobs at all? She made a point of picking her book up and seating herself on the single chair again. Huffing and moving the cushions about more than once. By the time she'd got almost comfortable the whistle was sounding and she did her best to ignore it but simply couldn't.

Ryan managed just fine – surprise. She got up and switched off the burner. If it was the smallest mug of coffee that she'd ever made Ryan was too sensible to point it out. She used the rest of the water to fill a pot of tea for herself. Well, after all, she was the one who'd made the effort. She sat back down with her book.

By the end of chapter two she had realised three things. The first was that sitting on the backward facing single seat of a camper van to read, especially when you had one leg folded under you, was not overly comfortable. The second was that broadsheet newspapers were capable of taking up a vast amount of space and making an unbelievable amount of noise. A bloody television would be quieter. The third was that no matter how delicious a fish supper tasted, once it was finished it didn't half reek – particularly in a confined space.

'Any pudding?' Ryan asked poking his head above the parapet of his paper. He was lucky that she wasn't holding anything that could have been used as a weapon in that moment. If she chucked the book she'd have lost her place and it just wasn't worth it. Almost – but not quite.

'Pudding? I didn't even manage to finish making the main meal. There's not a lot of room for cooking in here in case you haven't noticed.'

He glanced around. Of course he hadn't noticed. Why would he? He hadn't even made a cup of coffee yet on the miniature stove.

'Why don't you nip down to the shop and pick something up?' he said.

'Why don't you?' she retorted. The paper came down flat.

'I got the fish suppers,' he said. She glared at him fully aware that he was right.

'Is everything all right, Sarah?'

'Yes. Fine,' she snapped. The two of them stared at each other for a long moment.

'I'll go to the shop for something.' It was the most sensible thing he'd said all day.

She tried to ignore the rustling of the newspaper as he folded it, fixing her attention instead on her book. She even turned the page but had no idea what had come before nor what was printed on this page. After the door slammed shut behind him she put the book down and opened the fridge. Where was the Prosecco? All the booze in the fridge seemed to be beer. When had he done that?

Right! She grabbed a couple of bottles and pulled them out leaving them sitting out on the table. Three cupboards later she found a new bottle of Prosecco that she managed to squeeze into the fridge. She checked the tiny ice cube tray. Full. Result! Just how tacky was it to put ice into Prosecco? Who the hell cared? She popped open the new bottle and downed a glass of clanking Prosecco and wondered if the RV next door had a bigger fridge? What was she thinking? Of course it had. It would have bigger everything. And undoubtedly bigger knobs. A sudden memory of pouring the Prosecco while sitting on Ryan's seat hit her and she sat down on the warm patch and found it tucked down between the cushions.

'Thank god,' she said and swigged some straight from the bottle, looking round the tiny van as she finished it.

She couldn't believe how much she'd looked forward to this trip. As a child she had loved the way the stove opened up and the sink with its delicate tap and tiny plug. It had been like a working doll's house. She'd always been so excited to help her dad hook up the gas bottle and fill the water canister under the seat with a hose. This van had been adapted or had been different in the first place. Who knew? She'd to fill a canister at the nearby tap and then roll it over beside the van before plunging a weird looking valve deep into the tank. She'd lost count of the number of attempts it had taken to get the water to flow.

Ryan had been inside shouting helpful information through the louvre window while he pressed the little button and the mechanism whirred.

They had got it to work eventually. She supposed that she should be grateful for that. Plus it was easier to plug in an electric cable than it would have been to mess about with Calor bottles so she'd gained there.

The door slid open again with its now irritating roar.

'Here you go,' Ryan said cheerily. 'I thought we could have Cranachan. All you need is a grill for that. I know how much you love it and it seemed like you needed something to cheer you up.' He handed her the bulging shopping bag as she stood and stared at him, at the bag, at the camper van. Ten deep breaths and the rage almost started to slip away. Almost. Then she looked at the bag full of ingredients again and it was back.

'Cranachan? And what am I going to serve it in?'

Ryan grinned at her. 'I thought of that. I even bought plastic cups. No washing up.'

'There's twenty of them,' said Sarah peering into the bag and reading the label. 'And a whole tub of cream and raspberries. And a very large box of porridge oats. And no room in the fridge.' Even she could hear how shrill her voice had become by the end of the sentence.

'Oh, that's no problem. I got talking to the bloke next door and he's invited us round to watch the game. I said we'd bring a pudding.'

'Next door. In the RV?'

'Yes.'

'You didn't think that maybe you should ask me first?'

'You were going to make pudding anyway.'

'No, Ryan, I was not. And I really don't think that we can turn up on someone else's doorstep who owns a van that looks like that with some home-made Cranachan in plastic cups. Have you seen that thing? Have you seen them? They were watching us earlier. Sneering, I'll bet.'

'Oh, for goodness' sake. Who cares? Well, I'm going round. Hand us out the beer from the fridge.'

'Get it yourself.' She folded her arms.

'Honey, as you already pointed out there isn't much room for manoeuvring in here and you're already right at the fridge.'

She yanked open the door causing all the bottles to rattle and thumped them down on the table one after the other. How had he managed to get so many into that tiny fridge?

'See, you'll get the Cranachan in there now,' Ryan pointed out.

She blinked. Just count to ten. She counted the beer bottles.

'Well,' Ryan said. 'Just pop through when you're done.'

'You're not waiting for me?'

'Game starts in…' He checked his watch. 'Two minutes ago. Got to go.' He gave her a quick peck on the cheek and slid open the door. 'Want me to leave this open?'

'No!' But he'd already gone, leaving a draught.

She pulled at the door, which slid along, clunked with a dull thud then rolled back. Gritting her teeth she left it there and turned her attention to the ingredients on the table. Much as she hated to admit Ryan was right, this was her favourite pudding and there was no reason why she couldn't make it here. Maybe it would make her feel better. Especially if she ate the whole lot by herself and didn't bother sharing it. Sharing was overrated.

So she turned the heat on under the grill and covered the tiny grill pan with tin foil before scattering the porridge onto it. She washed the raspberries as the oats toasted, loving the nutty smell the oats gave off. If she just happened to find a caterpillar in the raspberries she'd make extra especially sure that Ryan got that serving.

There wasn't but, pleased at the thought of it, she smiled and began to whistle. She poured the cream into a bowl added some honey and, lacking a whisk, set about whipping it with a fork. Drat! She'd nearly forgotten. She opened Ryan's 'special' cupboard that contained his whisky, his cigars and some fancy flies for all the fishing he probably wouldn't get around to doing.

A nice single malt. Expensive. Delicious. She smiled and poured a generous amount into the cream then put the stopper back in and set it carefully back in its place. It took quite a while to get the cream to thicken and she'd had to stop to turn off the grill in the meantime but finally it turned and she was all set.

Hmm, quite a lot of cream but there were twenty cups after all so she set about fixing the desserts, layering cream and oats and squished raspberries. The last four cups had nothing but the whisky laced cream in them. She was about to start putting them on a tray to take them next door when there was a quick rap on the window. She nearly hit the roof.

'Hello?' Great. The neighbour. A slender well-dressed woman with coiffed hair and polished nails. Exactly the sort Sarah had envisaged. Exactly the opposite of Sarah.

'I'm Hilary. I just wondered if you needed any help.'

'No, thank you. It's all done.'

'Oh my, what a lot,' Hilary said. 'There's only the two of us next door, you know.'

Sarah shrugged. 'There isn't much of a fridge in this thing. Had nowhere to store the extra so we may as well eat it.' It wasn't quite true now that Ryan had taken the beer away but she didn't feel the need to explain.

'Oh, I can keep it for you if you like. There's plenty of room in mine.' Hilary put out her hands to take the tray from Sarah who was so taken aback that she handed it over. It wasn't what Hilary had said – she'd expected that. It was the way that she'd said it. Not boastful, not at all. If anything she sounded… sad.

'Yes!' A shout from the RV next door shattered the moment.

'Someone's scored,' Sarah noted rolling her eyes.

'Fancy that,' said Hilary. They made a face at each other and burst out laughing.

'I've got an idea,' said Sarah. 'Why don't we set aside a pudding for each of the men and we can sit here and have ours in peace.'

'I'll take them through,' Hilary offered.

'No,' Sarah put a hand on the other woman's arm. 'They know where they are. If they want them then they can come and get them.'

Hilary glanced towards her RV then shrugged. 'Yes,' she agreed. 'Yes, they can.'

Hilary sat on the main seat while Sarah sat on the backward facing chair.

'Here,' Hilary said. 'Lift the step inside and put your feet up on that. And if you turn the chair and put the seat back right down you can put pillows against the cabinets. It's much more comfortable.'

Sarah did as suggested and found that Hilary was correct. She let her head drop back and sighed.

'You sound as if you've been in one of these before.'

'Oh yes, we always had one when I was growing up. That's what I wanted but Frank wouldn't hear of it. So we ended up with that... thing.'

Sarah's head shot up and she stared then laughed.

'Want to swap? This is much more cramped than I remembered it being.' She reached for a dessert and Hilary did likewise. 'I really thought I was going to love doing this but... it's awful.'

As they ate, they swapped tales of childhood holidays in their family camper vans. Touring sites on the North Yorkshire coast, Cornwall, Norfolk, Lancashire and the Dorset coast.

'So much of it is so run down now,' Hilary said. 'And so expensive.'

'I haven't been for years. The kids always wanted to go abroad,' Sarah admitted. 'And I think we really needed some guaranteed sunshine too.'

Hilary was quiet.

'I thought that this year we'd get to spend some time as a couple,' Sarah continued. 'Without ending up at a theme park or standing around in play parks. You know.'

Hilary bowed her head, concentrating on her Cranachan.

'Not really,' she said quietly. 'We don't have any children. They didn't fit in with Frank's life plan.'

'Oh,' said Sarah. 'I'm sorry.' What the hell was a life plan? And what about Hilary's? She sounded sad.

'Ironic isn't it,' Hilary said, 'that when you don't have any you end up being able to afford the space and time to have them.'

'I guess…' Sarah wasn't sure what to say. She wouldn't swap her life with her children for anything.

'All Frank is interested in is his work and his sport.' Hilary shook her head. 'A wife's just for making sure the house is nice and entertaining his boss and doing occasional charity work. If I'm really lucky I get to make up the numbers for bridge.'

Sarah stared at Hilary with absolutely no idea what to say to that.

'It's okay now, though,' Hilary said. 'I've been taking some courses behind his back and have just got myself a job as a book-keeper.'

'That's what I do,' Sarah said and the conversation turned to Sarah sharing some of her experiences and tips with Hilary. They ate as they talked and before Sarah knew it there were only the two cups put aside for their husbands left.

'You know,' Hilary pointed her spoon at the last dollop of cream in her cup. 'This is really quite strong. What did you put in it?'

Sarah retrieved the bottle from the cupboard.

'Ooh, very nice. One of Frank's favourites.'

'I've also got a bottle of Prosecco in the fridge.'

'That's what Frank always buys for me.' They made a face at each other and with an unspoken agreement Sarah opened the whisky and filled two of the plastic cups. Hilary giggled.

'Frank would have a fit.'

'Ryan too. But they're watching the football and still waiting for their dessert to make it all the way to their mouths of its own accord.'

'Maybe we should just eat theirs, you know, before it goes off?' Hilary suggested.

'No, leave it. Then they have nothing to complain about. It was Ryan that wanted it, after all.'

'At least it was something you liked.'

'Yes,' Sarah said. 'It is. It's my favourite. That was why Ryan thought that I should make it. Of course, it would have been even better if he had offered to make it but…' She made a face. 'It might not have been particularly edible if he had. Somehow he follows the instructions and it doesn't seem to work.'

And all at once the day slid into a different focus. Not the rose-tinted glasses of her childhood holidays or through an unflattering comparison between a Caribbean cruise and the midge-infested campsite. Instead she was left with the straightforward view of a husband who'd come with her on this holiday because she'd been going on about reliving her childhood for years and who had gone out to get all the ingredients for her favourite pudding because he knew she was upset.

Okay, so it wasn't perfect. He could have just bought something ready-made and saved her the effort or… She looked at Hilary and thought about all the extra space she had in her life.

'Does Frank ever get you things… you know, just because he knows you like them. Even if it's something he can't stand?'

'No,' Hilary said. 'Not unless it's been recommended to him by his boss or someone at the golf club or the bridge club or someone-else-in-the-know about whatever it is.'

'Do you ever drop hints about things that you'd like to do?'

'No point,' Hilary said swallowing the last mouthful of whisky and pouring herself another cup. 'He never listens to anything I say.'

'That's a shame,' said Sarah.

'Not really,' said Hilary. 'It just means he's missed all the phone calls I've had with my lawyer over the past few months. Wanted to be sure I got the best deal in the divorce after all.'

'So, why are you on holiday together?'

'Let's just say I was advised that it would be easier for me to move out exactly what I wanted to take if Frank wasn't around to get in the way of the removal men.'

'That's…' Sarah stopped. What on earth could she say to that?

'…the best decision I've ever made,' finished Hilary. 'Should have done it years ago but it took meeting someone else, someone nice, someone normal, to make me realise how miserable I was. Now, you really must give me the recipe for this. I think I asked the movers to make sure they took a few select bottles from the drinks cabinet so at least I'll have one of the ingredients.'

The two of them were laughing and giggling when Ryan slid open the door of the camper van what might have been either minutes or hours later. Sarah hadn't a clue and couldn't have cared less.

'What the...' he said at the sight of the two of them sprawled on their chairs giggling and chatting. 'You never brought the Cranachan over.'

'No, we didn't,' Sarah agreed. 'Something wrong with your legs?'

'We were watching the game.'

'And we were talking.'

'About what? And is that my whisky? Do you know how much that cost?' Ryan stared at the mostly empty bottle.

'Yes, I bought it.'

'But the Prosecco was yours.'

'And do you know how much that cost?'

Ryan's mouth gaped open and shut a few times. 'But... but you like Prosecco.'

'Yes, yes I do. But I like this too and so does Hilary.'

A second figure stuck his head round the door.

'Frank, here's the dessert that Sarah kindly made for you,' Hilary slurred.

Frank looked at the plastic cup as if it were somehow contaminated with commonness. Then he seemed to remember his manners.

'Thank you,' he said staring at the contents again and taking a quick whiff of the cup. Then he nodded sagely as if understanding where the *Eau de Whisky* was coming from.

'Match is over, you'll be coming home now.'

Hilary looked at Sarah then smiled.

'Thanks for a lovely evening,' she said.

'You don't have to go,' Sarah said. 'You're welcome to stay a while longer.' Ryan made a noise but at a glare from Sarah he nodded.

'Stay as long as you like,' he muttered. He even managed a smile but Hilary gave them a quick wave and a smile then climbed out the van.

'I need to get an early start tomorrow,' said Frank. 'We have a holiday schedule to keep and I must admit I was terribly disappointed in this place. Didn't live up to its reviews at all. Thought they'd have higher standards in the sort of vans they allowed on the site.' Frank shook his head, oblivious. Ryan frowned. 'Come along, Hilary.'

Hilary rolled her eyes at Sarah then tapped the side of her nose and winked.

'What a dick,' Ryan said as soon as they'd closed the door of the van. 'Higher standards, my arse. It's a campsite for god's sake.'

'Ignore him. I think you summed him up perfectly. His wife would certainly agree. She's leaving him, you know. As we speak movers are clearing her possessions out of their house.'

'What? Are you serious?' Ryan plonked himself back down in his favourite seat and pulled the curtain open a little staring at the RV. He reached for the whisky bottle on the table and poured himself a glass drinking it in large gulps as he let the curtain fall back into place and stared at his wife.

'Look, I'm sorry you're miserable,' Ryan said. 'I thought this was what you wanted to do. We could have done something else. I'd have done something else, whatever you wanted to do. I just want you to be happy.'

'I know,' Sarah said and smiled at him. Ryan frowned at her in confusion then shrugged and together they cleared the table and set the bed up. 'I'm just at a loose end without the kids. Not sure what to do instead.'

'How about we forget about cooking and eat out while we're away?' Ryan said. 'The hotel next door has a nice restaurant.'

'That sounds good,' Sarah said. 'Better than fiddling with the small knobs.' She grinned and relief swept through her when he grinned back.

'And,' he said giving her a quick kiss, 'they offer a weekly Spa membership so we could sit about and relax for a bit. Just the two of us. Not really doing anything at all.'

'Sounds perfect,' Sarah said.

Grief Knots

RJ Ashby

Rain fell like the tears of perdition drowning Nina's grief. She sank to her knees, as if in prayer, in the muddied yard. Her shirt stuck to her and her hair hung like bootlace weed. She was hoarse from her heartache and bewildered. She called out once more, *'Why did you not take me...'* but the shout ended in a whisper and she crumpled, beaten. A few feet away her two dogs copied her cries. Nina scrambled to their kennel and lay in the soft warm hay. The dogs licked her dry and curled their warmth into her and she slept.

Her farmhouse was a few miles from the village of Crawley, on the side of a hill, cowering into a wood and was crammed with memories from her childhood to her motherhood: from her pony on the cobbled yard to the promises and plans for Millie. *'If only she had lived...'*

Early on the twenty fourth of November, the radio blared and Nina dressed. She raked the fire, boiled the kettle, filled a bowl for each dog – all automatic – while she remembered those she had lost and her heart filled, warm against the chill. In her head she revised the things she could have said, she should have said. She organised the day ahead, while her mind saw the past, sometimes talking out loud – to her ghosts.

She crossed the yard and unlatched the kennel door and two whimpering dogs circled her, sniffed her and licked at her hands. They scampered at her heel, obedient. They loved her.

With the bowls licked clean they, all three, marched off through the wood, down the hill to the back road. Memories met them. Once Nina had skipped here, hair bouncing, with Millie on her back, galloping free and fast. Laughter hiccoughing in them both, in the constant shaft of imagined sunlight.

Nina turned off the road and took a track along the edge of the forest. She climbed an old, rusted fence and bent low, as stray branches pulled at her hair.

Millie had scuttled through here too. She had found a brown enamel teapot and a china plate: delicate china, with flowers and a crack. She picked the first snowdrops. They had climbed up to peer into a bird's nest. She whispered to the fledglings.

'Mum, come and find me!' she squealed as she ducked behind a tree. Nina could always see her. Sometimes it was just her hands as they gripped the trunk, or her skirt was sticking out as she peered round the other side. Nina would pretend she didn't know and then creep up and shout, 'Boo!' Giggles echoed round the memory. Nina's smile slipped.

One dog was lured away, chasing a scent. The other one dug into the banking. Nina, glazed in her dream, didn't notice the dog's ears lift. He barked. He ran further into the wood. And he barked again and again. Nina followed. Someone had woven green branches together in a shelter. It was a very good shelter. The dog crouched. There was fabric inside, a sleeping bag, a floor of leaves – and two eyes staring.

'Hello.' Nina's heart leapt.

The eyes stared back.

Nina squatted down. 'This is very nice. It's cosy. That's what it is.'

The eyes watched. Nina put her hand in her pocket. She held a crumbled shortbread finger towards the eyes. The blanket dropped and a child came out clutching a torn, ragged toy. She ate like a starved animal.

'I guess you like my shortbread.' Nina found another two pieces in her pocket and offered them to the little girl. She put her hand into her jacket pretending there were more. A little hand came forward. Nina held it very gently. 'What a warm hand. Why don't you come home with me?'

The little girl didn't understand.

'Come with me.' She drew her on. 'Biscuits.' Nina pretended she was eating. 'Come.' She shuffled out and the little girl followed. She was layered up like a winter robin, a mud encrusted robin. Hand in hand they walked together along the track, back onto the road and up the hill. All the way Nina talked, entertaining and encouraging while one dog raced forward and back with excitement. The other stuck close to his new friend.

'How could someone leave a child all alone in the woods? Definitely illegal, negligent,' Nina told the dogs. She knew all about illegal immigrants travelling under those enormous trucks. This was not the first time she had found strangers on the back road. It was only miles to the biggest haulage firm in the country.

The house welcomed with warmth. Nina opened up the stove. The child sat in front until she glowed. She held her hands up to the heat. Her ragged doll was by her side. She ate a bacon sandwich. Soon her eyes drooped and she curled up on the rug, with the dogs, and slept while Nina scuttled upstairs.

Millie's bedroom was cold and uninviting. It had been empty for too long. Nina turned the radiator up and shook freshness into it. She selected some soft toys to throw on the bed. She plugged the illuminated globe in and wound up the clockwork clown so he would play at the slightest touch. Millie had liked to share. She collected a screwdriver and an old bolt from a box in the larder. She fitted it roughly on the outside of the door. Then she carried the sleeping child to bed.

The dogs and the child slept as Nina baked. It was a long time since she had held a wooden spoon in her hand and beaten butter and sugar and eggs. The recipe was second nature to her. She filled thirteen pretty paper cases with a dollop of cake mix and fifteen minutes later she was taking them out of her oven. She smiled, satisfied, enjoying the imagined pleasure of the little girl. Outside, the afternoon was gloomy, hinting at darkness. Nina found the child awake, sitting on the stairs, watching through the bannister, with her doll.

'Well there you are. You ready to have a glass of milk and a cookie?' Nina helped her down. A dog stretched, walked over and nuzzled the visitor, and then returned to his sleep.

'Come. Sit at the table. Now what am I to call you?' She pointed to the dog, 'Jack. That is Jack. And that is Fly. Fly. Me – Nina.' Nina pointed to herself then she pointed to the girl. 'You. Who are you?' She repeated, pointing in turn to the dogs and herself. 'Jack, Fly, Nina...'

'Jolanta.' She spoke with an accent.

Nina clapped. 'Jolanta. That's beautiful, Jolanta, milk and cupcakes coming, just for you!' Nina offered a plate with yellow and pink iced cakes. Jolanta touched the pink, then she changed her mind and took a yellow one. She licked the icing on the yellow one and then reached for the pink one.

'Take one at a time, Jolanta. You can have the pink one later.' Nina sat with a mug of tea, and a wide smile.

When Jolanta had eaten, she got down from the table and put her coat on. She picked her doll from the floor and cuddled her, 'Lalla.' She pointed to the door and said something else Nina could not understand.

'No. It's too dark to go anywhere my little one.' Nina reached for the key and locked the back door. She slipped the key into her pocket. 'Tomorrow. We can sort that tomorrow. You should never have been left – cold, hungry and tired. That is neglect in this country. It's an offence. But you'll be alright now.' Jolanta backed away from her.

'Come.' Nina led Jolanta back upstairs into Millie's room. Jolanta picked up a doll that lay on the floor and sat her neatly in front of the toy box. One by one she picked up all the toys that were scattered around and set them in the row. Then she took Nina by the hand and said, 'Podziekowonia.' She led Nina to the backdoor again, and pointed.

Nina knelt down at her level, 'No, sorry Jolanta. No it is too dark. It's too cold. You stay here tonight.' She shook her head the whole time she was talking. Jolanta understood, but she sat with her coat on and her doll held tight. When Nina went through to the living room the child followed. Nina closed the curtains, put the television on and sat to watch. The child sat too. They watched cartoon after cartoon. Jolanta cuddled into the cushions with her doll.

Later they ate again. Jolanta helped feed the dogs then they took them out to the kennel. Nina was careful to fasten the catch while Jolanta held the torch. 'Chee moja matk.' Jolanta said and pointed down the track.

Nina ignored her and took her hand. They returned to the front room to watch more TV. Nina selected Polish as the language and played a DVD. Local cafes were staffed by Polish workers. Nina watched Jolanta laugh, caught in the story.

Later Nina lifted the sleeping child, dropping a kiss on her forehead. She slipped the child into bed and watched from the shadows as the child mumbled, a smile held on her face and she too went to bed. Sleep slipped over her just as it used to.

Nina rose early. She kept herself busy until she heard a movement upstairs.

'Breakfast? Are you coming down, Jolanta?' She called out. At the bedroom door she saw something was wrong. The child avoided looking at her but she pulled at the nightdress. It was wet. So was the bed. And the dogs were sitting by the door waiting for their walk.

Nina enjoyed reverting to the work of a mother, but the reality of her wrongdoing was clear. The little girl had to be her prisoner.

'I am so sorry.' Nina said. Jolanta stood inside the bedroom staring. Nina closed the door and slipped the bolt into place. There was silence from behind the closed door.

At the road Nina turned left, away from the wood, away from the shelter. Both Jake and Fly ran together, racing together. In the distance Nina saw a young woman, looking this way and that. The stranger waved. Nina stood with her back to her. She rehearsed what she might say. The stranger spoke first.

'Good morning. I'm looking for a little girl.' The accent was strong and she was out of breath. Her face was white and her hair uncombed. 'Have you seen her?'

'This is the middle of nowhere, how would a child be out here and on her own?'

'She is so little. I am worried?'

'Try the police. Any neglected child would be taken to them. Have you got a passport?'

The young woman looked distressed. She didn't understand.

Nina felt her fear. She turned for home. 'Come on dogs, home!' The dogs raced back to her, Jack stopping to sniff at the stranger while Fly disappeared into the wood.

'If I see anything I'll phone the police.' She called back.

It was hard not to be touched by the pain in the young woman's face, but a voice sounded in Nina's head, 'Negligent. Unfit. Illegal immigrants …'

Nina didn't look back.

Her days were full again. Jolanta began to speak English and Nina forgot she was a stranger, forgot she was not her own daughter. One very cold December night Jolanta was snuggled up in bed. She cried out, 'Lalla. Nina, want Lalla?'

Nina hated that doll. It was missing again.

Jack would have it. Nina slipped on her wellies and grabbed a torch. It was frosty but she didn't stop for her coat. The ground sparkled in the moonlight. She shivered.

Ten steps to cross the yard. She called out.

'Right boys. Have you got Lalla? Jack?' There was a rustling of straw from inside the kennel. 'Come on boys. I want it now.' She flicked the torch on to see, as she unfastened the latch. The dogs peered from their coiled sleep. There was a rustle behind and Nina fell forward into straw. Her torch hit the floor. A soundless, heavy blow hit her head and darkness was complete.

A pulse of blue light revolved round the farmyard. Nina was carried into the ambulance. A paramedic sat with her.

'A short trip to hospital, Nina. Don't worry,' he said.

The doctors and nurses hovered with concern, but Nina was vague. Words tumbled from her – the lost doll, a first child, a second child, the key. She ranted like a mad woman, and the nurses whispered. She was given a small room by the nurse's station. Sedatives induced calm while she was fed from a drip. One night rolled into another. She slipped in and out of her nightmare, where two children ran round her in circles, and Steve, her husband, laughed his head off from a departing car.

'Nina,' Steve touched her face. He leaned close. He hadn't shaved. His eyes were red. He kissed her.

Nina turned. Her eyes flicked opened. He saw a smile on her snow-white face. 'You're back. When did you get back?' She spoke slowly with a slur.

'Today, I just got here today.' He patted her hand.

Nina tried sit up, she leaned towards him, she whispered, 'I didn't mean to steal her.' A tear trickled from her eye and rolled down her cheek.

'You didn't steal anything. You're bereaved Nina. You're going to speak to a counsellor this time.'

'Yes, but the little girl. I didn't hurt her.'

'I understand – little girls need their own mothers and mothers need their own little girls. Why can't we have our own again? Don't worry. You're the patient and you *are* going to get better. I'm not going away this time. Let's try again – a new baby.'

Nina smiled. She held out her hand and Steve wrapped both of his hands, knotting hers tight inside.

Favourite Soup

Sue Cook

'Can I have a word?' Rose's teacher steered Kitty to her desk. 'It's about your daughter's homework.'

Mrs Thomas pushed Rose's diary toward Kitty. 'Look at the last few entries, please.'

Puzzled, Kitty read. Mostly she read about what they'd had for tea. 'Is it the spelling?' Kitty asked.

'It's not the spelling, Miss Hamilton.' Mrs Thomas pointed to the wall displays. 'We're doing healthy eating at the moment.'

Suddenly Rose's words took on new meaning. *Sossij and chips aggen and chocclat biscits. My friend Lucy gives me her grapes. I like grapes.*

Kitty felt her cheeks redden. 'I got a BOGOF offer on the sausages. And microwave chips are so easy. It's not like they're deep fried or anything.'

Mrs Thomas looked over the top of her reading glasses and the lecture began.

On the walk home Rose held Kitty's hand tight.

'Mrs Thomas says if we don't eat 5-a-day then we get sick. Granny got sick and she died.'

Kitty glanced down and saw two big, trusting brown eyes staring back at her. Suddenly she felt pressure mounting in her chest, just like her mother must have done. 'Yes but granny was...' She'd been about to say 'old'. But she hadn't been. She was 57. 'Granny was unlucky.'

Unlucky was the word the doctor had used. 'Most people survive heart attacks these days.' But didn't doctors also say that prevention was better than cure?

Rose's hand gripped tighter. 'You're not going to be unlucky, are you, Mummy?'

Kitty forced a smile. 'We make our own luck in life, Rose.' And it started with adding peas to tonight's portion of 'sossij and chips'. She was fairly sure there was a bag buried in the back of the icebox even if she couldn't quite remember how long ago she'd bought it.

The following morning, Kitty went straight from school to the local supermarket. But the more she looked at the fresh produce, the more things seemed impossible. Everything was in huge bags. How on earth would she and Rose get through a kilo of carrots? That would last a horse a month!

She asked an assistant if she could buy one carrot.

The assistant looked at her as though she'd asked for a ticket to the moon. 'One bag, you mean?'

Kitty sighed. When she was little her mum used to go to the greengrocer, but the supermarket had put all those out of business. The only thing left was the market in town, which meant getting the bus and that was another expense she would struggle to afford. But Kitty knew she had to at least try — it was Rose's future after all.

She checked her purse while standing at the bus stop. There was only a tenner in it for the rest of the week. As the bus pulled up and the doors swished open Kitty made a decision.

'Sorry,' Kitty waved her purse at the driver. 'No change.' And she turned and started the mile walk to the town centre.

The man running the fruit and veg stall had a lovely smile. Open, honest, inviting.

'What will it be?' he asked.

Kitty ran her eyes over all sorts of things she'd never seen before. Jerusalem artichokes, papaya and, was that a purple cabbage? At least they weren't all in huge bags.

'Vegetables?' she said, wrinkling her nose with uncertainty.

The stall holder grinned. 'You've come to the right place.'

Encouraged, Kitty explained her new healthy eating streak, strict budget and total inability to cook.

The man nodded and suggested salad. He picked up what he later explained was an iceberg lettuce and bounced it off his biceps. 'No cooking involved. And I can quarter it for you if a whole one is too much.' He showed Kitty different types of 'salad leaves' and tore small bits off for her to try. Who'd have thought they'd taste so different?

Soon Kitty had peppers, onions, tomatoes and radish in her bag too and still plenty of change from the tenner.

'Now, what are you going to have with it?' he asked.

Good question.

'Sausage?' She still had lots of those. Eventually they plumped for tuna with boiled new potatoes, which he threw in for free.

'You don't get this service at the supermarket,' Kitty said as she dropped her change into her purse.

He smiled. 'I hope that means you'll be back?'

It did. Two days later Kitty returned for her next lesson. And again a few days after that. Soon she was one of the fruit and veg man's best customers. Kitty enjoyed her new diet as well as all the walking. She lost weight and felt an unexpected new lust for life. She particularly felt smug every time she thought of Mrs Thomas. But a few weeks later the thin-lipped teacher called her in again.

'It's about Rose's homework–'

'But we're eating really healthily now,' Kitty wailed.

Mrs Thomas pushed the book towards her. 'It's your daughter's moral welfare I have in mind, Miss Hamilton. I think you'd better read it.'

Kitty looked down and couldn't help smile: *'For tea we had rizoto with peas and sweat corn. Uncle Andy made it. He allways makes tea now. My favorit is favorit soup. It is orinj with green bits in called parssly.'*

'Andy runs the fruit and veg stall,' Kitty explained. 'He's been very helpful.'

Mrs Thomas peered over the top of her glasses, the word 'helpful?' writ large in raised eyebrows.

'He's teaching me to cook. It's not every day,' Kitty continued, encouraged by the warm, fuzzy feeling she got every time she thought of her fruit and veg man. He hadn't stayed over, yet. But life was looking healthier in all sorts of ways.

My Summer Holiday

Elves

When your mum and dad take you to the seaside for the day it's supposed to be fun — isn't it? Yeah, right!

It all went wrong just after twelve. Standing in the queue, waiting my turn, salivating as I watched the man working behind the counter, then moving forward as the person in front was served, until, at last, it was my turn!

'That'll be three and sixpence please.'

I handed a half crown and a shiny new shilling over the counter and gratefully accepted the warm paper package in return – not yesterday's newspaper as in my local chippy, but clean, white paper, bought in specially to give a much more upmarket feel to the fish and chips. I carried them outside, to where a wide grass verge lay between the street and the top of the cliff, and began to saunter in the direction of the river mouth, about fifty yards away. There was that familiar crinkling sound as I slowly and carefully unwrapped the paper and came to the greaseproof layer within. The fish was covered in a golden, crispy batter and the chips were deliciously firm, just like mum made them at home, and not at all like the soggy ones normally associated with a chippy. These were perfect. I brought the packet closer to my face and enjoyed the strong aroma of melted lard that carried so many happy and pleasurable associations. I breathed it in, soaked it up, then, unable to resist a moment longer, I picked up the first of those wonderful chips and placed it carefully on my tongue. It felt as if it would melt, but in fact it was exactly like a Rowntree's fruit pastille. You know what I mean — I couldn't resist chewing it. As my jaw worked, my fingers had already extracted a second chip from the package and were raising it to my lips where I could savour the salty tang: there is nothing quite like the taste of salt on freshly cooked chips. Only after enjoying this second experience of the fryer's art did I turn my attention to the fish. The batter was as crispy as it looked, and I pulled off a piece — this was the part of fish and chips they said would make you fat; well, that and the chips of course — and revealed the white flesh within, not the slightly wet feel of a large flake of cod, but the drier and smaller flakes and much superior taste — I thought — of a piece of fresh haddock, and put it on the front of my tongue. The sensation was exquisite. The savoury taste of the fried egg, flour and milk, coupled with more salt and the sharp tang of acetic acid.

It was a perfect day. I was at the seaside. Mum and dad were still at the caravan, leaving me free to wander. High above my head the sun shone in a light blue sky, unsullied by clouds. It was so warm, the best day of the year so far. The occasional car drove past me along the street, turning the corner where I now stood, looking down at the river mouth, its noisy fumes for a moment driving out for a moment that taste and feel of salt air, the aroma of my lunch and the sound of the wavelets breaking on the white sands of the beach. Then the car would be gone and I could resume my reverie.

There was a breakwater, doubtless built to protect the small fishing boats from the storms that presumably lashed the area in the winter, about as far from the present reality as it was possible to get. Just a short way from that was the old bridge, bypassed now but still used by those vehicles that needed to be on the seafront, carrying people and goods from one side of the river to the other.

It was there that I paused to watch the river traffic pass by: a couple of fishing boats, one returning and one leaving, a speedboat playing alone on the calm river water, even a small passenger ferry, carrying tourists along the coast and dropping in on the larger settlements like this one where they could buy model lighthouses for their bathrooms, or sailing ships in full sail, perhaps confined in a bottle, or, for the less adventurous, a tea towel with a picture of the allegedly picturesque old bridge printed on one side together with this — or next — year's calendar.

It all seemed pretty futile to me, though I smiled because I knew that mum and dad shared the same sentiments as these tourists. Then I placed another small piece of fish into my mouth, savouring it to the momentary exclusion of all my other faculties.

It was just a pity that I did that, since that was the moment when it happened, and it came out of the blue.

I didn't hear the loud screech nor did I see the dark shadow that rapidly grew larger as if it were my very own black cloud. There was no silver lining apparent either, just a pair of webbed feet, a sharp beak and a sharp blow on my head that sent my glasses flying at much the same speed as the remains of my fish flew off. But while my glasses hit the ground, my fish was already gaining height. A moment of terror and shock came and passed. Anger burned in its place.

It was just a pity that in that moment of madness I reached down for the nearest pebble I could find and hurled it upwards, towards the thieving gull that was already well beyond my range and was being mobbed by its fellows, all of whom wanted to share the spoils of his theft. The pebble missed the mark of course, leaving me with no further possible course of action other than to fume in impotent rage; to locate and retrieve my spectacles in the hope that they may have survived their flight and fall; and to gaze at the small pile of formerly lovely chips now lying on the ground at my feet, where the next swarm of carrion would doubtless soon find them.

It is a rule of physics that when an object — say a pebble — is hurled aloft, it will lose momentum owing to the drag of the air and will simultaneously feel the pull of gravity. The path of its trajectory is called a parabola. The pebble I had thrown followed such a parabolic course. I had thrown it upwards, towards the robber bird, but while I shifted my attention onto my glasses and my chips, it came, with an awful inevitability, back to earth. Well, that was what would have happened had it followed its path, and there would have been no harm done.

It was just a pity that an intervention prevented the logical end of the pebble's natural path. The fact is that it struck a cyclist who just happened to be crossing the old bridge at the time. At first, I was completely unaware of this. Too engrossed in my own more immediate affairs, I failed to hear the shout of sudden pain; or the sound of cyclist and car in a collision situation, the cycle and cyclist coming out of it by far the worse; or the squeal of brakes and the scream of agonised tyres as a number 14 bus, crossing the bridge from my side to the other, swerved to avoid the resulting carnage. I only became aware that something was wrong when the sound of wood, splintering in the face of an irresistible blow from a heavy moving object, the same number 14 bus, came to my ears. But it was the sound of the people nearby, screaming, that alerted me to the full scale of what had just happened. My glasses were seemingly none the worse for their little mishap. Now I hurriedly replaced them to my face and turned around to see what all the shouting portended.

It was just a pity that gravity continued to impose itself upon the actors on the bridge. A second car had appeared on the scene, seen what had happened — too late — and failed to apply the brakes in time. This vehicle only stopped after connecting with the rear of the bus, causing the bus to lose its tussle with the forces of nature and to plunge towards the river. Not a belly flop either. It went straight down. Nose first. A beautifully executed dive.

It was just a pity that the bus passengers had failed to leave the vehicle in time and were still inside when it performed its final and fatal manoeuvre. It was just a pity too, that the motor boat that had been playing alone on the river just happened to be nearing the spot, and was close enough to feel the full force of the tsunami unleashed by the dive of the number 14 bus. There were more screams, and a rapid, and unplanned, change of course.

The passenger ferry was really quite a small craft, driven by two paddles, one at each side. Colourfully painted in red, white and blue, its funnel reflected those same colours, and with bunting that ran from stem to stern by way of the two masts. I'm sure I don't need to record the colour of the bunting.

It was just a pity — no one's fault of course — that the ferry was passing under the bridge at the same time as the motor boat began its chaotic final voyage, it's engine screaming pitifully as it rode that fatal wave on its way to meet its Waterloo. It struck the ferry in just exactly the wrong place, tearing into the port side paddle with a ferocity one wouldn't have expected from such a tiny craft. The noise from its engine was suddenly and horribly drowned out in the resulting explosion, sending showers of burning splinters skyward and onto the bridge and any person who had the misfortune to be crossing it at the time. Reduced to a single paddle, and with water doubtless pouring into the gaping hole amidships, the passenger ferry's other paddle forced the boat to execute a very neat turn to port.

It was just a pity — just one of those things I suppose — that the passenger ferry was so close to the bank of the river. If it had been in mid-stream it might have managed to turn a full circle. But it had been approaching the shore in order to tie up at the breakwater and disgorge its passengers into the town. That closeness prevented a full turn. The ferry simply ran out of space and collided, head on, with the nearest object.

It was just a pity that the nearest object happened to be the fuel tender, engaged in its happy task of unloading spirit into the onshore tanks. One can imagine what happened. The resulting explosion destroyed the fuel tender, and the onshore tanks, and the passenger ferry, and the once picturesque bridge and everyone on it. It blew out windows on both sides of the river. It even knocked me off my feet.

As I lay there, not quite stunned, I reflected on how the blue of the sky and the warmth of the sun's rays had been replaced by a dirty black cloud, and definitely devoid of a silver lining, with flashes of flame evident, streaming upwards; and on how the sound of gulls squawking, people talking to each other as they promenaded along the front, and even the band playing some way off in the distance, had now all disappeared. Then came the next ear-shattering crash as a second fuel tank disintegrated and sent its constituent parts aloft. That lovely salty air had vanished completely, replaced by the acrid taste of smoke and the odour of burning diesel fuel.

The magistrate said that it was just a pity that I'd thrown the pebble at that gull and reflected that the probability of hitting the bird had always been regrettably small. There had been nearly two hundred people killed and several million pounds worth of damage that would take years to put right. Fining me ten shillings and sixpence — three times the price of my fish and chips — he recommended that in future, if I paid a small surcharge, I would buy the privilege of eating my lunch indoors, where I would be safe from the predation of marauding gulls.

Tyler Loves Parathas

Palo Stickland

We arrive in the afternoon, hug and exchange travel anecdotes. The motorway was blocked, the train was late or so busy, but isn't it great to be here, to meet up again after a year? I take a minute to look at the imposing facade of the beautiful town house we have rented for a week. It is on a sloping hill, a row of tall, red sandstone homes on four levels: a basement, two floors with a converted attic. I walk up the eight wide steps, lifting, and resting, my wheeled case on each of them. It must have been a family house, the pictures on the walls, some ornaments and the furniture tell us how they spent their days. I am speechless as I look around the living room. The coverings on the walls and sofas are in the colours of the savannah, pale green, light brown, sienna. Shades of Africa.

The paintings on the walls are beautiful. Lions lie leisurely on convenient flat rocks. The people are dusky, broad-featured, silent as they gaze into these rooms with a hot weather peacefulness. Children have grown up in this house. I've spotted the tiny picture, in the downstairs toilet, that gives away so much; two blond children, a brother and sister, their eyes sparkling as around their necks a python circles in sensuous motion. They hold its coils without fear while smiling at the camera. I tell myself, these people had a happy life in Africa, and money, to buy this house. We were not so lucky. Am I envious? Or bitter?

We now people these rooms with our own characters; with ghostly nannies, golden gods, Crimean nurses, special teddy bears and evil spiders. Our people tell of near death experience, of love and longing, true and imagined. We write at the dining room table as well as the living room. Deep in thought and creativity, we encourage and support each other.

The morning following our arrival, I am in charge of preparing lunch for seven, which does not include Jane's young black Labrador, Tyler, who is keeping me company in the kitchen, watching my every move. Jane has told me that he ate the last chapatti from the previous evening's dinner, which I had left on the worktop wrapped in a tea towel. He was too quick for her, much enjoyed the illicit snack, giving her a look that said, *you can't take it now, I've eaten it and it was good.*

I was apologetic. 'Oh, Jane, I forgot about him, leaving food on the worktop near the door was silly. You can tell I've never owned a dog.'

Now, Tyler sits by my side, wide eyed with longing and much patience for the parathas he hopes I'll let him eat. I love how his eyes follow my every move; how he seems to listen to my words.

'I don't think parathas are good for you, Tyler. You're not a vegetarian.' I lean over and whisper to him as he stretches his neck towards me. 'But I have known dogs who would eat anything. When I'm finished perhaps there will be one for you.'

I chat to him as I prepare the parathas.

'That's the potatoes on to boil over there, and on this worktop, I'm preparing the dough. I've been doing this since I was twelve, I could do it with my eyes closed. Isn't this a big house, Tyler? The kitchen doesn't remind me of

Africa, but all the other rooms do. I'm from Africa too, I don't talk about it. But since you're such a good listener. I'll tell you. Some people call it being twice-migrated. First from India, then from Africa. My father was brought up in Uganda, my mother in India. She took me back to see her parents when I was a toddler. I think that's why I love parathas, Tyler. They're probably the first food I ate, mashed up with lots of butter. Let me check the potatoes.'

I leave the dough, which is now waiting to be kneaded, and move across to the cooker. The potatoes are ready, I pour the water out of them, leaving them to cool. Tyler, who has followed my floured hands towards the cooker now pads over to the worktop with me, keeping his eyes on my hands unless I look at him, then he gives me an intent gaze, as if my every word was important to him.

'You remind me of how I must have followed my mother around her cooking area when she cooked parathas for me. She cooked on a low fire seated on a stool with her flour, her dough, the potatoes all around while I would have sat outside of that circle with my mouth watering, waiting for her. She would have let the paratha-mash cool before giving it to me. Or perhaps my grandmother fed me. That's the dough kneaded. Now, to take the peel off the potatoes. Where was I? My father had lived in Uganda all his life, my grandfather worked for a British company, which was very fortunate for us, when Idi Amin gave all the Indians three months to leave Uganda. My father applied for permission to settle in England.'

I hear footsteps coming down the corridor. It's Jane. 'Are you okay? Is Tyler being a nuisance? I'll take him away, if you like.'

'No, Tyler is fine. In fact, he's very good company. How is the writing?'

'We're still working on the story that you managed to finish last night. You're not missing anything. Are you sure you don't need help?'

'No, I'm about to spice up the potatoes, then it's putting the parathas together.'

'Right, see you later. Smells great in here.'

I have spread the cumin seeds on the griddle to toast and shaken them on to the worktop to press under the rolling pin. They give off a delicious aroma. In they go with the spices on to the mashed potatoes. Then, a good mix before dividing into fifteen balls, one for each paratha.

'Yes, I remember the sense of fear that there was around that time. I was nine years old, Tyler. My mother still talks of the 'blacks', she still uses that word, who had been friendly servants but became so fearsome when they knew we had been ordered to leave. She said they were all eyeing up our possessions. It's amazing what humans will collect in a home, Tyler. Let's get some flour to make the chapattis. Two tiny ones for each paratha. Just like in this house. So much stuff. Did you see when I opened the tall wall cupboard in the dining room? It's full to the top with board games. And you'll have spotted all the toys in the basement. Jane has put them high up because you've got your own. I was allowed one doll when we left Uganda, even she was lost in the busy airport: I cried during the whole flight to London. What's more, Tyler, my mother had sewn gold chains and bangles into the hem and bodice of my dress, as she had done with all the family. It was the only way to take some of our wealth with us. Are you watching? I'm placing a round of potato in the middle of the chapatti, moistening the edge with water on my fingers and placing the other tiny chapatti on top. Then I'm rolling it out to about twenty centimetres, a bit bigger than my hand, then placing it on the griddle. There's a rule for cooking chapattis and it works for parathas too. A little heat, then turn, about twice as long on the second side, then turn and oil and press down. Then oil the other side until both are cooked. I'm going to leave this one to cool.'

Tyler's nose is twitching at the sight of the first cooked paratha. He's so good, sits patiently, looking and listening.

'Do you remember the homeless man we met yesterday on our walk to the town, Tyler? You liked his dog, didn't you? When we came from Uganda we had nothing. Our relatives who lived in England took us in. We worked hard to catch up. I have a bad feeling about homeless people, part of me says why don't they try harder, we did? It's a kind of prejudice, just like my mother's attitude towards Africans, I suppose. Perhaps, I should try harder. I'm always embarrassed by street beggars, even when I'm in India. Nearly done now, Tyler. A pile of parathas! A good morning's work. We've got natural yogurt with lime pickle to eat them with. And we're ready for lunch.'

I reach for the cooled paratha, Tyler follows as I peer down the corridor, his head towards my hand. 'Okay, let's go into the back garden.' I whisper and lead the way out of the back door.

I step out, Tyler's gaze is on my hand that holds the paratha. He's right beside me.

'You have earned this, Tyler. Having to wait, not to mention my making you listen to my memories.' His nose twitches as I hold the paratha lower for him to take and it's while he's eating that I hear the steps over the gate at the end of the garden. It is only a low wall, I can see the homeless man leading his dog to the park bench across the road.

'Oh. I was talking about him, Tyler. Aren't we lucky to have parathas to eat?' I look down at Tyler who is finishing his treat. That's when I decide to try harder.

I take six parathas out to the park bench.

'I've been cooking,' I say to the homeless man. 'Parathas. They're like potato scones, only spicy, but not too much. Would you like one?'

'Yes, thanks.'

I put out my hand, 'I'm Naina.'

'Michael.'

We shake hands.

'Your dog will like them, too. This is Tyler, and he loves parathas.'

Darkness

Julia Chalkley

Last night, Josh had hit Emma in the face. Twice.

This morning, she'd woken groggy and with a throbbing dull pain in her cheek and nose. Not broken, but probably bruised. As she lay there gathering alertness, Josh began to break out of his sleep. And she remembered.

No point in asking him whether she had a bruise on her face. Best not to tell him at all that he thrashed around and hit out in his sleep, grunted and wailed, that she didn't want to sleep with him.

Josh sat up and shouted 'What's the time?' He looked wildly at Emma and then at his clock.

'It's ten past eight,' Emma said.

Josh was silent.

'Breakfast in bed?' Emma asked.

'No.' Josh shut his eyes. 'I'll only spill it on the duvet.'

They lay there for a few minutes. Emma tried to find something to say that wouldn't set him off.

'I dreamed last night that I couldn't see anything,' Josh said. He put his hands over his eyes, then dropped them onto his stomach. 'Then my dad came along. I was in my bedroom back home, I mean, with my parents – and he switched the light on and told me not to make such a fuss, everything was fine.'

He sat up. 'It's not, though. I really thought, when I woke up, that – '

Emma swung her legs out of the tangle of duvet and her feet hit the floor with a thud. 'I'll make breakfast,' she said. 'Come down when you're ready.'

As she set out the bowls, she heard Josh coming downstairs one heavy step at a time. No point in repeating that he could still see out of one eye. The blind eye now ruled his life.

It had been easier to deal with the initial panic, when he'd woken to the alarm one weekday morning and opened his eyes on blindness. His puzzlement first, then growing panic barely controlled as he stumbled to the bathroom mirror and tried to peer into the right eye with his still-functioning left eye, seeing nothing obvious to block his sight. He'd rushed back into the bedroom, misjudged the position of the bed and had run into it with a force that tore skin off his shin. As he collapsed onto the bed, Josh had screamed at her that he was blind, blind, ring the doctor. By the time she reached the phone, he was crying.

Six weeks later, the medical profession had swept over them like a giant wave of surf, all noise and tests, and had left Josh and Emma beached in a suddenly quiet house with a collection of leaflets about adjusting to sight impairment. He picked them up by their edges and held them at arm's length like bags of dog turds before dropping them on the floor. Emma read them when Josh wasn't around. She had learned by now that she couldn't discuss their contents with him.

The phone rang. Emma looked at Josh, suddenly nervous. He had to pick up the phone. She couldn't keep lying to his manager. The first time, she'd been fluent. 'He's asleep right now, the tests – exhausted him. I'll ask him to call you back.' The second time, she knew that Jacquie knew she was fibbing. They'd ended the call politely and formally. Jacquie had told Emma she'd call Josh in three days' time. Emma understood what Jacquie carefully hadn't said. Josh had to talk, or Jacquie would start formal proceedings regarding his continued employment.

'Josh,' Emma said, tentatively.

Josh stood up, slowly. The phone rang on. Seven rings. Eight. He walked slowly to the hallway. Emma moved quietly to the doorway of the kitchen to watch him. Nine rings. Ten. Just as he put his hand on the handset, the ringing stopped. He lifted his hand, and Emma could see the shape of his palm written in sweat on the handset.

'You'll have to answer her, love,' Emma said.

Josh pulled the phone out of its cradle and threw it. It hit the jackets hung on the wall and made no sound at all. 'WHY?'

Emma retreated to the cooker and gripped the rail on the oven door.

'WHY?' Josh yelled at her. 'What can I say? I'm blind in one eye. The other eye might go blind soon. I can come back to work as soon as she likes, but I won't be able to see what's on the computer. Won't be able to input numbers, can't read new accountancy standards, can't add up – which is a fairly important skill for an accountant, wouldn't you say?'

Emma clamped her jaw shut. Yesterday she had pointed out that he could still see out of his left eye. Today she knew better. She'd let him scream until he cried, then they'd both pretend it hadn't happened.

Josh sat down on the chair by the phone. 'My left eye just went dark,' he said. 'Oh God. This is it.'

Emma turned and started to walk slowly back along the hallway. 'Stay calm,' she said. 'Yelling won't help.'

'Stay calm?' Josh shouted. 'Easy for you…' He put his hands over his face and whimpered 'Oh God…'

Emma turned away. Whatever she said wouldn't help. She wished suddenly that he would go blind completely, right now, so she could stick her tongue out at him without him knowing.

Josh came to eat his breakfast, and reported that the sight had come back to his left eye 'for now.' Emma refused to respond. They ate in silence. Josh shoved his empty bowl away, stood up and left the room. Two minutes later, Emma heard their bedroom door slam.

After thirty minutes, Emma went upstairs with a cup of tea for him and a determination to say nothing inflammatory – to say nothing at all, for safety's sake. It was a relief to see him snoring away in a tangle of bed sheets, even though he hadn't bothered to take his shoes off before rolling up in the duvet. She crept away, shutting the door quietly behind her.

For several minutes she sat holding her tea in both hands, staring at the phone. Then she put her mug down, took the phone into the sitting room and dialled the number Josh was too scared to call.

Josh woke five hours later. Emma heard his footsteps thumping slowly down the stairs. Right on time. She checked the clock – five minutes to go – and went on dicing the onions piled on the chopping board in front of her. Almost there.

Josh slumped down in the chair in the kitchen. He wouldn't look at Emma. She wouldn't say anything to him. She diced steadily, threw a piece of onion into the pan and smiled as she heard it sizzle. She swept the rest of the onions into the pan and stirred with a flourish.

The phone rang.

Emma put the pan off the heat and went quickly down the hall. By the time Josh said 'Leave it,' she'd swept up the phone.

'Emma Harkinson – oh, Jacquie, hi! How are you? Yes, he's here, I'll call him.'

She brought the handset down to the kitchen and thrust it at Josh. 'It's Jacquie,' she said. 'She wants you.'

Josh wouldn't take the phone. He looked up at Emma, furious, scared, uncertain. Emma jammed the phone against his ear and glared back at him. 'She wants you,' she repeated.

Josh took the phone. 'Jacquie, hello.' He listened. 'Who? No, I haven't heard of him. Did he? Has he! Well, look, I might not be able to… One eye, yes. They've told me the other eye might go blind as well, so… Is that right? Well, sure, if he has the time – yes, I'll wait.'

Emma put the pan back on the heat and stirred the onions, looking back to the jug of stock. Ready, all ready. There was a short pause.

'Yes, Josh Harkinson. Hello there. Jacquie tells me you've had a similar experience to me.' Josh was standing now, walking around the kitchen as if he couldn't keep still. 'Really! God, that's rough. Yes, it is a shock.'

Then he was silent for a long time, listening to the tinny voice at the other end of the line. The soup was almost done before he said, 'Thank you. I will. Please do. You must come over to us. It would be good to talk to you. Bring your wife. Sorry, yes, partner. He'd be welcome. She, yes, she'd be welcome. Emma would love the chance to talk this over with her. It's been hard on us both.' Josh wiped his eyes, and added, 'Is Jacquie still there? Oh, sure. Please tell her I'll be in tomorrow at nine if she'd like to discuss this. Thank you. Bye.'

He hit the disconnect button and put the handset down on the worktop. Without looking up, he said, 'Jacquie had someone from the Warwickshire branch on the line. Did you hear that?'

'I got the gist of it,' Emma said. She tasted the soup. Not bad. A bit more pepper. 'He's had the same problem as you?'

'Both eyes,' Josh said. He looked up. 'Both eyes, blind within the space of a month. They got him this software, speaks to you as you type, and sent him on a course to sharpen up his touch-typing skills. He missed two weeks at work and some people don't even notice he can't see them.'

Josh pulled out his handkerchief, wiped his face. 'Jacquie doesn't think there's a problem. She wants me back.' His voice cracked. 'I'm going in tomorrow to talk it over.'

'Brilliant,' Emma said. 'See?' This time Josh didn't shout at her for saying it. 'They want you. You're a good accountant. They'll do anything to get you back.'

'I thought she was going to fire me,' Josh said.

'You should have just talked to her,' Emma replied, with an edge to her voice. Steady, girl.

'You will drive me in tomorrow, won't you, love? I mean, I could call a cab, but...'

Emma thought of the few days she had left before she had to go back to school, and the pile of marking she hadn't had a chance to tackle yet. 'Sure,' she said, keeping her voice casual. 'Lunch is ready.'

'Onion soup. Oh, Em, that smells wonderful.' He closed his eyes and breathed in deep.

'You haven't lost everything, Josh,' Emma said. She put the bowl in front of him. 'Take yours in. No, *you* take yours in. You can see well enough. Spoons and bread are on the table. Now go.'

'Bossy,' Josh said. 'My brilliant, bossy wife. I'd be lost without you.'

'Scoot,' Emma said, smiling.

After Josh had gone, her smile disappeared. Jacquie had stuck to their agreement. She hadn't told Josh that Emma had called her to bargain for his job. This was her future. Lie after lie, building over the years. Married to a man who collapsed in the face of a setback and waited for someone to rescue him.

She poured soup into her bowl, then stopped and put her hands down on the counter and squeezed them into fists. The bowl was part of the Doulton crockery set that she had put on her wedding list. This time last year, she was counting down the days to her wedding, trying to organise everything with Josh giving the occasional order about which of his nieces must join the bridesmaids' crew. This year she was fighting to stop herself from smashing the crockery piece by piece, walking out and running down the street until she found a solicitor's office.

'Emma?' Josh called from the dining room.

Emma breathed in deep and held it. She couldn't divorce him, not right now. Maybe not ever. The stupid thing was, everyone would think it was the sickness and health vow she was breaking, and it wasn't. A blind husband, she could cope with that. A different husband, no. She'd agreed to marry Joshua Charles Harkinson, a forthright, commanding and positive young accountant. Not this whining little bully.

'Emma!' Josh roared. 'Are you joining me for lunch or not?'

Emma picked up her bowl of soup, put her chin up defiantly and went to join her husband.

The Cleaning Programme

RJ Ashby

Mr Simon Brown, now retired, sat hunched in his old parka on a cold park bench at 8:30 am, as his family finished their breakfast in their comfortably warm town house. Simon had slept in, and rather than face his daughter-in-law, he had headed into the park. His daughter-in-law had taken him in after his wife had died. Her gesture seemed generous and Simon had tried to get things right.

He kept trying. Like the morning when the twins had got up so very early. He saved the day. Grandfather's Special Cinnamon Toast was a winner. He followed HER rules and got the kids involved, beating the butter, mixing in sugar and dusting cinnamon on top. The cinnamon went up their noses, they were so good at the dusting. He carefully cut out bread shaped letters, T for Tom and D for Denny. They ate every last scrap.

That was just before the robot arrived. The box had lain in the hall. He had studied the label: deluxe model, multi-skirted, six armed cleaning robot, programmable, with automatic timing. *Cleans while you play.*

It was a Dalek, with a skirt that could widen and narrow as required. The six arms rotated, at every angle, to lift, dust or polish. It could fill the dishwasher in seconds. Under that skirt it hid sponges and pipes. It could wash. It could suck. The suction fired everything to a tank in the garage.

It was phenomenal.

The rule was he had to eat breakfast at 8 am. The cleaning programme started when SHE left for work. Once, when he overslept, he came down in his night shirt. SHE didn't like that.

One day he missed his breakfast deadline and, when the family had gone, he crawled on his knees into the kitchen, below the robot's radar. His mission failed. He gawked as the robot's skirt raised and sucked in the socks and shoes that he had placed by the door. They were soon to be followed by his toast and jam. The robot removed his freshly spread feast which fell from the plate, as it was whisked from the table to the dishwasher.

One day he had tried resetting it, but it refused an automatic restart and rescheduled everything – for later. Then the embarrassing incident of the rubber chicken that flew up its pipe and filled with air like a balloon, blocking the flow. He had taken the robot apart that day, but the engineer had to be called out. Simon should have owned up. He knew that SHE knew it had been him.

Now, back from the park, he watched from the back door as the creature cleared everything from the table and filled the dishwasher, while the suction from its skirt lifted every speck of sand from the floor. Then it began the steam clean and more suction.

He decided to eat in the garden. He dashed in for a bowl, then for milk, then cereal, but the step was cold to sit on. The robot moved on to the hall. Simon padded over the warm damp kitchen floor in his socks. He threw his parka onto the hall seat and climbed the stairs.

The high pitched thrum, as the robot got stuck into something big, alerted him and, from the landing, he saw the last corner of his beloved parka sucked from view with a gut wrenching rip and a burp from the machine.

That was when he decided – it was time to move out.

Walking Wounded

RJ Ashby

Jen stopped outside the exclusive hotel. Was she ready? Her regret was growing. Why did she think she could walk from Scotland through the Cheviots into England? She felt sick at the thought of all the miles that lay between her and the end of the week. If only she had a friend to share the adventure. The doubts that usually overwhelmed her, surfaced. She felt her cool begin to slip. A shiver ran through her. It was too late for that. She set her shoulders back, lifted her chin and marched in, trying to look as if she did this every day. It was time to heal some wounds.

'We don't have a booking under that name. You did say Mrs Croft?' If Jen was honest she had expected a problem.

'Yes, Jen Croft – Jennifer…' her voice quavered. She frowned. 'It… it is the 16th?'

'No sorry, there's nothing.' The girl ran her finger back down the list. 'I have a Jennifer – Jennifer Moore, *Miss* Jennifer Moore.'

Jen's face flushed crimson. 'I am *so* sorry, that is me. You see I… my maiden name… ehm divorce . Trust me to be dumb. 'She was embarrassed at herself.

'You must be part of the walking group. Melody, Melody Sloane.'

'Yes, that's right. I am so sorry.' A tight smile emerged and she let her bag fall to the floor. 'I thought I'd come on the wrong day. What a relief. I usually get things wrong…'

'You're the first. You're sharing, is that right? You're with a Geraldine Miller. Room 23. Here's your key-card. I just need you to sign in. Here please.'

Jen leaned forward to write. Her handbag dropped from her shoulder and the pen juddered across the pristine page. She apologised again.

'Dinner is at 7:30. The dining room is just there.' She pointed. 'You are on the second floor. I'll ring for the bell boy.'

'I'll find it. I can see the stairs. Twenty-three you said. Thanks.' Jen caught the strap from her handbag placing it back onto her shoulder, clutched her neon jacket to her side and lifted her bag. She struggled up the staircase, clumsy with her bags. The corridor had a sweet scent – flowers. A breeze drifted through the open window bringing quiet conversation from unseen guests.

She struggled with the door, her bags and her jacket. Somehow she bunched everything in. She scrutinized the room but quietly reprimanded herself, 'Why did I say I would share. I bet *Geraldine's* a pain.'

She found the single bed discretely round the corner. That suited her. She tested the bounce, then lay for a moment. She pulled her magazine from her handbag. It had a cover picture that matched the cool charm of her room: style and colour; and a model reclined. Scent rose from the pages. She scanned a few pages before she was distracted by the silence. Her eye settled on her well used suitcase. She slid it behind the bed and folded her garish jacket into a drawer, aware of her unsophisticated origins. She flicked through television stations then found a radio station before she returned to her magazine.

Time passed but no one else arrived so she soaked in the bath and dressed, sticky in the steam. She was not going to dress in front of a stranger. Bare feet felt good on the thick carpet but she still squeezed into her shoes. If only she had... high black heels, and long, languid legs, flashing a taut thigh from a full length split in her skirt... the magazine lay open to show exactly that and the photo-shopped glamour challenged her comfort. She stood in front of the mirror, white blouse, cream skirt, American tan tights. She tried the shirt tucked in. It was better loose.

At 7:30 she sidled down the grand staircase eyeing the rich oak, the mirrors and the paintings. At the door of the dining room she hesitated. No Melody! She froze.

'Madam, your table,' a waiter urged her in.

'Oh. No. My friends... I...'

A shrill voice from the room opposite caught her attention, 'Jenny, Jenny we're in the bar. Come!' Melody stood among a group of women who raised their champagne glasses and beckoned.

'Lovely to see you. This is Jen, she's going to be the sensible one. I can tell. No time for introductions we need to go through. Come on girls.' She leaned towards Jen, kissed the air and offered one arm in embrace as she sailed forth, to the dining room. Jen took the offered glass and followed.

Their table was set for six. The group divided left and right and took up seats in order of arrival. Jen sat. The seat to her right was empty. On her left was a chubby woman, intent on conversation with her neighbour. Soon wild shrieks of horror focused on that neighbour as others listened to a tale of disaster. Jen didn't know how to react so she busied herself with the menu and her champagne fizzed in her nose, she sneezed.

'Now ladies, Jen... She's a real walker. She'll keep us right. And she's a nurse. Gerry's going to be late, some kind of crisis. She should be here about 10:30. Hostel tomorrow – anyway you all have the itinerary. Remember the bus is 9:30. Let's drink to the expedition. Cheers.' She raised her glass.

'Not done much walk...' Jen flushed, excluded from the camaraderie. Her new walking boots, her fluorescent jacket, her borrowed waterproofs and her threadbare socks – did they fit the picture of experience? She took the full gaze from four faces, all of whom now saw her as a person of merit, someone to aspire to... She shifted, uncomfortable.

Melody chirruped her way through the meal then led them to a private lounge for coffee and drinks. Everyone relaxed. 'We need to get to know each other, so think of something to say about yourself. No pressure. No more than two minutes each. Gerry will introduce herself when she comes. You'll see... Who's first? Fiona?'

Fiona nodded to each of her companions. She was slight, pale skinned, with a short cut to her greying hair. 'I'm Fi. I've escaped death once this year. This is my recuperation. I've had operations, therapy, the works, but I'm better now. The dreaded big C... I *am* going the whole way. I would say if it kills me but that would be stupid. A walk can't kill me, can it? How dangerous is it Melody?'

Melody shook her head and rolled her eyes.

'Don't laugh at my stick. It should keep me on my feet. It's to save you dragging me up the steep bits.' She tipped her drink at each of the group and grinned.

Fi's neighbour stood to speak. Her cheeks were picked out in pink. 'Sandie McVey. I am very unfit, totally unqualified and not convinced I can make it all the way. It'll be a miracle if there are no tears! I give in very easily. When I get home, I've threatened the kids that the school run is history. It's the 'walking-bus' for them. But listen, we can do it together, help each other. I have been training. Round the park, twenty times. So my boots know how to walk on the flat. I hope it is just as easy on a slope! But I never thought about a stick... I need one!' She nodded to Fi in recognition of her foresight, and sat down. 'Just please don't leave me behind!' She looked right at Barbara when she said this. 'And thanks, Melody, for this.'

'Here! Here!' four voices agreed.

Melody turned to Jen and nodded for her to speak.

'Jen. Divorced. Now Miss Moore. This is my new start. I am having a proper holiday – a whole week off. I've not done that, well, ever. They joked at work – the place would fall down without me cos I am always there. But I'm not going to think about anything but myself, *all week*.' She lay back in her seat.

'I suppose it is my turn now. Sorry.' Barbara's brummie accent was strong. She half stood, shoulders round, nodding to each of the women in the group. Her voice was quiet. 'Me, Barbara, the beached whale!' She sniggered. 'My other half introduces me like that. I'm on a journey.' She marked the word with a finger gesture. 'I want to be me again, just plain Barbara, Barbara from Birmingham. A path to thinness: Walk Yourself Fit. I've read the book and now I'm here.' She perched back on her seat looking to Melody. 'That do? Or do you want the full story. Might come with tears...'

'Great, Barbara... oh dear I didn't mean it that way. We are going to have fun. Yes fitness. Yes brave. But mostly we'll have fun. All for one.' Melody punched her fist up.

'We are five, not three.' Fi called.

'Sorry, I was brought up with three brothers and I did want to be one of them. Anyone got a better slogan. We can work on that tomorrow. Raise your glasses – to the week,' and the others chirruped an agreement.

The door opened and a woman entered. She stood for a moment and took in the group. She was out of breath looking excited. 'Hi everyone, Geraldine, Gerry. Have I missed anything?' She sipped at her drink. 'Best way to get to know someone is buy them a drink. So what is everyone having?'

Gerry returned from the bar, settled in and soon her conversation hypnotized them all.

'When I told him I was going away on the 16th he thought... God knows what he really thought. My bag was packed and my boots polished both by the door and he says – *those boots needing repair?* I say no, they're walking the Pennine Way. He says *that's more a run than a walk.* I say no I'll be back on Saturday. He says, *What! The party is tonight. Are you taking the kids? Does Mum know?* At that point my handsome sophisticated silver fox became a deranged wolf, you know, almost frothing at the mouth! Whatever I said he just kept on ranting. *Are you kidding me? – winding me up?* No I say. I am going away this afternoon and I'll be back on Saturday. *What about the kids,* he says again? That's your problem I say. And he, well he can do a good meltdown. That's lawyers for you. Sometimes I think English must be a second language to him, or maybe it's Asperger's. So I've parked the kids with a friend, showed face at the party and made all his arrangements...'

'And him – what has he done?'

'Work, you know the mantra, 'you like to spend my money... Silly bugger. Wait till he tries to phone.'

'What would he have done if you had just gone?' Barbara asked.

'The kids would have had the problem. Anyway, I've deleted my number from his phone. That'll confuse him for a bit.' She laughed and downed another drink. 'He'll be so pleased to see me on Saturday.'

Tales of senseless husbands were shared. Jen could have joined in, only her stories were not funny. A grin disguised her hurt. She chilled at the memory of a bare fist into her stomach or her back and his grip on her hair. 'Take his money and run.' She spoke louder than she meant.

They all laughed.

Jen took that as her chance to escape. She didn't want small talk and happy families.

'I told you she was the sensible one.' Melody sighed as Jen disappeared upstairs.

The next morning at ten past nine the walkers filed back upstairs from the dining room. In room 23 Geraldine pulled a second pair of socks on and then took time to lace her boots, tensioning the lace at every loop. She worked her ankle and last of all she stood and stepped back and forward.

Jen had pulled her old hockey socks on. The wool was rough on her feet. She laced her new boots pulling the laces tight to the last loop and flexed her ankles.

'They look the part.' Geraldine admired. 'I don't use mine enough. They will outlast me at this rate. I think they are about twenty years old. Do you think Barbara is up to this walk? Bet she has to give in?'

'I'll watch Barbara. I can go at her pace.'

'You got kids, Jen?'

'No. I don't think I was meant to be a mother – no patience.' But it hadn't been patience she lacked. Turning her back on Gerry she busied herself with the zip on her bag and hoisted it onto her shoulder. 'You ready?'

There was a queue at reception and an untidy clump of bags both inside and outside the door when their minibus pulled up.

'Now one final question ladies, have you got your boots on, your jackets, and enough cash for lunch and coffee.'

Jen tapped her bum bag and shared grins.

'Right, to the bus.' Melody stayed. She was paying the receptionist when Jen, red faced, scurried back in.

'My jacket, sorry I've left my jacket in the room. How stupid!'

The bell boy led the way back to room 23 and waited by the open door as Jen rushed in. She pulled the fluorescent pink and green jacket from the drawer. 'Guess why it was in there?' The boy said nothing, but he laughed.

More laughter greeted her in the minibus. Someone called out, 'Easily forgotten, Jen!'

Forty minutes later they stopped in the middle of a deserted car park on the lower slopes of the Cheviots.

'Has anyone not got their phone?' Melody held her phone up. Each of the others followed her example. 'Everyone got my number? We've a five mile hike before we get to the coffee/lunch shop. Bags will be delivered to the hostel. Make sure you have everything you might need – pills, jacket, Jen?'

'I'll never live this down.' Jen held her jacket up, pointed to her bum bag and said, 'Heroin and Ees, but probably won't need them until this evening. Sunglasses, phone, think I'm set.'

'Are some of them for sale?' Fi called from inside the bus. She was looking round for her purse which had fallen out of her pocket. 'Got it! How much is it for a happy pill then, Jen?'

'Good idea to bring a nurse along Melody.' Sandie said giving thumbs up to Jen.

Jen was flustered, 'No, I'm a care worker not a nurse. I could do injections though. I just need your permission...'

The women began to move out. Melody trotted to catch up with Gerry. Gerry's voice somehow disturbed the peace of the hills that rose all around, edging the pale blue morning sky. The landscape was a carpet of well-worn velvet: patches of luscious greens through to browns and from time to time a rock face had worn through. A few sheep were scattered across the hillside like extras. The girls spread out in an untidy line as they followed a narrow worn track along the side of first one hill, then another, keeping to the south side of the River Bowmont, which flowed like a ribbon of silver, shimmering as it flowed downhill. Two hours later they would cross at a bridge, to the north side, for lunch at the Black Swan.

'How far did you say, Melody? Five kilometres?' Sandie called from the front of the group.

'Miles, five miles. It should take about an hour and a half, maybe two hours. Jen, wait up.' Melody hurried close and spoke quietly. 'Just wanted to say Barbara might need a bit of encouragement.'

'Yes, sure, I thought that.'

'The hostel is eight miles beyond, so if we make good time on this bit we could take a longer lunch break.'

Jen breathed deeply as she scanned the hillside below.

'Glad you came? You will soon make friends. I'm hiking in Spain next month. I have to have evidence of four days continuous walking or they won't let me go.'

'Sounds like a real adventure.'

'Then maybe the wilderness.'

'What's wrong with Lanzarote or Turkey?'

'Jen, look at that. A buzzard isn't it?'

They watched as a large brown bird rose. It climbed higher and higher then dropped like a stone. It rose and dropped again before they lost sight of it.

'Some people always end up on top. I want to be one of those for a change.' Jen stumbled.

'You alright?'

'Sore heel, that's all.'

'I thought you were limping. Are your boots alright?'

'I bought them last week. My old ones were falling apart when I dug them out.' She had found the boots in a charity shop. They were a bit tight, but the girl in the shop assured her they would stretch. 'It is just this foot.' She waggled her right foot. 'One foot is bigger than the other.'

'Sit down right now, sort your socks and loosen those laces. Here's some Vaseline. Rub it into the leather. I'll slow the others down till you catch up.'

Melody hurried on. Jen sat on the grass and unfastened her boots. When she fastened them up again she left the laces looser. She waggled her feet. The nip on her right heel returned the minute she stood, but she set off at a brisk pace to catch up.

'Oh no, break over. Here she comes.' Barbara stood. Her breathing was laboured. 'How many calories do you think I have used up so far? I have to work off the calories from last night before the real fat gets moving. I should jog up here.'

Sandie laughed and gave her a slow handclap.

'Slow and steady Barbara. Nothing done in a hurry lasts.' Fi was up leaning on her stick.

'Lead the way, Jen.' Melody took the Vaseline and used some to add a healthy sheen to her lips.

One by one the ladies fell into line. Jen thought she must look good as she strode on with her bright jacket hanging diagonally from her shoulders. Behind her Fi walked, her stick propelling her on. Barbara bounced in after her, with pink cheeks and a broad smile of determination.

Melody stood gazing down the valley. She waited for Sandie to shuffle off. Geraldine was the last to move. She was peering through a small set of binoculars towards the river watching a heron guard the river bank. From time to time her voice cracked across the hillside with her endless amusing commentary.

An hour and a half later they dropped down to a track, then to a narrow road that led them to the village of Burnside and the hotel. It was a rustic pub with a bar that was full already. The dark crowded room was airless and warm to the walkers but outside the scent of roses hung round the tables and birds perched silent amongst the greenery, grasping onto the prickly stems and hiding beneath the pink, red and yellow blooms. The birds sauntered out when there were crumbs to steal.

Jen's heel was sore. She was sure she had a blister that might have already burst. She confided in Melody. 'Melody, my heel is raw. There's a bus to Langford.' She pointed to the bus parked across the street. 'I'll get some stuff there and meet you at the hostel later. Ok?'

'Yes get it sorted now. Give me a ring if there's a problem. We'll see you at the hostel.'

Jen almost skipped out of the door and onto the bus. The engine idled while the driver waited for passengers.

'Oh. Oh. Wait. Wait.' A voice carried in from the street. Another passenger clambered on. Jen sat back and closed her eyes. For a moment a smile curled onto her face.

'There you are.' Barbara landed heavily beside Jen, more than filling the space. She was out of breath. 'Couldn't let you go alone. Melody gave me this.' She thrust a tightly folded map at Jen. 'Here, more use to you than me.'

Jen snorted, 'As if I need that!' She crushed it into her bag. Barbara's chatter obscured everything else. Jen gazed out of the window and she discovered it was easy to ignore the conversation. There was no space for her to answer anyway.

Barbara assumed control as they stepped onto the High Street at Langford.

'Right, this looks promising.' She sidled Jen into a charity shop, Mountain Rescue. 'We need trainers. They'll have something here.'

Barbara engaged the young assistant in their problem while Jen stood like an errant teenager. The assistant was a volunteer for the local mountain rescue team. She knew the answer to any hiking issue. She had special blister packs and the shop sold woolly socks and trainers. Jen bought the lot, including the medical attention, for six pounds fifty. Barbara selected a walking pole for herself, and one for Sandie. Then, the very helpful girl informed them of a shortcut to the hostel.

Jen felt better. Her mood improved and she suggested they stop for coffee. She even smiled. Her walking boots dangled from her shoulders, jerking at a different pace now. Barbara too, stepped out stronger. She marched with two poles.

'This is easier walking. Better for me.' Barbara set a good pace. 'Great exercise. How far do you think?'

'We should be there by five. It's half two now.'

'And with the shortcut, we might beat the others.'

At four o'clock they came to a junction.

'Across the bridge?' Barbara asked.

'Sure,' said Jen without halting.

They had followed a narrow path on the south side of the river for a mile or two when a forest sprung out of nowhere. The bank of the river was steep here and it flowed quickly into the thick growth of trees but the path turned uphill and disappeared over the brow.

Barbara's face crumpled, 'I can't do that. Too soft. Too steep.' She was already out of breath.

'This is wrong.' Jen stretched the map out as Barbara lay back on the rough ground. 'We've taken the wrong path.'

Barbara stared at her companion. 'You are joking me. Not from that bridge?' Her face grew red.

'I'm afraid so. We should be on the other side of this river.' Jen's laugh was nervous.

'You told me you knew. I asked. You idiot.' Barbara shouted. 'It's hard enough you know. Now this! Double, no triple the distance! I hate you. I hate this stupid walk!'

'You can do it. Come on.' Jen managed to keep her voice light. She looked back along the path hiding the pain that had crossed her own face.

'I knew it would be hard. Greg said. I should have listened. I'm the laughing stock again. Did you want to have a go at me too? You didn't want me to come with you did you? Is this the pay back – get me lost. Next you'll be leaving me out here. Go on, just like him, leave me. I don't want to go any further. Just go!' Her shouting became a wracking howl.

'Absolutely not, Barbara! That's not true.' Jen's tone changed. She moved closer and put her arm round her shoulder. She sat very close to Barbara .

'Greg's been laughing at me for years. Now he's gone!' She sat hunched, letting tears wash out the truth.

'Barbara, I thought this was just to lose weight.'

'He's got a young thing – at the office…'

'Well it's his loss, Barbara. You're better off without him. You'll see.'

'Mmm.' She blew her nose.

'Listen, you've got a plan. You are usually so positive. I can see that. Get fit, lose the weight and he'll come back.'

Barbara stopped crying. 'Do you really think that?'

'Well he should do!' Their faces were close. Jen wiped Barbara's tears. She said, 'Do you want a laugh?'

'I never did a hill walk in my life, Barbara.'

'But, I thought … Melody said …'

'I lied… I'm always lying.' Her voice was almost a whisper.

'Well, you've never done any walking!' Barbara burst into gales of laughter. Soon the two lay helpless, hilarity overtook distress.

'You mean it's not just me that's lost. We… both…' She changed her position so she could look into Jen's eyes. 'So this might be it then.'

Jen nodded. She sat hunched over her knees and cried into her hands. 'I haven't got any friends. My husband used to beat me up. I lie to keep people away. I lie. I've got nothing.'

Barbara struggled to her feet. 'Then we have both got something to prove, haven't we. We're not giving in. Come on, on your feet. I'd make you walk across that river but those blisters are what started this and you and I are going to do this whole bloody walk if it kills us, so those blisters better stay dry – for now.'

They returned the way they had come, sometimes arm in arm.

The hostel was empty when they arrived. They chose their beds and relaxed until Fi came to find them.

'Next time you are taking a bus I'm coming with you.' She flopped onto Jen's bed.

'You're worn out. Take that bed and tell Barbara about your ordeal. I'll get you a cup of tea.'

The rest had gathered in the kitchen.

'What time did the bus get here?' Gerry called.

'Ignore her, Jen,' said Melody. 'Are you sorted?'

Jen lifted her foot to show the neat bandage.

Sandie groaned. 'The bus sounded so much better than an eight mile hike.'

'Well tomorrow is short and there are no roads, no buses. We'll have a picnic on the top. I'm going for a shower. Tea is booked for eight. Can I carry one of those mugs for you, Jen?'

Gerry was already in the pub when the others arrived.

'Cocktails anyone?' She chirped from the bar. 'Anthony has everything!' She flashed a wicked wink at the girls.

A waitress called to the group, 'You're in the snug.'

Gerry returned to the bar throughout the evening to drink more cocktails.

The following morning they gathered outside the hostel. Jen stretched her aching muscles. 'I feel tired all over.' She yawned.

'Okay ladies. It's a short walk today, a ramble.'

They set off in companionable silence and climbed a style that was marked with various coloured discs. They were scaling the tussocky slopes of Haverslaw. From the top they would pick out the route east, to their next halt in the village of Whitholm. There were fields of wheat in the lower valley. It swished in the breeze, an undulating sea of grass hiding the river from the walkers until they were higher. Barbara and Jen took steady steps.

Fi spoke as they caught her. 'She's quiet this morning.' She pointed her stick at Gerry.

'Cocktails have a sting in their tail I think!'

'Or maybe Anthony?'

The three giggled.

'Perhaps her old man isn't so wonderful.' Barbara raised her eyebrow and made a face. Fi laughed.

'She said Anthony had everything, I could do with a bit of him. It would be worth the hangover…' Fi stopped to look back down the valley. 'Can we take a rest?'

'I want a picture.' Jen said.

Fi leaned on her stick and studied the path they had come. She pointed out the hostel and the pub.

Barbara's phone beeped. 'I've got a signal.' She read her message. 'Good timing… He wants to put the house on the market. What the…' She concentrated as she typed into her phone.

Fi and Jen walked on. Geraldine was tramping on at the front, with her head down and her shoulders hunched. Sandie waved her stick and Fi moved on to talk to her. Jen held back waiting for Barbara.

'You alright?' She asked.

'Primed to kill! Why can't he leave me alone? Give me a few days without his crap. What was your husband like Jen?'

'I don't talk about him. You need a lawyer, Babs. The best advice I got was to get a good lawyer. Don't think about the expense. You need the best advice. Then you tell him to speak to the lawyer. I ended up in a women's refuge. They told me that. He was guilty. He had to pay. If my baby had lived he would have paid maintenance. He beat that baby out of me. You don't get money for that.'

'What, a miscarriage?'

'He beat me up, just happened that I was pregnant that time. The doctors tried to save my beautiful little girl. She was beautiful. She would have been just like me... Angelina...'

'How can you bear it, Jen?' Barbara reached for her hand.

'We had a funeral. She was herself for just a short moment, a beautiful moment.' She held Barbara's hand and let her tears fall as she walked on. She felt like a real mum.

Two hours later they halted by a scree slope.

'We can stop for lunch.' Melody pointed ahead to a rocky outcrop. 'What about a table up there?'

'The best tonic on a day like this is iced coffee. I've made extra. Anyone want one?' Sandie offered.

'You're an angel. When did you make that?' Gerry held out her hand to take the first cup. She sipped it. 'That's the best coffee I've ever had.' She whooped.

'I don't suppose you can keep the volume down?' Sandie asked.

'Who, me?' Gerry bellowed. She had recovered. They laughed.

'Remind me to buy you a cocktail when we get down, Gerry.' Barbara teased.

'I might give them a miss tonight.'

'That means the barman *will* be available.' Fi winked at Jen.

'Where can you find a better restaurant: a view like this, lungs full of fresh air and iced coffee?' Melody raised her cup.

'All for one! One for all.' The chant drifted across the hillside.

Jen winked at Barbara.

Snowbound

Annis Farnell

It's gone quiet out there, Janet thought.

Usually, there was a near-constant hum of traffic on the busy dual carriageway, but she was aware, now, of silence. She drew back the thick woollen curtain, raised the blind, opened the shutter; so many barriers to winter's pervasive cold in this old house. She peered out.

It must have been snowing for quite a while; the front garden was a mystery of lumps, humps and hummocks under its white coverlet, the drive a level white trench between them. A lorry ground past on the roadway, a camouflage of snow plastered to its bodywork, hiding its owner's identity. Where it passed, the wheel tracks were white channels.

And it's not stopping any time soon, either, Janet thought, seeing the broad white flakes dancing in the strengthening wind; the night sky was heavy with unshed snow. The lorry's crisp tracks had already blurred at the edges, were growing shallower as she watched.

She closed the shutters, pulled blind and curtains, and threw another log into the stove. A couple of snowflakes, melting down the flue, hissed as they touched the hot coals. She made cocoa, laced it with rum, and settled down with a seed catalogue. The snow was early, usually it coincided with the need to prick out tomato seedlings, but this year, she hadn't even ordered the seeds. San Marzano... she'd give them a try this year. Her mind wandered off down a dream lane of tomatoes dried in the solar drier and bottled in olive oil; perhaps add some thyme? Puréed and frozen in ice-cube trays... bottled for soups... Tumbling Tom, that was a nice little tomato for salads... Janet ticked the entry, moved on. A tiny, striped aubergine caught her eye... *I wonder if it tastes as good as it looks? Might be fun to try it...*

A brisk metallic tattoo from the door-knocker brought her back to the real world. *Who on earth ... ?*

'And a fat lot of use you are,' she apostrophised the German Shepherd, who had roused enough to yawn. 'You're supposed to be a guard-dog, not a hearthrug. Come on, then.' At least Rika looked imposing.

The dog looked mildly interested. *Walkies? Odd time of day, but humans are strange beasts. Oh, no, it's that noise at the door.* She came to her paws with a convulsive heave, and assumed an air of alertness.

There were six of them huddling together along the narrow path.

'Do I get a choice of carol?' Janet asked, 'or just a rousing chorus of "We wish you a Merry Christmas"?'

The two tall men at the front of the queue, their peaked chequered caps and Hi-vis jackets already crusted with snow, grinned appreciatively.

One said, 'Mebbe once we're out o' this snow, ma'am. I'm sorry, the road's blocked just past here a wee bit, and we cannae turn round, either, there's an artic jackknifed a couple o' miles back. It's a lot to ask, but would you mind... ?' He waved a hand at the crowd. 'I wouldn't ask, but there's nane o' them equipped for a night out in these conditions.'

'I suppose,' she said; so much for a quiet evening. 'At least with you two here to keep an eye on them, the family heirlooms are safe.'

The copper grinned again.

'More like the PC and the telly, these days.'

A radio crackled, the words almost unintelligible; Janet supposed that eventually, one's ear became attuned. The other policeman stepped back to answer it, stumbling as his foot found the edge of the path.

'Right, folks,' the first policeman said. He wore sergeant's stripes on his uniform. 'This good lady's taking you in until the road's cleared, so in you go, quick as you like, let's not let too much cold into the house.' He frowned as a middle-aged man thrust himself forward. 'There's no sae much o' a rush, sir, that you havena time to get rid o' some o' yon snow first; nae need tae drag it through the house.' He stood, solidly commanding, in the doorway.

With reluctance, the man obeyed. One by one, the others followed suit: a tall man, his fair hair a barely-visible fuzz, a Hi-vis fleece hanging open over a T-shirt; and a mother-and-daughter pair, both skinny rather than slim, their hair in identical mousy dreadlocks. The mother was wearing the sort of hippy, floaty garments and ropes of beads that had gone out of fashion when her own parents were still young, while the daughter wore jeans, topped off with a chiffon blouse and a welter of chains and bangles.

The man in the suit had seen Rika, and extended a fist for her to sniff. It seemed he wasn't afraid of large, hairy dogs.

In the light of the porch lamp, the big man with the nearly-bald head had, Janet thought, the sort of face old ladies cross the street to avoid. He gave her a gap-toothed grin.

'Thanks,' he said. 'It's good of you.' He kicked off his rigger boots, and left them tidily in a corner of the porch. The grin widened. 'I'm like the dog, I'm house-trained.'

The mother-and-daughter duo, hand-in-hand, edged in next, each mirroring the other's wariness.

'We don't like dogs,' the mother stated. 'I hope you're going to lock it up.'

'No,' Janet said, 'I certainly won't. She's very well-behaved; if you don't bother her, she won't bother you.' Ignoring the flattened ears, the ruffle where hackles were beginning to rise.

'I really must insist -'

'My house, my dog, my rules,' Janet said. 'You can be warm in the house or freeze in your car: take your pick.'

Finally, Scotland's Finest were able to shake off their crust of snow, and make their way inside. Thankfully, Janet shut the door.

Assembled in the sitting-room, the crowd found places to sit. The mother-and-daughter combo bagged the two-seater settee; *If that girl was any closer to her mother, she'd be in her lap,* Janet thought. The businessman took one of the two Queen Anne-style wing chairs.

Janet said, 'I've got some folding chairs for the rest of you, if you'll give me a moment to fetch them.'

'I'll give you a hand,' the obliging Sergeant offered.

Out of earshot of the sitting-room, he said, 'I shouldna say this, really, but that's a right lot we've dumped on you.'

She grinned. 'They could be worse. Some of them.'

There was a flurry of activity as everyone was seated; Rika returned to her favoured spot, and resumed duty as a hearthrug.

'Right, first things first,' Janet said. 'It's going to get confusing if we're all calling each other "you". I'm Janet Mollison'

'Sergeant Dewar', and

'Constable Stott'.

'Mike Beattie,' the thug said.

'Garfield Birkenshaw,' from the businessman; someone sniggered, though whether at the name or the man's pomposity was unclear.

'Moonbeam and Lilith,' the hippie mother said. 'We don't believe in surnames, they're only there so the state can control us.'

Now there's a conversation-stopper, Janet thought. Aloud, she offered hot drinks.

In the middle of taking orders, the lights went out. Anguished squeals came from the hippies, to a background of surprised 'Ohs' from the rest.

'Just stay calm,' Sergeant Dewar's crowd-control voice came out of the darkness. 'It's only a power cut.'

'Don't move,' Janet ordered. 'Stay where you are till I get a light.'

Both policemen produced torches, and smaller lights showed where mobile phones had been switched to torch mode. She lit night-lights and candles, and a hurricane lamp; together with the firelight, the warm glow gave the room an almost festive air.

'We won't be able to have a hot drink, now,' the younger hippie whined. What was her name again? Oh, yes, Lilith.

'Away and dinnae be daft,' Mike Beattie said. 'There's more ways o' boiling watter than an electric kettle.'

'Do you have herb teas?' Moonlight said, in evident expectation of a negative.

'Rosehip, peppermint or chamomile,' said Janet, wondering why she was bothering. Two chamomile teas, one English Breakfast, one coffee and two hot chocolates later, Janet settled into the other Queen Anne chair the younger men had courteously left for her. She glanced at the wag-at-the-wa' clock. *If I'm going to have something to eat myself, I suppose I'll have to offer them a meal.*

'Has everybody eaten?' she asked; a chorus answered her in the negative.

'We're vegans,' Moonlight said.

Why am I not surprised?

'I'm allergic to nuts,' Lilith added.

Birkenshaw started to say something, but Janet interrupted.

'This is a private house, not a hotel, and I'm not geared up for an invasion like this, so it's the take-it-or-leave-it school of catering. If you don't like what's on offer, hard luck.'

Moonlight said, with the air of one much put upon by Fate, 'We can just have a plate of fresh vegetables, you don't need to cook for us.'

'Really? And where are those going to come from? If you think I'm going out in this snow to pick you some Brussels sprouts, you've another think coming.'

Moonlight and Lilith looked confused, as though the concept of growing vegetables was wholly alien.

'We get organic vegetables delivered,' Lilith said. 'That way, we know we're not eating anything contaminated with chemicals.'

Janet shrugged. 'I don't use chemical fertilisers or insecticides either, but you'll just have to take my word for it.' *Or go hungry. Better not mention what I do use for fertiliser, they'll probably think it comes under the heading of exploitation of animals.*

'I'll have to come with you, and make sure nothing we eat is contaminated with animal products. Exploitation of animals is evil,' Moonlight said.

'I'm coming too,' Lilith chipped in. 'I need to be sure there's no nuts in anything. Even a trace could kill me.'

'Oh, for crying in a bucket,' Constable Stott said, not so very sotto voce.

Birkenshaw said, 'I shall be fascinated to see what you can produce to feed such a diverse crew at such short notice.' Oddly, he did sound genuinely interested. 'Is there anything I can do? I'm quite handy in a kitchen.'

Life's full of surprises, Janet thought, accepting the offer, and to the chorus of (male) voices that arose, 'No, thanks, one helper in the kitchen's enough. But if somebody could set the table, the dining-room's through there. Cutlery's in the top drawer, table mats one drawer down. Soup, meat and pud.'

Moonbeam began, 'But I've already told you, we don't eat meat -'

'So what? You're going to use your fingers? It's a figure of speech; get a grip!'

Janet picked up a candle-lamp, and headed for the kitchen, Birkenshaw and the two vegans in her wake. *Good job I've got a big kitchen,* she thought, with grim amusement.

'You two stand there,' she directed the women. 'If you won't help, at least stay out of my way.' She handed Birkenshaw a black apron with a wine merchant's embroidered logo, and pointed him towards the larder. 'If you could chop some onions and leeks, please. And I'll need some mushrooms as well. I don't think the lion's mane are quite ready yet, but you should get enough shiitake and oysters.'

She opened flues on the big Rayburn, glad she had stoked it a short time before; stacked plates in the lower oven. She dragged a large pressure cooker containing three small perforated pots out of a cupboard, set it on the hotplate, and poured in water from the kettle sitting at the back of the range. Two more pots joined it. Green and red lentils and barley went into simmering water to cook, and polythene bags full of green things emerged from the big freezer in the corner.

Birkenshaw came back, laden with vegetables; with approval, she noted he had selected one of the big chef's knives.

'Oh, put it away!' Moonlight begged, panic in her voice. 'Big knives are so dangerous! We're scared of them!'

Birkenshaw thumped three large leeks onto the green chopping board. 'If you don't like it, bugger off and annoy somebody else,' he snapped. It seemed his handiness in a kitchen was no idle boast, as thin slices of leek, finely diced onions began to fall from the flashing blade.

Janet peeled potatoes and celeriac, which, sliced thinly, went to join the other things bubbling on the hob. The leeks and onions were sweated down. Soon, the pulses and vegetables were cooked and drained, and layered in a large, deep pie dish with the onions, mushrooms, a couple of tins of kidney beans and some ice cubes, faintly yellow.

'What's in that?' Moonlight demanded.

'Vegetable stock,' Janet replied, curt with this foolish woman. 'Nothing goes to waste in this house.'

'You're not very nice to us,' Lilith said, pouting. 'I don't think you like vegans.'

Exasperated, Janet said, 'Frankly, I don't care what you are; I just get very annoyed with complete strangers who wander into my house and think they can start making demands.' She was aware of Birkenshaw chuckling softly. For some reason, she found his unspoken support encouraging. She finished the dish with a topping of potatoes, sprinkled with oatmeal.

Seven bags of frozen greenery were turning to soup in yet another pan, and Janet unrolled a sheet of puff pastry, while instructing Birkenshaw to prepare apples.

'Yes, chef.' He grinned at her, and she saw for the first time, that behind the surly exterior lurked a very attractive man. 'Tarte tatin, I take it?'

'That's it,' she said, tossing sugar into one large cast-iron frying pan, and emptying a bag of frozen lamb chops into another.

'We don't eat meat -' Moonlight began.

'So you keep telling me, but the rest of us do.'

'But the smell... how can you stand it? And those poor little lambs...'

'You don't think we slaughter those pretty little things skipping about the fields in spring, do you?' Birkenshaw weighed in, backing Janet up.

Apparently, that was exactly what Moonlight and Lilith thought. Birkenshaw gave a snort of derision.

'Lamb, to a butcher,' he explained kindly, as to a couple of four-year-olds, 'is a young sheep. Killing the little ones would be a waste: you'd maybe get tenderness, but not much meat and very little flavour.'

This was an explanation too far; the two women gave identical faint moans, and fled. Birkenshaw's grin became positively wicked, and even more attractive; Janet found herself wishing it was just the two of them.

'That's got rid of them,' he said, satisfied. 'Where's the bread kept?'

'There's a loaf in the bin in the pantry, but I'll need to make more for tomorrow; I hadn't bargained on six guests for breakfast!'

Once they were seated round the big table, Sergeant Dewar said, 'This fairly beats a piece and a cuppie in a lay-by! It smells fantastic.'

It was true; in some mysterious way, the low light shed by the candelabra seemed to intensify the rich, savoury smell of the food, as though, being partially deprived of vision, their sense of smell was enhanced; the scent of beeswax and burning wick, the resinous smell of logs, the hint of sulphur from the coal in the Rayburn, percolating through the house, provided base notes to the appetising perfume.

Moonlight and Lilith sipped their spinach soup, and picked daintily at their vegetable pie. The two policemen and Mike Beattie attacked their larger helpings with enthusiasm, and came back for seconds. Birkenshaw ate slowly, savouring each mouthful.

Moonlight and Lilith rejected the tarte tatin with every appearance of loathing.

'We don't know if there's animal fat in that pastry,' Moonlight said.

'That's fine,' put in Mike Beattie. 'There'll be mair for the rest o' us.'

'And we don't eat sugar, either,' Lilith chipped in. 'Our bodies are temples -'

Mike guffawed. 'Mair like a chapel of rest.'

There were subdued sniggers from round the table, the sounds of men trying – and failing – to remain marginally polite. Sniffing, mother and daughter shared an apple for dessert.

Dinner over, the men cleared up, while Moonlight and Lilith huddled together on the sofa in the sitting room. Janet opened the back door to let Rika out, and gasped.

'Come out here and see this!', she called over her shoulder to the men in the kitchen.

The snow had stopped. The power cut was evidently a large one, there was no distant glow from towns and villages to pollute the night sky. Across the moor, the snow gleamed, stretching to the distant peaks. No movement, no sound disturbed the stillness, except the soft noise of their breathing, the dog's paws crunching through the crisp top layer of white. And above it all, the midnight sky arched winter-black, its velvet glittering with a myriad pinpoints of silver light; to the south, Orion stood out, Betelgeuse on his shoulder, and Rigel at his heel; but to the north, Polaris and its pointers, Cassiopeia and the two bears, Great and Little, faded, for above the horizon the night sky flimmered and gleamed in shifting curtains of green and gold.

'It's the Merry Dancers,' Constable Stott said. 'I hinna seen them as good's that since I was a wee loon.'

They stood silent after that, a group of humans feeling awestruck and very insignificant, until the biting cold drove them back to the fire's warmth. Rika, unimpressed by the wonders of nature, was already sprawled on the hearth. There was no sign of the women; Janet suspected that the dog's return had sent them scurrying to the sanctuary of their allotted bedroom.

Janet poured drinks, and gave Rika a bone-shaped black biscuit; in companionable silence, they sat listening to the dog's jaws crunching her treat.

Birkenshaw fished in a pocket, producing a small card wallet; he handed Janet one.

'One good meal deserves another,' he said, with that oddly attractive smile. 'Just give one of the staff my card, and they'll let me know you've arrived.'

The card bore his name, and that of a very upmarket new restaurant in the city.

'And I know it's a bit of a cheek,' he added, 'but might I put that pie on my vegetarian menu?'

Murder Most Foul

Sue Cook

The old woman who consulted Horatio Lande on a relatively minor legal matter assured him that his fee would not be a problem, that she could repay it many times over no matter what her outward appearance. But when business was concluded and it came time to pay, she admitted she did not have the money.

'What's this, Mistress Sittingbourne?' he bellowed, a sound incongruous from a frame so shrivelled from subsisting on meagre fees. 'You said you could pay.'

'And so I can. I can earn you your fee many times over, and enhance your standing as an advocate greatly using this.' She placed on the shabby desk which stood between them a small glass vial stopped with a sliver of wood, the like of which Horatio Lande had not seen before.

'You offer me some potion? Or is it poison to stop me pursuing my claim!'

'Your cases have not gone well of late,' she said. 'You have lost some that you should have won. Clients are looking elsewhere, which is why you have taken on poor widows like me.'

Horatio Lande felt his mouth hang open as the crone spoke words he knew only too well to be true.

'Besides, you do not drink it,' she continued. 'You dab a little behind each ear, like this.' She removed the stopper, placed one finger tip over the opening of the vial which she then inverted. She placed the finger tip over each mastoid in turn before replacing the stopper.

'If it were poison I should not use it myself.'

Lande noticed a faint herbal smell. He took the small bottle and sniffed. It was quite pleasant.

'How will this repay me?' he asked, replacing the stopper and regarding the vial as though it were some strange bat, one which could not be trusted to refrain from sucking his blood in the night.

'Use a little each time you wish to improve your performance at court and it will greatly enhance your ability.'

'What? You wish me to stand before a judge and fellow advocate and apply some sort of perfume?'

'The courts can be hot and full of bad odours from ne'er-do-wells who of necessity are present, are they not?' she continued. 'You would merely be using a pleasant smell to protect you from bad ones. You could claim, if asked, that an apothecary made it to your own special formula, to help protect you from the malodours which propagate the plague and such like. You do not, of course, need to name your apothecary. A little mystery is never a bad thing.'

'My very own burglar's blend,' Lande mused, thinking that such a ruse might work, though he was by no means certain that her 'perfume' would.

'Burglar's blend, sir? I'm sure I know not what you mean.'

Lande leaned over the desk and lowered his voice. 'It is rumoured that in France a band of thieves used a mixture of herbal oils to protect them from infection when they entered the houses of plague victims for the purpose of robbery.'

The woman brushed seemingly imaginary specks off her rough woollen skirt. 'I'm sure I don't know what an old widow what lives in the English countryside would know of such matters.'

Lande gave her a thoughtful look. Was she old enough to be the originator of the burglar's blend? Probably not. Her mother might have been.

'But if in six months my mixture has not repaid my debt twice over,' she continued, turning her wizened yet surprisingly bright eyes on him once more, 'you may pursue me by any means you wish.'

The lawyer rested back in his chair and stared at the little bottle. 'What does it do?' he asked.

'Do, sir? Why it simply promotes clearness of the head, strengthens the vocal abilities and powers of reasoning,' she replied. 'All essential qualities in the modern advocate.'

Doubtful, but having little choice, Lande decided to try the old woman's formulation. It smelt nicely enough and she spoke the truth about Elizabethan courts of law: they were crowded, hot and stank.

The first time he used the mixture the result was a miraculous change in fortune; a certain defeat became a famous victory. Thus it happened the second and the third time. Soon his reputation was so greatly enhanced that he had more clients than he could accommodate and was able to choose only the most lucrative. The potion cleared Mistress Sittingbourne's debt in weeks, not months.

He soon developed the habit of keeping a few drops of the potion on a handkerchief so that he could apply it under the auspices of dabbing away sweat when under pressure. Questions of what was in his peculiar perfume stopped.

After some years of unmitigated success, Horatio Lande grew fat and rich. He was also bored. He was so selective in his cases that he might only need to work once a week and his thoughts turned to other pursuits. In particular, he felt a strong urge to write a play, one about a successful lawyer.

None of the London troupes of actors, not even the struggling ones, showed any interest. Some were openly scornful.

'Where is the tragedy?' one director asked, tossing the carefully penned papers into the air. 'Where is the political comment? Who wants to hear about nothing but success?'

Another fellow in passing added, 'And it rhymes. No one writes in rhyme anymore.'

Lande tried the last of the crone's potion before presenting it to yet another company, with no success. It seemed her herbs, whatever they were, only worked in the courtroom. Frustrated, he travelled into the country, to the address in Kent which the old woman had given him, in the hope she was still alive and would be able to help him with this matter, too. He also needed to purchase more of the potion that kept his coffers so full.

His rich London garb raised a few eyebrows when he asked in the village after Mistress Sittingbourne's house, though the directions given to him brought him there directly. She did not seem surprised to see him.

'Come in, Mr Lande,' she said, holding open the door of her tiny cottage. 'I've been expecting you.'

'You have?'

'News of strangers travels faster than the stranger himself. Will you take some ale after your long journey?'

The house, he was pleased to note, was clean if basic. He readily accepted a cup of ale from the woman who seemed to have aged not at all since they last met and found it quite acceptable, although the rough wooden chair on which he was forced to sit creaked ominously under his bulk.

'You have done well since we last met,' she said.

'You did tell me you would repay my fee many times over and, thanks to your magic potion, that has certainly happened.'

'Magic?' she said with surprise. 'There was no magic in that, Mr Lande. Just a few simple herbs and some wise words.'

'Come, come,' he said. 'Surely it was more than that.'

'More than that would be witchcraft,' said the widow. 'And you would have been readily profiting from it.'

'Well, I'm sure it wasn't witchcraft. No, not that.' Mr Lande backtracked hastily. His eyes fell to a marmalade cat, which at that very moment stalked into the kitchen from another room. 'What a... um... an unusual pet,' he added.

'There's many as don't like them, true,' said Mistress Sittingbourne. 'But he's a good mouser and the dogs my husband had when he were alive made me sneeze terribly.'

Hmmm, thought Lande as his host got up to let out the cat. Nobody kept a cat these days for fear of being accused as a witch.

'Nonetheless,' he continued as she closed the door again, 'your wise words improved my fortunes immeasurably. And a few simple herbs for luck would be construed as white witchcraft, wouldn't it. Simple folk knowledge used to help others?'

'But to my material benefit and yours. What would a good lawyer make of that argument? Your gain was had at the detriment of others. Each win for you meant some other lawyer's loss. Will there be none of your fellows who would argue against you if accusations were made?'

'No, no, I'm sure it won't come to that,' Lande blustered.

'Indeed,' she seemed mollified. 'Because essentially my mixture did nothing but give you self-belief. You thought, or hoped, it would work and it did.'

'Of course! Self-belief! That's all I really needed,' said the lawyer. 'Wise words indeed, Mistress Sittingbourne. And now I could do with another few wise words, if you will.'

'And what would that concern?'

'Thanks to your... um... previous wise words, my career is everything I could have hoped. What I wish to do now is to make my name as a playwright. But I cannot interest anyone in my work.'

The old woman frowned. 'But I am no playwright, Mr Lande. Nor do I have a troupe of players who could perform your work. I don't understand what it is you think I can do.'

Now that she asked, he wasn't sure either. He just felt that she would have something for him.

Into the silence she said, 'I have a stew on the hearth. Plenty for two. Perhaps you would consent to dine with a poor widow this evening and we can discuss the matter and see what can be done?'

Horatio Lande looked towards the black pot which hung above the fire in the grate and for the first time noticed the smell of cooking. He inhaled deeply, thought about many things such as enchantment and bewitchment before smiling broadly and stating that he would be delighted to share a meal with such a wise soul as she.

The pot proved to contain a most sustaining lamb stew with plump white dumplings suspended within it.

'What are these green specks?' asked the lawyer as he divided one of the dumplings with his spoon.

'Leaves of the parsley plant,' came the reply. 'For cleansing the blood.'

'Delicious, too.'

'Now, tell me about your play,' said the woman. So he did.

When both their platters had been wiped dry with bread, Mistress Sittingbourne summarised the plot thus: 'In other words, this play is the Life and Times of Horatio Lande?'

'Yes, I suppose it is,' came the reply.

There followed a long silence during which she collected his platter and filled cups with a cloudy juice which she said was made from apples. Lande sipped and found it most palatable, if somewhat mild compared to her ale.

'Tell me,' said Mistress Sittingbourne when she had regained her chair. 'When I was last in your office, you told me a tale about some burglar's brew or other.'

Lande nodded.

'I remember you being most animated, as though the story fascinated you greatly.'

'It did,' he said. 'Does it not you?'

She inclined her head slightly but did not reply. 'What is it about the tale which engrosses you so?'

Lande had to think. 'Firstly, we do not know for sure if it is true or not. If it is then it is highly audacious that men should risk their very lives to gain from the dead. Shocking, too.'

'So there is an element of, shall we say, myth?' Mistress Sittingbourne waited for Lande's nod. 'Of scandal and also of heroism?'

'I'm not sure I'd go that far, Madam,' Lande objected.

'Is it not heroic to risk one's life in search of riches?' she asked.

'Yes. No. I mean... I see what you mean, not that I would call theft an act of heroism. Normally. I certainly would not have done it, not even for another flask of your ma-, your marvellous potion,' Lande finished with a nervous laugh.

'Have you ever done anything illegal?' she asked.

'Me? Certainly not. I uphold the law, not break it.'

'Hmmm' she said. 'Tell me about your childhood. Were you perhaps from an uncertain background, or poor folk?'

'Heavens, no. My father was also a lawyer, my mother the daughter of a grain merchant.'

'They perhaps died young, leaving you the ward of an evil aunt?'

'No, no. My father lived to a good age and my mother still resides at Cambourne. She writes to me often on the subject of marriage and issue. Why? What is this about?'

'You recall First Minister Cromwell?' asked Mistress Sittingbourne.

'Who could not!' retorted the lawyer. 'One of the most talked about men in London until his execution. And for some time thereafter.'

'What can you tell me of his parentage?'

'No one knows. Some say his father was a butcher, some a brewer, and that he was beaten regularly and ran away.'

'And yet no one who quizzed him on the subject received an answer that satisfied either proposition.'

'Indeed.'

'And what did he do after he ran away?'

'No one really... knows...' Lande's answer trailed off into thought.

'So we might say that there is an element of mystery, an element of myth about his origins, too?'

Lande sat back in his chair with a thoughtful expression. 'Indeed, I believe you are right.'

'And what of Mistress Boleyn?'

'The mother of our glorious Queen?'

Mistress Sittingbourne nodded.

'What of her?'

'Was she not talked about as much as Cromwell? Much more than, let's say, the first of King Henry's queens, the faithful Catherine?'

'Goodness me, yes. But what a lot there was to talk about. That extra finger of hers marked her as being one made for witchcraft, and that this was how she managed to entrap Henry into marriage, by bewitching him to fall in love with her.'

'And she tried it on Cromwell, too, some say.'

'Indeed,' Lande warmed to the topic. 'Yet he managed somehow to resist her charms despite being recently widowed and hence, some might say, more susceptible to the comforts offered.'

Mistress Sittingbourne next asked, 'Why do you think people like to gossip about these two?'

'Because there is so much to gossip about.'

'And what is there in your life to gossip about, Mr Lande?'

Suddenly Horatio Lande could see where all these questions were leading. 'Nothing,' he admitted then added to himself, 'save that a cat-owning client once gave me some herbs and some wise words.'

'So, what your play needs is intrigue, some myth some, dare I suggest, witchcraft influencing the fate of mighty men?'

'But...'

'Writing plays is about weaving a fiction, Mr Lande. A fiction that will engross the public. Like Cromwell wove a fiction about his early life, like the enemies of Mistress Boleyn wove a fiction about her captivation and betrayal of King Henry.'

'Once again, Mistress Sittingbourne, you speak wise words. I see now why my play has failed to garner interest. But what can I do? I know nothing about weaving these fictions you speak of.'

'As once you knew nothing about the law. You were not born a lawyer any more than you were born a playwright. You must learn the craft from those who have mastered it.'

Mr Lande jumped to his feet, seeing the way clearly ahead. 'You are right! I need to find a playwright who will act as master to my apprenticeship. But where to find such a one?'

'I have heard of a brilliant but troubled writer who might be persuaded to help you for a small sum.'

'You, Mistress Sittingbourne? How have you heard?'

'Because, Mr Lande, all I have left in my life is my cat and to listen to gossip. Besides, Mr Marlowe is a local man, from Canterbury just three miles hence, though he spends most of his time in or about London now.'

Horatio Lande spent the night at an inn before returning to London with the express wish of making contact with this C Marlowe, Esq. The journey was difficult as, far from cleansing his blood, Mistress Sittingbourne's repast seemed to have muddied his head. The innkeeper had told him it was her apple drink that was to blame, though it seemed difficult to believe. And yet his head was in a terrible fug and felt like it might explode with every jolt of the carriage. Perhaps the man was right after all.

Once he reached London, Lande made enquiries about the playwright and discovered that the man was indeed considered brilliant but prone to drinking and keeping bad company. He had recently been called before the Privy Council and was apparently under orders to present himself to the authorities on a daily basis. Exactly what he was accused of was in itself the stuff of legend. Some said atheism, others that he was a Catholic sympathiser intent on sedition, others still that he was a spy or that he was suspected of immoral liaisons with other men. Whatever the truth of it, Horatio Lande saw that there might well be some benefit for him. Could such a man afford a successful lawyer? He doubted it and so he, Horatio Lande, one of the most prominent legal minds of London, would offer his services in return for literary tuition.

He went to view one of the man's plays, a most controversial tale written in this new-fangled blank verse — poetry that didn't rhyme, unlike Lande's own more traditional work. The man somehow even managed to make devils appear on the stage. A genius indeed, or perhaps there were very real and abominable reasons why the man was before the Privy Council... Either way, Lande had to meet him.

He managed to track down Marlowe to the south side of the river, to Deptford. He made arrangements to meet him there in the house of a lady by the name of Eleanor Bull. By all accounts she ran a private hostelry of some sort. With his manuscript in his bag he set off early, intent on first visiting the remains of the Golden Hind, which was moored at Deptford docks and open to visitors.

He found the ship both enchanting and disturbing. He marvelled that such a tiny vessel could sail so far and was repulsed that men might survive so long bound so close together in its sunless innards. He was happy to leave, to regain the fresh river air, and set off through the streets of Deptford in search of the widow Bull's house. And all the way there he mused on the theatrical possibilities of life aboard a ship of discovery. It might be caught in a huge storm, a veritable tempest. Shipwrecked! What stuff of legend and intrigue might be found there.

A serving woman opened the door. She seemed rather timid and, on Lande's explanation as to why he was calling, admitted that Mr Marlowe was within, with friends. She showed the visitor towards a room but did not usher him in or introduce him in any way. Instead she left him outside the closed door and immediately bustled away back to the servants' quarters.

Lande, not having met with this sort of behaviour before, hesitated at the door. There were raised voices within. He checked that he still had his poniard about him for safety's sake, removed his play from his bag that he might have it quickly to hand to explain his presence, and then, after some deliberation as to whether to knock or not, decided to enter the room unannounced.

The scene which greeted him was not one he could have foreseen in any life, especially not his current one. Of the four men in the room, two were holding down a third on a table where sat the remains of three meals. A fourth man was in the act of thrusting a dagger into the trapped man's eye. With a crunch, which was not quite covered by the victim's cry of distress, Lande heard the blade penetrate the skull and embed itself deep within the brain matter.

The lawyer felt the blood drain from his own face just as it now welled from the dying man's socket. A cry escaped his lips, from where he knew not, and the three perpetrators turned to look at him as one.

'Who are you?' the man with the knife asked.

Horatio Lande had enough wit not to give his name. He said, 'I have an appointment with a Mr Marlowe. But I can see it is inconvenient,' and he starting to turn with a view to exiting as fast as his size would allow.

He had barely raised one foot off the ground before the three were on him.

Two seized him and held him tight by the arms while the third thrust the bloodied knife against his neck.

'You weren't here,' the last said. 'You saw nothing. And if you say you did, the same fate will befall you. Do you understand?'

Lande tried to nod but found the knife dug deeper into his flesh. 'Yes,' he whispered.

'And do not be fooled into thinking you can gain justice by speaking against us. We three will have the same tale to tell. That Mr Marlowe came at me first with my own knife.' At these words, the knife was removed from Lande's neck and thrust into the scalp of the holder by his own hand. Blood coursed over the man's face and Lande felt his knees start to buckle. Had he not been held so firmly he would have fallen to the floor.

'Understand?' the man with the knife asked again.

Lande's eyes flicked to the still twitching corpse on the table, the one which he now knew belonged to the man he had come to meet. He nodded in small rapid oscillations. The hold on him was released and he was surprised to find that he could support his own weight. His legs were working so well, in fact, that he fled from the house and was at Deptford steps awaiting a boat to take him back up the river before he realised that his play, bearing his name and occupation prominently on the title page, had been left strewn on the floor at the scene of the crime.

It was only when he reached his own home, back in Chancery Lane near the Inns of Court, that he felt he could slacken his pace. His heart began to slow from its breakneck pace and the sweat in which he was bathed began to subside.

He waved away his housekeeper's cries of concern, locked himself in his study and poured a large helping of wine. This he downed in three gulps and collapsed into a chair to reflect on his experience.

He had witnessed the most heinous of crimes and would not report it. He would remain mute and watch silently as the deliberate murder of London's pre-eminent playwright was dismissed as self-defence. He, Horatio Lande, would be guilty by association and by omission. He, Horatio Lande, hitherto possibly England's most law-abiding gentleman, would be committing a crime. He, Horatio Lande, one of London's most distinguished and incorruptible lawyers, was planning to aid and abet murderers who possessed papers which bore his particulars.

It was, he acknowledged, the germ of a story, one which might best be nourished by some homely stew, some potent apple juice and many wise words. Horatio knew the ways of the likes of Marlowe's killers. He must get away, change his name, or forever be in their grip.

He gave an ironic laugh as he understood at last what Mistress Sittingbourne had been trying to tell him at their last meeting; that all the world's a stage, and all the men and women merely players. And he, now reached the age of slippered pantaloon, at last would play his part.

William.

He'd always wanted to be called William.

Moments in Time

Mairibeth MacMillan

The past, Sorcha had discovered, was more of a series of memorable moments than one continuous memory. In her ten years so far there had been a number of them that had helped to define her – not many of them positive.

There was the moment last year when her Dad had opened the door to the two policemen who had sat them both down and told them that her mother wouldn't be coming home thanks to a man who'd had so much to drink he'd driven onto the motorway heading in the wrong direction.

Then there was the moment when she'd met the new housekeeper. Mrs Wilson had wasted no time after Sorcha's dad had left for work in telling her that little girls with messy rooms were dirty and would be going straight to hell and then she'd never see her mum again because she was an angel in heaven now. That thought made Sorcha feel sick every time she left a book sitting on her bed or noticed a piece of lost Lego on the carpet as she closed her eyes to go to sleep.

Then there was the moment she'd watched the bin lorry drive away chewing up her favourite jigsaw all because Sorcha had left it on the dining room table, not wanting to break up the picture she had spent a whole day putting together. She hadn't thought that a finished jigsaw would be considered 'mess' but Mrs Wilson had thought differently.

Now, every night all Sorcha's dolls were put carefully back into their box and every piece of jigsaw puzzle was, too. Often Sorcha decided that it was better not to take the toys out rather than risk losing them forever. An untidy room wasn't going to keep her from seeing her mother again. No way. Sorcha had had enough taken away from her.

At the end of that summer there was another moment. A different sort of moment. Followed by a whole series of moments.

The house next door was a manse. The minister had retired and moved away and a new one was moving in. Mrs Wilson never missed church and heartily approved of the fact that she worked next to a manse and spoke to the minister on a regular basis – even if it wasn't the minister of the church she actually attended. 'Polishing her halo,' Mrs Wilson called it.

Sorcha found it hard to believe that Mrs Wilson would ever be an angel but then, according to Mrs Wilson, Sorcha didn't seem to know a lot about the difference between good and bad. Odd, considering her mum had always told Sorcha that she was her wee angel.

Sorcha watched from her living room window late one summer afternoon as burly men carried furniture into the manse which had been empty for a couple of weeks now. Mrs Wilson's halo must have been getting tarnished while she waited for the new minister to arrive. Sorcha grinned when she saw a pink wardrobe being lifted out of the back of the van, followed by a pink dressing table and a pink chest of drawers. Could it be another little girl? A friend next door? Sorcha hoped so.

Mrs Wilson never let any of her friends from school come round more than once – every one of her friends had committed some unmentionable sin according to Mrs Wilson.

'Your dad wouldn't consider me a suitable guardian if I allowed children like that to come and play,' Mrs Wilson had told her more than once and she was never allowed to play at anyone else's house. 'How can I say to your dad that I'm looking after you properly if you're off gallivanting somewhere else doing who knows what?'

A little girl next door would be hard to say no to, though, wouldn't she? And surely the daughter of a minister couldn't be a sinner in Mrs Wilson's eyes. Perhaps she would even help her to polish her halo. Sorcha waited and waited and waited and finally, just as Mrs Wilson called her for tea, a car pulled into the driveway and a little girl about her age got out. Her dad got out of the car and slammed the door then Sorcha got a shock when a third figure got out from the passenger side. A woman. This little girl still had a mum. Sorcha stared for a moment then smiled. Maybe they could be friends. She wanted to knock on the window and wave or run outside and say hello but Mrs Wilson came into the lounge just then.

'Don't stare, Sorcha. It's rude,' said Mrs Wilson. 'Now come and eat your tea before it gets cold. You shouldn't be wasting good food.' But she came and stood next to Sorcha and looked at the people next door as she spoke. Maybe staring was all right for grown-ups.

Just as they were about to turn away from the window the mother turned and looked straight at them. She smiled and waved over at them. Sorcha waved back and gasped when she saw the black shirt and white dog collar the woman wore. Mrs Wilson toyed with the cross around her neck and tutted. She turned away and headed for the dining room.

'Sorcha! Now, please.'

Sorcha raced through to the dining room eager to finish her dinner and go outside to see if she could get another glimpse or maybe even speak to the new girl next door.

'Go back out and come in properly,' Mrs Wilson barked at her. 'We don't come running into the dining room. What if I'd had hot food or a hot drink in my hand? You might have been burned.'

Sorcha sidled back out the door and waited for a minute before she came back in. Slowly, quietly, carefully. Sorcha's dad wandered through from the study and Mrs Wilson served the food as soon as he'd sat down, then left them to eat. Sorcha never spoke at mealtimes, not because she wasn't allowed to but because her dad couldn't seem to hear her through his paper. Or maybe it was because it rustled so loudly when he turned the pages. It was pointless, anyway. Sorcha picked at her food as she thought about the little girl next door. What was she called? What school would she go to? Then her stomach clenched. What if she didn't like Sorcha?

There was no pudding. There was never any pudding these days. She'd asked Mrs Wilson once and the woman had frowned at her.

'Rot your teeth. That's all that puddings will do for you. Rot your teeth. Good healthy food that's what I'm employed to cook and that's what I'll make. Doing you a favour, you know. You'll thank me when you're older.' Sorcha wasn't sure. Her mum had baked for her regularly.

Her food had tasted better than Mrs Wilson's too although Sorcha didn't dare point that out.

At the end of the meal, Sorcha cleared her plate and cup into the kitchen for Mrs Wilson to wash-up and headed for the back door.

'Where do you think you're going?' Mrs Wilson asked, arms folded across her chest.

'I just wanted to see—'

'The new neighbours won't want you disturbing them when they've just moved in, Sorcha. Have some respect.' Mrs Wilson shook her head. 'Whatever would your mother say?'

Sorcha's shoulders sagged as she climbed the stairs to her bedroom instead and sat in the window recess to read. There was no sign of anyone outside next door anyway. At exactly eight o'clock the front door closed behind Mrs Wilson and her dad came up to tuck her in.

'Daddy?'

'Yes, sweetheart?'

'The new minister's the mum not the dad,' she said. Her dad stopped fixing her sheet for a moment then patted it into place and stood.

'That's nice,' he said. 'Good night.' And he was gone.

The next morning Sorcha watched the clock, skipping rope at the ready, until it was exactly ten o'clock. It was dry but Mrs Wilson never let her play outside until after then so that she didn't disturb any of the neighbours too early. She took out her skipping rope and skipped round the garden a few times sneaking glances at the house next door. Even after she'd gone through every single skipping rhyme that she knew all the curtains were still closed and it was after eleven.

'Some folks,' she heard Mrs Wilson mutter when she came out to hang out the washing and noticed the closed curtains.

It wasn't until after lunch that the curtains were drawn and it was nearly three before the back door opened and a little girl came outside. She was dressed in jeans and a T-shirt. Sorcha stared. Mrs Wilson didn't like her wearing common clothes. She was surprised a minister allowed it.

'Hello,' the girl said and waved at her across the fence. 'I saw you yesterday. I'm Verity.'

'Hello,' Sorcha skipped closer to the fence. 'I'm Sorcha. Verity – that's pretty.'

'Thanks,' she smiled at her. 'Mum says to ask if you want to come and play. Can I come with you to ask your mum?'

'No,' said Sorcha. Verity's smile faded. For a moment she didn't want to tell Verity the truth then she realized that was silly. She lived next door. She'd find out soon enough. Then she'd whisper about it like so many people did even when Sorcha was close enough to hear. She took a deep breath pushing the familiar sadness aside.

'My mum died last year.'

'Oh.' Verity looked at her and didn't turn away or drop her gaze like most people did. 'I'm very sorry. My mum talks to people all the time when their husbands and wives and children die.'

'Children die?' said Sorcha.

'Yes, sometimes. Those are the worst. I know my mum cries when that happens.'

'She cries?' Sorcha was puzzled. Mrs Wilson was always telling her that she shouldn't cry. 'But doesn't she believe that they're with Jesus in heaven?'

'Of course they are. But that doesn't mean that we can't miss them now.' Verity stated with confidence. Sorcha felt something uncurl within her. A fear that if she cried it was because she didn't believe her mum was in heaven. 'I miss my Uncle Max,' Verity continued. 'Sometimes I cry because I miss him. And he's only in Africa.'

'Only...' said Sorcha. 'Africa's a long way.'

'Yes, but he'll be back in a year or two so it's not as far away as heaven,' Verity said. 'He's a missionary. Anyway. Should we ask someone if you can come and play? Mum said she'd get a drink and a biscuit ready.'

'I'll meet you at the gate,' Sorcha said but Verity had already climbed the railing and dropped down onto the grass missing the flower bed by a couple of feet.

'You are not allowed to climb the railings, Sorcha.' Mrs Wilson's dour voice burst Sorcha's little bubble of happiness.

'But I didn't...'

'I saw your friend on the railings. What your friend does is a reflection on you so always remember to choose your friends wisely.'

Sorcha looked at her feet and scuffed a toe through the grass. Verity, however, seemed uncowed by Mrs Wilson and smiled a bright sunny smile.

'Hello, I'm Verity. My mummy's the new minister.'

'Yes, well,' Mrs Wilson half turned away but Sorcha distinctly heard her mutter, 'Some things can't be helped, I suppose,' under her breath.

'She's invited Sorcha to come through for a drink and a biscuit. Just to say hello.'

'Really?' Mrs Wilson humphed. 'Well, I suppose, she is the minister... You can go, Sorcha but don't be a nuisance and mind your manners. I don't want to be getting bad reports about your behaviour especially from the minister.'

'Yes, Mrs Wilson.'

'And don't climb the railings. Go round the proper way and ring the doorbell. In fact, I'll come with you.'

Sorcha was a little deflated that Mrs Wilson was coming too but she was so excited about being allowed to go to a friend's house – even if she'd only just met her – that she could hardly keep still and skipped along beside Mrs Wilson.

'Do you need to go to the toilet, Sorcha?'

'No.'

'Are you sure?'

'I don't need.' Sorcha wished Mrs Wilson would stop talking about it in front of Verity.

'Then stop jumping about.'

'Okay,' she said. And she tried, she really tried, but it was just so exciting to think that Verity lived next door. She skipped another couple of steps and then Mrs Wilson's hand clamped down on her shoulder so she stopped. They walked down the driveway past the neat flowerbeds that surrounded the small square of front grass.

'Could do with a good weed.' Mrs Wilson sniffed. 'Wonder who does that sort of thing in this house? Not really the thing.'

'What isn't?' asked Sorcha staring at the flowers.

'Nothing,' Mrs Wilson said and rang the bell.

It gave a loud ding-dong deep in the house but Verity had the front door open before the noise even finished.

'Verity, either don't ring the bell or just wait–' The minister was half out of the kitchen, tea-towel still in her hand when she noticed Mrs Wilson and Sorcha in the doorway. 'Oh, hello.'

'Mummy, this is Sorcha from next door, you said I was to ask her if she wanted to play.'

'Yes, but I thought you would just, well, never mind.' The minister frowned and looked at Sorcha then at Mrs Wilson and smiled a different smile. 'Hello, I'm Anne.' She held out her hand towards Mrs Wilson who stared at it for a moment before reaching for it. 'You can call me Reverend Anne,' she said to Sorcha.

'Elspeth Wilson,' Mrs Wilson replied. Sorcha shot her a glance. She'd never heard her first name before. Mrs Wilson scowled.

'This is Sorcha. Your daughter invited her to play.'

'Yes that's right, Verity was so happy to see she would have a friend next door.'

'Well I hope she won't be a bother.'

'Not at all. It'll keep Verity out from under my feet if she has someone to play with.'

'I'm the housekeeper,' she said. And the minister nodded. 'Sorcha's mother died last year. Drunk driver.' The last phrase was always whispered and always struck a mix of fear and embarrassment into Sorcha. She felt her cheeks heat and stared at the floor.

'Girls, you can go and play upstairs or outside, if you like,' said Reverend Anne then turned to Mrs Wilson. 'Please, come in for a minute.'

'No, I have work to do. Just send Sorcha home in time for dinner at six, please.'

Reverend Anne nodded at her and started to close the door.

'Come on, Sorcha,' Verity said and grabbed her hand, pulling her towards the kitchen.

Once they were back out in the garden – this time on the other side of the fence – they played at skipping for a while. Verity knew a whole different lot of skipping rhymes which she taught to Sorcha and then for a while they ran round the garden and explored the different areas from the broken down hut to the expanse of rhododendrons that you could get lost in.

Sorcha had never been in this garden before and had only seen it from across the fence. She was having a great time exploring it despite Mrs Wilson glaring at them the whole time from the kitchen window. Finally Verity's mum came out with a tray containing a drink and a chocolate biscuit each. Sorcha's eyes grew round at the sight of it. A whole chocolate biscuit each. Verity was so lucky to have a mum like that.

'Do you miss your mum?' Verity asked as they sat on the wooden bench munching on their biscuits.

'Yes,' said Sorcha. 'Of course I do.'

'Is your dad still alive?' Verity asked after a pause.

'Yes.'

'So, Mrs Wilson doesn't look after you all the time then?'

'Just when Dad's at work. She goes home after tea.'

'That's not quite so bad, then,' Verity said. Sorcha didn't ask her what she meant. She knew she should be grateful that Mrs Wilson was there at all. Otherwise she might not get to stay with her dad either. Mrs Wilson had told her that more than once.

As the weeks passed, Sorcha and Verity became inseparable. They were in the same class at school and always sat beside each other on the bus every morning and afternoon.

One morning in the October break the two girls were playing very quietly with a jigsaw in Sorcha's bedroom. Mrs Wilson had been in three times already to make sure that they weren't making a mess. Sorcha envied the fact that Verity was allowed to have a little mess in her room and Verity had been horrified when she heard about Mrs Wilson throwing away Sorcha's other jigsaw.

'But... does your dad know?'

Sorcha stared at Verity. 'I don't know,' she said. She had always assumed he did and had agreed with Mrs Wilson, but maybe he hadn't.

'Maybe you should tell him. She shouldn't be allowed to do things like that,' Verity said. 'It's not nice.'

Sorcha said nothing although she secretly agreed. Maybe she should try to talk to her dad. Would he even hear her if she tried to speak to him? Would he care? And if he did speak to Mrs Wilson would she just throw some more of Sorcha's toys away to punish her? Sorcha wasn't sure if she wanted to take the risk.

'Are you coming over this afternoon?' Verity asked.

'No, I'm not allowed out. The Women's Guild is having a committee meeting and Mrs Wilson is the new president so she's having it here. Dad said it was okay. She's doing some baking this morning.'

'I thought she didn't approve of sweet things?'

'She doesn't.' Sorcha frowned. Verity was right. She had smelled lovely smells coming from the kitchen this morning – biscuits and fairy cakes at the very least. Smells she hadn't smelled since her mum had died. 'I guess it's okay for grown-ups,' Sorcha said.

'I guess,' Verity said frowning then she brightened. 'My mum's coming to the meeting. Maybe she'll let me come too and we can play.'

'I've to stay in my room and be as quiet as a church mouse,' said Sorcha.

'Okay, I'll bring a board game to play or another jigsaw.'

'Okay.'

Sorcha smiled as she ate her lunch. It would be nice to have company when she had been expecting such a dull afternoon, terrified that she would make too much noise and make Mrs Wilson angry. When she finished she took her plate and cup through to the kitchen and put it next the sink. She stopped and stared at all the baking on the table.

Mrs Wilson was using Sorcha's mother's two china cake stands and the lazy susan. They were piled high with scones and biscuits and tray-bake and fairy cakes but what really caught Sorcha's eye was the plateful of Melting Moments. As she approached she noticed the recipe book still open on the table. Her mother's recipe book. There was her mother's handwriting. Looking at it made Sorcha's eyes itch and her nose feel all clogged. She took a quick sniff to make it go away, but that only intensified the familiar, comforting smell of the baking.

All this baking and yet when Verity came round Mrs Wilson gave them a glass of water or milk if they were very lucky and had point blank refused to allow them anything to eat other than bread and butter. Jam, Mrs Wilson had told her, was a sinful indulgence and so looking at the pile of scones richly slathered in butter and jam Sorcha wondered if maybe the Women's Guild didn't care about going to hell.

Sorcha turned to leave the kitchen but her attention was drawn once more to the Melting Moments. Her favourite. And they'd been made from her mother's recipe, in her kitchen, using ingredients her dad had paid for. Surely she and Verity were entitled to one each? As a special treat. Sorcha stared at them for a long moment then she made her decision. She and Verity deserved a treat for having to be so quiet. She opened the cupboard as quietly as she could and removed a tea-plate then put the two smallest Melting Moments onto it and headed for her bedroom.

If she had just been a moment faster Mrs Wilson would have still been in the lounge when she reached her room. But she wasn't and Mrs Wilson stepped in the hallway level with Sorcha's position when she was only halfway up the stairs.

'What's that?' Mrs Wilson's voice was sharp.

'Melting Moments,' Sorcha said.

'Those are for the ladies attending the meeting today. Are you stealing from the ladies of the church?' Mrs Wilson said. Her voice was as cold and hard as the china plate clutched in Sorcha's fingers. Sorcha stood on the middle stair as Mrs Wilson came around and started to come up towards her, one step at a time.

'After me spending all morning in the kitchen baking for this meeting, you're in there stealing?' Mrs Wilson's voice got louder with every word.

Behind her, framed in the glass doorway, Sorcha could see Verity's shadow. The visitors had started to arrive. She felt sick. Would all the visitors agree that Sorcha was a terrible person and a thief and never going to heaven to be with her mum and... No, Sorcha straightened her spine and stood her ground for the first time. Verity's presence outside strengthening her resolve.

'It's not stealing,' said Sorcha. 'This is my house. My daddy bought the food. That's my mummy's recipe book and she wrote that recipe in it for me. It's only one each for Verity and me. I'm not stealing.'

Sorcha held her ground even though the plate trembled so much in her hands that the cookies nearly fell off as Mrs Wilson took one step towards her at a time.

Mrs Wilson's expression made Sorcha worry that she was about to wet her pants, but she knew that would only get her in more trouble and she was sure that she was right about the Melting Moments. Right about the fact that her mother would have wanted her to have some.

'How dare you? Your mother will be crying in heaven when she sees what an evil child she has,' Mrs Wilson roared and grabbed for the plate.

Sorcha screamed and jumped back. The plate flew into the air over the banister, smashing on the hall floor below. Sorcha's fingers still clutched part of each of the Melting Moments and she turned to run with them to her room. She screamed again as she felt Mrs Wilson grab her hair but pulled away from her as the front door flew open.

'Mrs Wilson, is there a problem?' Sorcha heard Reverend Anne ask just before she slammed her bedroom door. A few minutes later there was a soft knock on her door. Sorcha ignored it, but the door opened anyway and Verity stuck her head around it.

'What happened?'

Sorcha pursed her lips and held out a piece of broken melting moment for Verity. 'I wanted to give you one of these. It's my mum's recipe and Mrs Wilson had made them for the meeting. But I took them without asking and she's very angry.'

Verity sat on Sorcha's bed and patted the seat beside her. Sorcha sat and together they bit into their partial Melting Moments. Even through her tears the taste made Sorcha smile. It reminded her of cold winter afternoons baking with her mother in the warm kitchen. Then she started to sob and couldn't stop. Verity put an arm around her while they finished eating.

Sorcha had no idea how much time had passed before there was a soft tap on her bedroom door.

'Come in,' called Verity and Reverend Anne came in followed by Sorcha's dad.

'Time to go home, Verity,' said Reverend Anne and held out a hand to her daughter. 'You can come through and play anytime, Sorcha. Or if you want to talk I'm always here to listen. That's my job.'

'Okay,' said Sorcha although she had no idea what she would have to talk about.

Sorcha watched her dad as she listened to the two sets of footsteps going down the stairs and across the hall. The outside door opened and voices could be heard then it closed and the voices faded away. Her dad sat down on the bed beside her and lifted her onto his knee. Sorcha put her arms around him and held on tight.

'I'm sorry,' Sorcha said. 'Mrs Wilson said that Mummy would be crying because I stole the Melting Moments.'

'She's not,' her dad assured her running his hand over her hair. 'She would have given you one. Or made you a whole plateful just for you. Don't ever forget that. Your mother loved you.'

'But Mrs Wilson–'

'Is gone,' said her dad. 'I'll find someone else to help with the house and pick you up from school but I'll look after you myself as much as I can.'

'Can we bake?'

'Er...' her dad froze then started to laugh. 'I don't know. Let's just see how it goes, okay? I can always ask someone else to bake for us.'

'Okay.'

Sorcha closed her eyes and let her head rest against her dad's chest. Another moment that she would remember forever.

Searching for Grandma

Annis Farnell

She mounted the shallow steps, passed through the portico. The courtyard was larger than she had imagined, the linden trees casting welcome shade over the scattered tables set for four, for six, for eight, all with customers, or reserved notices; a popular spot, then. At one table sat an elderly couple, at another, a clique of youngsters in their late teens; in the far corner was a boisterous family at a large table cobbled together from several smaller ones. Some sort of family celebration, she surmised, feeling a pang of envy; there had to be four generations there, all obviously enjoying being part of a family circle.

Why couldn't my family be more like that? she thought, remembering the simmering silences, the outbursts of viciousness, Grandma sitting silent and withdrawn, with the family, yet not of it; she herself, separate from them, too, but all too often abruptly recalled from her thought-wanderings to the discomfort of her surroundings. Christmases and birthdays were the worst: the knowledge that the gifts she would receive would be anything but the books and art materials she craved, that she would be forced, as always, into a show of gratitude for the tights and woolly hats, the respectable cotton knickers. And constantly, the pressure to find 'nice' friends, to be more 'normal'.

She had rebelled, of course, in small and secretive ways: she had gone without school dinners, used the money to buy books – that was foiled, when her parents found out, and made her take sandwiches; forged excuse notes on games days, so she could spend the afternoon in the school library; invented outings with classmates whose parents her mother didn't know, in order to visit museums and art galleries.

Nursing, her parents' preferred choice of profession for her, lost out to a place at St Andrews, supported by a sizeable bursary. There, for the first time, her hunger for books and thirst for knowledge was not viewed as a slightly embarrassing abnormality. Instead, she found friends among like-minded people. She cropped her curly mane, took to wearing comfort-fit jeans, Weird Fish tops and rugby shirts, which suited her slender frame, and stuck her feet into solidly supportive and comfortable footwear, in place of the pretty-but-flimsy slip-ons approved by her mother, sister and aunts. She also disproved, quite frequently, their dictum, that men only liked feminine girls, though, almost twenty years down the line, she had yet to find one she liked enough to commit to.

And then, aged nearly ninety, Grandma had died, quietly and without fuss, much as she had lived. And had left everything to a surprised granddaughter, on the grounds that 'she is more like me than any of the rest'. Her father had been furious, raging about his mother's 'ingratitude', and had contested the will. Then railed against a legal profession that had not only refused to grant him more than his legal due, but had obliged him to share it with his sisters, then added insult to injury by charging him a sizeable fee. *Serve the greedy bugger right,* she thought, chuckling at the memory. If she really was like Grandma, maybe here in Germany, she could find a family she might relate to.

A waiter was balancing a laden tray one-handed, distributing drinks with the other. She let her eyes wander, searching.

'Sit at the table for two under the big tree', his email had read.

Just as well nobody's claimed it, she thought, a wry smile tugging at the corners of her mouth, as she wound through the tables towards it. A middle-aged couple were also making for the shady spot, but she beat them to it. A young waitress, too, tried to head her off, but gave up as she pulled out a chair.

She settled in the seat facing the entrance. What would he be like? His response to her advertisement had given very little away. The butterflies were crawling in her stomach; excitement? nervousness? She had no idea. Perhaps she would feel better after she had eaten something. As though reading her mind, the young waitress came up, handed her a menu, and went away again.

She studied it. She wasn't particularly hungry, in fact, despite her earlier thought, she wasn't at all sure she wanted to eat anything, and seeing a platter with what appeared to be the best part of a leg of something set before a diner at a neighbouring table, made her feel slightly nauseated. She wished she could read German, at least enough to know what she was ordering. *Damn my family and their racism!*

'Suppe'. Soup, possibly, but then ... 'Gulaschsuppe'? Goulash was a kind of Hungarian stew, so how could it be a soup? And why did they run all their words together like that, it made it so difficult to read.

Perhaps the safest thing would be one of the other cheap options, then at least she could leave it without feeling she'd wasted too much money. 'Obatzda und Brez'n' No clues there, at all.

'Do you speak English?' she asked the waitress.

'A little. What I have learned in school.'

'What is this?' She pointed to the Obatzda.

The waitress frowned in concentration, trying to recall the word.

'Käse ... cheese? Und Brez'n ... is bread, ja?'

Bread and cheese. Not much to go wrong there. She ordered a beer to go with it, the September heat had made her thirsty.

A young waiter delivered her beer, and the waitress brought her snack, wishing her 'Guten Appetit.' She smiled her thanks.

Ah, she thought, looking at the knots of bread on the plate; *so Brez'n are pretzels. But ... this is cheese?* The bowl contained something lumpy and cream-coloured, too liquid to be served on a plate, too solid to be truly a liquid. Dubiously, she broke off a piece of pretzel, and scooped up a little of the stuff.

The flavour of the simple dish surprised her with its intensity. The rich, soft cheesiness contrasted with and complemented the bread, with its crisp, salty crust. The beer had been a good choice, too, the bitterness of the drink enhancing the creamy salinity of the food.

'Frau Doktorin Guthrie?' a male voice somewhere above her head enquired. He pronounced it 'Goot-ree'.

She swallowed hastily, embarrassed to be caught with her mouth full.

'Elspeth Guthrie, yes.'

He wore a lightweight grey suit with a matching tie, the brightly-striped shirt lending the ensemble an air of gaiety. A tall man with light grey eyes and fashionably cropped grey hair, he had the sort of rough features that manage to be attractive, while falling short of being handsome.

Elspeth was glad she had opted for a summer frock and a touch of make-up, and knew a twinge of regret that she hadn't visited a hairdresser lately. She gave herself a mental shake; this was an appointment, not a date. Without waiting for an invitation, he pulled out a chair to join her, setting his slim briefcase on the paving beside the table.

'Meyer. Theodor,' he said, reaching across to shake hands.

The waitress appeared, and placed a beer in front of him.

"Tag, Herr Kommissar,' she greeted him.

Kommissar? Elspeth thought; *he's a policeman?*

"Tag, Magda. Obatzda, bitte.'

She turned to Elspeth. 'I am sorry, I do not know you are a friend of Herr Meyer.'

That explains that, then, Elspeth thought, remembering how the girl had moved to head her off. *He's a regular, and I came and sat at 'his' table, but they couldn't shift me, because it wasn't actually reserved.* She smiled.

'Don't worry about it.'

'Did you have a pleasant journey?' he asked.

'Thank you. It was – interesting. I've never flown before'

He looked a little startled. 'What, never?'

She shook her head. 'The only time I've ever been out of Britain was a school trip to Normandy with my French class, and then we went by coach. If I'm honest, I never really felt the need to travel abroad, I was always too busy exploring Scotland, so I've clocked up a fair mileage by road, and on boats and ferries, I've just never had the need to go by air.'

'"Nur wer die Heimat kennt ..."' he murmured.

'I beg your pardon?'

'It is a quotation,' he explained. 'From Goethe. "Only he who knows his native land, has a yardstick for other countries." I, too, have spent much time exploring Germany.'

They smiled at one another, two strangers caught in a moment of kinship.

In a sudden burst of confidence she said, 'I was really worried about getting to Berlin from Frankfurt, but it was so easy, everything is so well signed.' What was it about this man that invited confidences? Normally, she hid her uncertainties beneath a veneer of assurance.

He acknowledged the arrival of his food with a nod and a smile, and attacked the plateful. He chewed and swallowed, washed down the mouthful with a swig of beer.

'So,' he said. 'What is your interest in Erna Rehfeldt?'

'I told you in my email,' she said. 'She was my grandmother.'

He studied her, calculating.

'But why? And why now?'

She answered the last question first.

'Because she died a few months ago. Because she said I was like her. Because she left me enough money to pay for the trip, and because I knew nothing about her, only that she was German; it seemed to me, learning more about her, and perhaps about myself, was a good way of spending the money. One of my aunts once told me that the family called her "Bob's little war souvenir". Not that he got to Berlin until 1947, he was just too young for the war. But – but there seemed to be – I don't know, a-a sort of feeling, an attitude, that somehow she'd taken advantage of him being so young, that he was just a meal ticket, a way out of Berlin.'

'Ach, so,' he said, uninformatively. 'Did you not think to ask her yourself before she died? This – curiosity – seems very sudden.'

She nibbled her pretzel, thinking.

'It wasn't as simple as that. There was always this – this atmosphere, as though she should be ashamed of being German. As if they all held her personally responsible for the war.' She looked up, blue eyes meeting grey. 'My family hates all things German, in spite of the fact that in two world wars, none of them was killed, maimed, or even taken prisoner. Mainly because they were all too old, too young, or in reserved occupations. Our bit of Scotland hardly ever saw the Luftwaffe, and we were never bombed. It's almost as if the family feel it was all done deliberately to inconvenience them, they take it so personally.' She shook her head. 'Even my generation doesn't seem to have escaped the taint.'

'Wars leave long shadows,' he said. 'So why are you different?'

She smiled, a faint twitch of the lips.

'Probably because I became a history teacher. I learnt to look at events from a distance, without getting personally involved.'

He pounced. 'And now we are in September. Do you not have classes?'

Again that faint smile.

'I teach in a university. And I'm on a sabbatical.' The cool grey eyes acknowledged a hit. She chuckled. 'I'm supposed to be working on a book about Christian missionaries in post-Roman Scotland. I'm afraid at the moment, Grandma's history looks like being a bit more interesting!'

'And so you are taking, what, a historian's interest?'

She thought about it.

'Yes, I think that's fair. Grandma never talked about the war, or the time before she met Grandpa, so I'm really tackling it as an intellectual exercise, if you like, rather than a family thing. Come to that,' she added, 'the family haven't been so much unhelpful as obstructive.' The row, following the revelations of Grandma's will, had been nothing compared to the furore after she announced she was going to Germany. So far as Elspeth was concerned, the rift was final; in the last few weeks, she had often wondered why she had put up with them for so long.

Interest stirred in the impassive, craggy features.

'You think they are hiding something?'

'Hiding something?' She was puzzled. 'No, they were just – I suppose, "ashamed" is the only word. You know, that Grandpa let the side down by marrying an enemy.'

'That is all?'

'What more is there?' she asked. 'They hated her, and she, them. She must have been very unhappy for most of her life, poor woman. I've never really understood it; I've known other people with a German grandparent, and most families seem to have accepted them, so why not mine?'

'This is why you speak no German? Or — ' she realised those grey eyes were cold, penetrating, ' — sprechen Sie besser Deutsch, als Sie vorgeben?'

The sudden switch to German threw her; she looked blank. Ignoring it, she met his eyes squarely.

'Even my generation wasn't allowed to learn German at school, so I did Spanish as a second language. I'm afraid my school didn't teach classics, which would have been far more useful to me. And I'm sorry – this feels more like an interrogation than a conversation.'

'I had to be sure,' he said, 'that you were all you claimed to be.' He smiled, without humour. 'When I can discover nothing about a person, it can be a bad sign, as well as a good one.'

Shock held her silent for a heartbeat, then: 'You investigated *me*?' He bowed his head in assent. 'But *why*?'

'Because your grandmother was flagged up as a Person of Interest.' She gaped at him. 'You must understand, Erna Rehfeldt was not a native Berliner. She came from East Prussia, claiming to be a refugee from the communists, and she came late, not until 1948. It was the time of the

Airlift, tensions were high between Russia and the Allies, and there were a lot of spy scares. And apart from her late arrival, there were other reasons for believing she was working for the Russians; she had several boyfriends among the Allied soldiers before she fastened on your grandfather. You see, he was going back very soon after they met.'

'You're telling me,' she said carefully, 'that Grandma was a Russian spy?'

'After a fashion. She was, we think, what they called a sleeper; her job was to lie low, become an innocent member of the community, live a normal life, until she was called. In her case, it never happened, but now, with the situation in the Ukraine and the Middle East, and tensions building again, you can understand that we were … interested, to know if she had passed the torch on to you.'

She shook her head. 'Perhaps this explains why she never tried to get close to her grandchildren, either. I suppose it would have seemed too much like a betrayal.' She was aware of the ambiguity of the statement, but let him make of it what he would. 'It's all a bit much to take in.' She paused. 'I thought, when you replied to my advertisement, that you were a – oh, some member of the family, a cousin or something, but you're not, are you?'

He shook his head. 'I am sorry if I have misled you, but I never claimed to be related, did I?'

'No,' she conceded.

He reached down to his briefcase, and produced a thin envelope.

'I put together what information I have that is of public record,' he said, handing it to her, and waving away her thanks. 'I am afraid I was unable to trace any living relatives. Do you intend to stay here long?'

'I'm here for two weeks,' she said. 'I didn't know how long it would take to trace her family, and besides, I thought I should make the most of my first trip to Germany.'

He grinned at her. The grey eyes were warm now, sparkling like Aberdeen granite in sunshine.

'Very wise. Berlin is a beautiful city. Perhaps you will allow me to show you around a little? We could start with an evening cruise on the river and dinner?'

A holiday romance had not been one of her plans, but so what? And if investigation, not romance, was his plan, so what again? There was nothing to find, so nothing to fear.

Hamster

Julia Chalkley

Of all the decisions I made that day, the one I most regret is that I called my husband a hamster.

He earned it by snuggling deep into his sleeping bag and tying the neck of it so tightly that it covered all but his eyes, nose and moustache like a hamster rolled in cotton wool. Dan shouted 'Hamster!' and I joined in. Greg endured the storm of teasing without comment.

We can dish out the teasing, Dan and I, but we can't take it. We argued at least once a week as children. Mum used to separate us whenever the arguments went as far as kicking and punching. When I was six I gave him an impressive black eye. Two years later, he threw me off the sofa – I couldn't move my arm, and Mum thought I'd broken it. She had to take us both to A&E, as Dad wasn't home yet. The doctor found it was a severe strain to the shoulder muscles, not a break, but he told Mum he had a duty to report any suspicious injuries to children. He gave that up when Greg and I resumed battle, me clonking Greg round the ear with a clipboard and him throwing a glass of water over me, both of us replaying the original disagreement full volume in the A&E cubicle.

We don't throw punches now. We're good enough friends to spend our spare time sailing together, though we still argue. Greg goes quiet whenever we reminisce over our childhood battles. Growing up without siblings, Greg had been treated gently by his parents and always gives in hastily whenever I argue with him. Hamster, I thought. Very fitting. Soft, sweet, not tough enough to fight.

He certainly wasn't facing up to the sail home very well.

'It's howling out there,' he said.

We listened to the wind rattling the halliards. The words of the latest shipping forecast stuttered across the page of the logbook in my own shorthand.

'The wind is going to be dying down, though,' I said. 'Force 7 at the moment, coming down to 5 or 6. We've sailed in a 6, it's a bit lively but we can cope.'

'And it's a northerly,' Dan said. 'It'll blow us home.'

'We need to get home by Monday, and that means starting now,' I said. 'It took us nearly four days to get here – today's the last day we can set off and still be back at work on time.'

'We could ring up and ask for another day's leave,' Greg suggested.

'No,' Dan said. 'All my leave's used up for this year. We'll go out of the estuary and see what it's like in the open sea. If it's really rough, we can nip back in. Agreed?'

'Yeah,' I said. 'Come on, Greg, don't be a jessie.'

Greg's eyes swivelled between us. We looked back at him, ready for a battle if that's what he wanted.

'Okay,' he said. "But I still think… Okay.'

'I'll get the stew going,' I said.

I spent the trip from Egersund marina to the estuary entrance peeling vegetables, frying onions and adding the lot to a quart of thick stock. It was our traditional first meal on passage – a chunky vegetable stew, hot and bland. We kept it simmering on the stove at a low heat for a day or two, taking a ladle of stew out to warm up the person on watch and adding more stock and vegetables to it to keep it full. With a few hours to go before landfall, we'd heave to and finish the lot, with all the bread we still had on board.

By the time the stew was ready to eat, we were three miles off the coast of Norway and heading south with a furious wind pouring relentlessly over our stern, the yacht pitching in seas rougher than any we had seen before. The cooker swivelled on its gimbals, keeping the surface just close enough to horizontal to keep the stew in the pan. I was hanging on to the bulkhead as I stirred the stew. Dan was taking the first turn on the tiller. Greg was up in the cockpit alongside him, fighting off seasickness by staying out of the cabin.

'Lively!' Dan shouted down to me.

'Yeah,' I shouted back over the clatter and snap of the shackles on the deck. 'It'll calm down. Are you both clipped on?'

Each of us had a webbing leash with a secure clasp at each end — one clipped to our chest harnesses and the other clipped securely to a safety line, a length of thick stranded steel wire running the length of the yacht on both sides. I was fanatical about it. During rough sails, solo watches and night watches, I secure my leash to the safety line before I take the last step up into the cockpit, and I don't unclip it until my feet are on the top step of the ladder on my way back down into the cabin. The other two are less cautious, and I can't help but check on them.

'Maybe we should turn back,' Greg said.

Dan looked back at the coast of Norway, and I took another step up the cabin ladder to see over his shoulder. The break in the cliffs where the estuary led to the safety of Egersund marina had disappeared. As the waves reared up behind us we lost sight of the cliff altogether. I realised that we couldn't turn safely to head back into the wind and that even if we did, our chances of finding the estuary entrance were small.

'We should go on,' Dan said. 'The wind's going to die down soon. We'll be safer at sea than being blown around close to those rocks.'

Greg's eyes widened, but he didn't argue.

Later that night a wave broke over the stern and slapped into the cabin, covering the cabin floor in an inch or so of water. We set the bilge pumps running and heard them choking on a throatful of seawater. We'd closed the hatch between the cockpit and the cabin to keep the sea out. After that, the world was divided into those resting on the damp, salty bunks in the cabin below and the lone person on watch in the cockpit. At every change of the watch we looked first at the wind speed, hoping it had started to decrease. At every change of the watch, we recorded the wind speed and direction in the log. We found that the wind increased as time went on, with sudden hard gusts that sent the needle flying crazily around the scale as the helmsman fought to hold the course. It touched 50 knots just before the yacht was flipped hard onto its side.

I don't know why I didn't react straight away to Greg's silence. Maybe I hit my head on the engine panel. I say it to myself as an excuse, but all I do remember is my shoulder hitting the panel hard with a crack that must have been the sound of the wood panelling splitting into a shallow dent. My head missed everything, I think.

Dan wasn't so lucky. I saw him float across the yacht's tiny cabin in mid-air and hit his head hard on the ceiling on the opposite side, crashing into the table on the way and tearing its bolts loose from the floor. He dropped onto the bunk below him and real life came back into focus.

The yacht had stopped churning. The waves outside had gone still and flat, though the wind still played the hellish orchestral on the yacht's rigging and we bobbed in a random ugly dance. The table lay on the floor sliding port to starboard, starboard to port. The exposed nails of its shattered base raked scratches into the polished surface with each slide.

'Are you all right?' I asked Dan.

'I don't know,' he said.

Those words were more surreal than watching him fly across the cabin. This was my big brother, always loud and sure of himself. I wanted him to smile, tell me he was joking. Instead he grabbed the bulkhead, hauled himself to his feet and reeled around the corner to the heads, where he threw up noisily. I stood waiting for him to come back, physically and mentally, and tried not to think that without Dan we were all lost.

The wind twanged the rigging, the voices in the wind began snarling and cursing again, the waves began to slap the boat to and fro. Dan climbed the ladder, opened the hatch and looked up into the cockpit. There was a short silence. That's when I realised that I hadn't heard Greg make a sound since he'd screamed Dan's name twice, just before the yacht skewed crazily sideways and the world turned upside down.

If he'd been washed overboard – the webbing leash wouldn't snap. Would it? Would the clasp unhook itself? Had the safety line snapped? How long could he survive being towed behind a yacht?

Had he remembered to clip his leash to the safety line at all?

In the long silence, I remembered how the cliffs of Norway had disappeared behind the waves as we dropped into the troughs between the wave crests. A fully dressed man washed overboard into the North Sea floats chin-deep in water, and the wind pushes a yacht harder, sends it on a different track from a man in the water. If Greg had gone overboard, we would never find him, and he had less than thirty minutes before his body temperature dropped to fatal levels. I thought of making the decision to stop searching and carry on home and felt as if I were looking down from a narrow ledge at a great height.

Then I heard Greg's voice, high and panicky, saying to Dan; 'I heard that wave hissing behind me. It broke over the stern.' Dan said something soothing and climbed up into the cockpit. I yelled, 'Clip yourself on!' and Dan stuck his head back through the hatch to say; 'All right! Don't nag!'

I sat at the chart table, wondering how I could have ignored the chance that Greg might have been washed overboard.

Dan came back down the steps into the cabin and sat down heavily on the bunk. 'I have a real headache,' he said.

I stood up to get him some water (discovering vaguely that I had the tap stem gripped hard in my hand, that I had grabbed it and ripped it out of its socket as I was thrown across the cabin). Shoved the tap back into its socket. Drew water. Found paracetamol. Knelt on the bunk beside him.

'Greg's okay up there?'

Dan gulped down the tablets. 'He's fine. The boom's broken, so the mainsail's out of action. We've strapped the boom to the deck, don't want it crashing through the hull.'

I went back to the chart table and logged our GPS position onto the chart of the southern North Sea. Halfway across. A full day's journey before we came within sight of safe English harbours.

'Can we make a run for it to Denmark?' I asked.

Dan shook his head and grimaced as his headache bit hard. 'No. We'd have to go through the Kattegat Strait, and that's dangerous even in calm weather. Turning east, we'd be sideways on to these waves – we'd have no chance. We'd be knocked down every few minutes.'

I sat thinking of our options. None. None at all. Except to keep going. Thirty hours ago, I'd been peeling the vegetables for the stew as we pottered down Egersund's estuary channel. I'd turned the gas back on half an hour ago to be ready for the change of watch, and the stewpot was still miraculously locked onto the stove-top, its contents bubbling on a heat as low as a candle-flame. I stirred it and reached for a bowl.

'Have some stew,' I said to Dan.

'I'm not hungry,' he said.

I poured a ladleful of stew into the bowl and passed it over to him. He took it and said again, 'I'm not hungry.'

'When was the last time you ate or drank?' He took the spoon I handed to him. 'Eat now. It'll take the edge off your headache.'

'Bossy cow.' He began to spoon the stew into his mouth and slurp it down.

'You can tell Mum I nagged you next time you see her.'

Immediately, I regretted saying that. Mum might not get the chance to referee between the two of us again, and Dan knew it. Dan got to the bottom of his stew, refused seconds but took another glass of water. As he retreated to his bunk, I poured a second bowl of stew and went up the steps to the cockpit.

Greg sat with his hand clamped white around the tiller. He had pulled the hood of his jacket over his head and tied it tight, so that the edge of the hood formed a circle around his face. Only his eyes, nose and lips were visible. Just as it had been a day ago, when Dan and I had teased him. With another huge wave rearing up behind him in the darkness and his eyes wide, he looked small and scared. He didn't want to be up there, but if he asked to be relieved of the watch he knew Dan or I would have to take his place. I was ashamed of calling him a hamster.

'Stew,' I said, handing him the bowl.

He leaned forward and took it from me.

'Do you want me to take the tiller so you can eat it?' I asked.

'No,' he said. 'I can manage the tiller with one hand if I concentrate.'

My eyes followed the rise and rise of a wave behind the boat. Greg saw my eyes lift up and up and widen.

'I'm not looking around,' he said. 'It just scares me... That big wave lifted our stern right out of the water – I couldn't steer with the rudder flapping in the air. We got turned around and the wave broke over us.' He settled the bowl in the pit of his lap and dug the spoon into the thick stew. 'The mast hit the water for a minute. I thought we were dead.'

'I'll stay here,' I said. 'If you want more stew...'

'No,' he said. 'Shut the hatch. We have to keep the sea out of the cabin, or we'll sink. This is enough stew for me.'

I hesitated. The wave behind him hissed as its top began to break into spray.

'Close the hatch now,' he said. Quietly said, but as forceful an order as Dan had ever issued.

I took one last look at him sitting in darkness. Light from the masthead shone faintly on the wave that filled the air behind his head. I checked that his line was safely clipped to the ring set into the cockpit wall and reluctantly shut the hatch.

As I went to finish filling in the log I could still sense him, steering us safely home.

Witches and Whales

Enza Vynn-Cara

Mom has brought out all the best pieces including the green damask tablecloth, Grandma's silverware, and the gold-plated candlesticks like the ones you see at the altar. With their chubby, unlit, red candles, they stand at each end of the table guarding the oval trays filled with provolone, ham, pitted green olives, roasted red peppers and artichoke hearts. At the centre of this food bazaar, a white ceramic dome safeguards Mom's best Christmas Eve dish: fried baccala.

We're on schedule, all Dad has to do is fetch his pièce-de-résistance. He's about to leave when he sees Rita snatching olives and rolled pieces of ham off the trays. My sister has a mammoth's mouth. All she wants to do is eat, eat, and eat again. Stealthy, like a bird of prey hovering low, she has been around the table once or twice. I've been watching her closely, guarding the table really, and even so, I didn't notice her hands reach out or her mouth at work. But Dad catches her red-handed and, this time, her whining doesn't work.

'Damn it, Rita.'

He holds her by the shoulders, shouts the taboo word. In my head, it echoes louder than Dad ever said it. She has done it again, I think, good for Dad to give it to her, finally.

'Did I hear it right?' Under the mistletoe hanging from the top of the arch that separates the plain white of the kitchen from the yellow daisies of the dining room wallpaper, Mom stands, firm and heavy, holding her wooden spoon like it's a sword. Her sweaty face glows a healthy pink and the bare light bulb dangling from the kitchen ceiling tinges her copper hair with gold. St. Michael the avenger, I'm thinking, seeing the spoon magically reshape itself into a winged Arthurian sword gleaming with the same hue of copper and gold as the halo around Mom's hair.

Mom casts a charcoal stare at Dad. 'You called your daughter a whale?'

'A fat whale,' Rita whines.

'A fat whale. Nice, Frank, really nice.'

Mom's voice has an edge that makes you want to hide, but there is no place to lie low. Dad has moved everything to make space and now the room is bare but for the dining table and Grandma's damask armchairs. He shakes his head in denial.

'I didn't say that.'

He is right. He didn't call Rita a whale— he called her a *fat baby orca*.

Orcas aren't whales, but that won't make any difference to Mom. She's been on the warpath all day. Nothing we do is right, nothing we say she wants to hear.

'Mrs Ashton, our science teacher, says orcas are dolphins not whales.' As I say this I shy behind the dining table as if that will keep me safe from Mom's anger. 'They're dolphins. Orcas are dolphins, right Dad?'

'They're dolphins.' Dad gives a sigh of relief and draws Rita to him. 'Like the one you have on top of your bed, honey. You like them don't you?'

'Oh yeah.' Welcoming Dad's embrace, Rita stands all graceful and girl-like: shoulders straight, tummy tucked in, chest pushed forward so that her Brussels-sprout breasts push against the white and red beaded sweater, another hand-me-down I'll be wearing come next winter. She brushes a blond curl away from her forehead and gives Dad the stare — the Marlene Dietrich stare, Grandpa calls it. I don't know how she does it, but everything about her changes. Even the baby fat that makes her look like the hump of a whale suddenly moulds into curves. Grandpa likes Marlene's curves, says the Witch has got plenty of them too.

'It's true, Mom.' Rita glances over her shoulder, a beaming smile warming her face. 'Orcas are dolphins and very beautiful. Whales are beautiful too, no matter how big they are, like Moby Dick. Even the Witch says so.'

Besides swallowing anything within reach, Rita's mouth can spit out the silliest things at the worst possible moments.

It's no secret that Mom can't stand the Witch, especially after cooking for her all day. It's no secret that Dad hates us calling her that. He clenches his jaw then slowly draws in breath. The air is sizzling from the heat of the oven that has been on all afternoon, the heat from the radiators to counter the cold of the snow falling all day, the anger that makes Dad's mouth twitch, and the bullets fired from Mom's stubborn stare.

'Moby is the most beautiful white whale ever.' I echo my sister's words, and sound as silly as her. I jab my elbows on the table, fists tucked under my chin. 'Ahab is a fool to want to kill her.'

'Is that so?' Mom points an index at me. 'Stand back from that table, Elise. That's my girl, shoulders back and straight. The Witch likes you being skinny and straight backed, and maybe she won't mind us orcas.'

'Stop calling her that. You're getting the children to do the same.' Dad releases Rita, leans with his elbows on the back of the armchair. His green eyes become narrow slits. 'You could help me a little, be nice to her.'

'Nice?' Mom lifts up a hand and finger after finger starts counting. 'I cook for her, listen to her telling me how to educate my children, what should they read and eat, stand aside while you chauffeur her back and forth, morning, evening, and weekends. What else, Frank, do you want me to do? Please tell me.' She's yelling now, something Dad hates. 'I should let her take care of the children. That should do it. Let her have the run of the place here and come and help you.'

'What's wrong with that? What's wrong with lending me a hand?' Dad hits the back of the armchair and then grabs it to stop it from tumbling forward.

Rita steps back, the green eyes widening, while Mom drops her spoon, puts a hand on the pit of her stomach. Her lips quiver. It's as if Dad's fist has hit her stomach and not the chair.

'It would, wouldn't it,' she whispers, glancing at the table. 'If all this won't make her budge, we'll consider that too.'

I don't like what Mom says. I don't like Dad's reddened face. A scream soars inside my head.

You're a fool, Dad, just like Ahab.

Dad stares at me like he has heard my scream. And I think he did because Rita and Mom glower at me too.

'I'm out of here.' He turns, snatches his coat and the wide brimmed hat from the hat-rack and stomps out the front door.

'Daddy,' Rita calls after him, but the door slams shut on her face. She hides her double chin in the turtleneck of her sweater and looks at me sideways.

'You messed up,' I tell her.

'Huh, huh.' She shakes her head at me.

'Yes, yes, yes.' I jab a finger at the table. 'It's your fault, your big mouth's fault. But it's better full of food, at least it shuts up.'

Rita stamps her feet. 'You're mean and jealous because Daddy likes me more.'

'Oh yeah, Miss Dolphin Princess, I'm really jealous, like I want to be an orca.'

'Dolphins.' Rita pouts. 'They're dolphins, Ma, they're dolphins.'

'Enough.' Mom straightens her shoulders.' It's enough,' she whispers, hands reaching to her back. She unties the strings of her apron and lets it fall to the floor. 'We got work to do, girls. It's Christmas Eve and we have guests. I'm going to get dressed.' She walks across the room on flat heels that seem to find no solid ground, and hollers over her shoulder. 'Rita, you fix those trays the way they were before you messed up. Elise, you go after your father; make sure he's back in time for dinner.'

'But Mom, don't think Dad—'

'Now, Elise.'

Coat flying over my shoulders, I'm out of the door, calling after Dad. He is down the hall, hovering on the edge of the stairs half turned as if unsure whether to plunge down or come back. When he sees me approaching he tells me to go back inside.

I keep my pace; reach him by the stairs as he begins to climb down.

'Mom said to come with you.'

'And I say you stay.'

'I'm coming.'

'Damn it.' Dad slams his hand against the rail. He takes a deep breath. 'Just... stay put. I'll be right back.'

He rushes down the stairs without looking back. I hear a Christmas jingle bell and the front door of our building slamming shut. Everything goes silent, dark, but I don't want to go back inside. I sit Indian-like behind the rubber plant that smells like an ashtray and begin to count the cigarettes butts everyone leaves behind, thinking I could figure out which are Dad's, but I can't. They're all different sizes, twisted and dirty. The lights on the landing dim down. They won't flick on again until someone walks past them. Soon Grandpa and his witch will get here and if Dad is not back then she'll know—she always knows when Mom and Dad have a fight.

She doesn't like Mom. And Mom doesn't like her. She calls her *Witch* and *Anorexia* and the Witch calls Mom *Moby Dick*. When she reads from the illustrated books she buys for us, she always chooses the one that Rita likes best and screams the words Ahab and Big Moby Dick as if we are too far from her to hear. Then, looking askew at the open door to see if Mom walks by, she whispers, 'You two, watch what you eat: she's beautiful, yes, but you don't want to be fat like her.'

If Dad is around, the Witch lies, says Moby Dick is beautiful. She always finds a way to take Dad by the elbow, pull him down to her height and say things like, 'Those delicious creations you bring home, Frank, don't help Angela any. Too sugary, too fattening, even for me. But darling, they're so, so tempting.'

Dad is a pastry chef. He works in the largest bakery in town, 'The Baker's Word.' And he is indispensable. They even named some of his creations after him: Frank's Chocolate Fingers, Frank's Rum and Gin Baba, Frank's Lobster Tail. But now the pastry shop is closing down, and Dad needs money to buy the place and be the boss. That's all he thinks about. He doesn't bring any pastries home anymore and says to watch our weight, that Rita and Mom are well built and on the heavy side, but not fat.

Until today.

Today Dad said Mom and Rita are as big as whales. That's what he meant when he said orca.

I know he would never say that on his own. The Witch made him do it. She has him under a spell, can get anybody to do what she wants. She's got Grandpa smoking again—the best cigars from her native Cuba, she says. She herself smokes too, long thin cigarillos always hang from her strawberry mouth like Dad's Marlboros, and—like Dad— she can speak and puff at the same time. And she drinks as much as Grandpa. But he did that even before he married her so, I guess, the Witch is not to blame. Still, like Mom says, 'Does she have to keep filling the glass up for him?'

The skylight above my head is a blackboard without stars. It's so dark now, I've become invisible to my eyes. I draw my knees to my chest and listen to the faint ticking of my Mickey Mouse wristwatch. It's the only sound I hear until the Christmas bell jingles again and the downstairs lights flick on.

A shadow slithers up the stairs. Someone is thumping a beat on the worn carpet. I hole up behind the rubber plant that smells like an ashtray. It must be the Witch, I think, with Grandpa trailing behind her. A familiar sweet smell of chocolate and Marlboros sifts through the air. Footfalls on the landing trigger a burst of light. Through the heart-shaped leaves I see a man, his wide brimmed hat low over the forehead, a cigarette in his mouth, and two large white boxes in his hands.

'Dad.'

Startled, he tilts his head to see past the rubber plant. 'Elise.' Smoke puffs through his parted lips. 'You're still here?'

'You told me to stay put.'

His left eyebrow rises. 'I said that, didn't I?' He stabs the cigarette in the soil that feeds the rubber plant and gently hands me the boxes. 'Careful with my creations.'

He sits next to me. His legs are too long. Even after he bends his knees the snow-caked boots slam against the rail. 'Okay, you can take a peek.'

I flip open the cover on the top box. Inside is a delight Rita would die for: chocolate covered cannoli, Rum Baba, struffoli, Frank's Chocolate Fingers, and more. My dad is the greatest pastry maker ever and one day he will own his own shop, sooner if the Witch and Grandpa lend him the money. I glance up at him. He tosses his hat at the rubber plant, where it teeters uncertainly before sliding to the floor. On his left brow runs a scar that curls upward into his temple. It's been there as long as I can remember. He got it that time Grandpa lost it—the only time he really lost it, Dad always says.

'Can I have one?'

'You're not supposed to. They're for the Witch. '

'You said not to call her that.'

'And we shouldn't. She isn't that bad, likes you a lot, says you think way too fast and too much.' He takes a chocolate finger, pops it whole in his mouth, then shuts his eyes. 'Just right. Try one.' He points at the ones with the yellow wrap. 'Cream and chocolate, your favourite.'

They're huge. I sink my teeth into the first one, and I'm in heaven. I eat a second one and it's even better than the first. I'm Ishmael hearing Christmas jingles in high seas.

'Dad, we're going to be fat like Moby Dick.'

'Suits me just fine.' He pops another chocolate finger into his mouth and then links his fingers. 'Whales are beautiful and wild and you know what else?'

'What?'

'They mate for life.'

'That's not really true, Dad. Mrs Ashton says they like being a family though.'

Dad grins. His teeth and chin are caked with chocolate. 'Kind of like us, huh?'

I point at the smears on his face.

He wipes his mouth with his handkerchief, runs his tongue over his teeth and grins.

'How's that?'

'You're good.'

'Chin up.' With a clean corner of the handkerchief he wipes my chin and mouth, and then shifts his weight around to give himself more room. One by one, he resets the pastries inside the box to hide the gaps left by the ones we ate. 'They're good.'

'Good enough for the Wi... I mean Grandma.' I sigh. 'She doesn't like that either. What do witches want to be called anyways?'

'By their first name, maybe? She'll like that.'

A New Life

Palo Stickland

Glasgow 1965
He alighted at George Square, leaping from the open back of the bus, waving a cheery goodnight to the conductor. It was drizzling, even the statues looked downcast, he turned up his collar, pulled down his cap. Exiting the square at the City Chambers, he walked up the hill towards Martha Street, stopping at the Registry Offices to check if their names were posted on the banns. Yes, *Malkeet Singh to wed Brenda Murray*. Tonight, he must tell his brothers. He kept a steady pace up the hill, crossed Cathedral Street, heard the hymn singing from the Baptist Church, which was a reminder to make a final visit to the Sikh Temple, and continued up the hill to Grafton Square.

When he reached the entrance to the close at number eight, he turned to look out at the garden, the focal point of the three-storey tenements that surrounded it. How many times had he seen these trees drooping like this all around the neat paths, the benches all empty. He'd lived here for a few years, before giving the kitchen of the one bedroom flat to his brothers, newly arrived from India, and willing to take over communications with their mother. He wouldn't do what she wanted any more.

Their estrangement was their mother's fault: she married them off too young. He had been fifteen, but now he wouldn't do what she wanted. Shaking his head as if to physically remove the memory, he turned to climb the stairs to the second floor. The aroma of spices wafted down to him long before he pressed the bell to the flat.

It was Jeet who opened it shouting, 'Brother, come in! We been waiting. Come.'

He wanted to say, we are not in your Punjabi fields, no need to raise your voice. Instead, he lied about the bus. 'The traffic was bad. Wonderful smell in here.'

'Bally's new recipe. Special spicy lamb. Give me your coat, Brother.' Jeet ushered him through the tiny lobby to the kitchen.

Bally, the youngest of the three brothers, stood stirring the pot on the two ring cooker which was on a spindly legged stand next to the white sink. A short, dirty cream curtain covered two feet of the window above the sink. Beside the cooker there were shelves set into the wall cupboard on which they kept a few dishes and pots; on the opposite wall a modern, freestanding unit with a flap-down section in the middle held the groceries, part of the top shelf was kept for letters. Next to that was the old iron range, no longer used but a lot of work to remove, so it stayed. Both brothers slept in the alcove, opposite to the window, on a solid wood, wall to wall, bunk bed arrangement; their clothes were hung on pegs or were in the suitcases under the bed. A blue, Formica-covered table stood in front of it; two chairs were placed with their backs to the sink and cooker.

Malkeet stepped over to Bally and peered into the pot, 'Ah, almost done. What's this?' He lifted a bottle.

'The new waiter at the restaurant gave me the idea, Brother. Red wine to put in when meat is cooked, isn't it? Special for you tonight.' Bally grinned, leaning into Malkeet's hug.

'Very good, Bally. Any letter from home?'

Jeet placed his arm between them as if to stop a fight that hadn't started. 'No talking about Ma and India. We only argue when we do it.'

'Then what's to talk, Jeet?' Bally insisted, turning to Malkeet.

'Brother. Yes. We have letter, same as before, Ma make demand, *"Why is your older brother not sending for his wife and sons?"*' Bally mimicked his mother's voice and raised his eyebrows, shrugging his shoulders in mock dismay.

'The usual then?' Malkeet took the glass of whisky offered to him by Jeet and settled himself on the lower bed in the alcove, a good place to observe his brothers. He sniffed the whisky, 'Another special? Macallans. What are you boys up to? Softening me up for something?'

'No, Brother! Nothing up! No up, no down. That woman in Off Licence, she say, this, Best Whisky!'

'Yes. And she'd know. I agree. It is very good.' Malkeet sipped his drink.

'Ma's letter say your boys now fifteen and seventeen, will be late for them. She say, *"What's wrong with Malkeet? He not reply my letters!"*' Bally was not for letting go.

Malkeet slapped his thigh and laughed, 'She hasn't found a wife for them? She did for you both. I remember Ma saying, *"Oh, Bally is taller than me now, I have to find him a wife."*' Malkeet poured another drink for himself and a bigger one for each of his brothers.

Bally placed the pot of lamb on a wooden stand in the middle of the table and spooned out the meat into bowls for each of them. They tucked in.

'Yeah, I was fourteen. She no ask me. But I did want a wife,' Bally grinned.

'And what a coincidence, that she had a sister who was just right for me. Ma was in the luck, getting two for one, yeah?' Jeet relented and joined in.

'It will be good when Brother's boys are with us, isn't it, Jeet? They can work as waiters because they're good looking and clever,' Bally added, wading into trouble.

'I left them when they were babies. You know them better than I'll ever do,' Malkeet said. 'It will be difficult for me if their mother comes here. There's Brenda.'

Bally and Jeet ate as if the meat was so delicious they couldn't answer. They waited for their older brother to continue.

'I'm going to marry Brenda — and go to Canada. I don't want the old life.'

'You too long away from India, Brother. We understand. It good to have the boys with us,' Jeet said. 'We want to open restaurant,' Bally nodded.

The evening passed in a haze of Macallans, exquisitely cooked lamb and much laughter. Jeet produced papers from the cupboard while outlining the plan for a restaurant, careful not to make any more references to Malkeet's sons. As he refilled their glasses, Malkeet noticed the blue air mail letter which Jeet had stuffed back into the cupboard.

'Of course, I'll s — s — ign. It's no prob — lem. I'm your big brother, what wouldn't I do for you? Remember when those r — ruffians from the next village accosted the two of you in the fields. How I made them pay? Remember that?' Malkeet thumped his hand on the table, the glasses jumped, the whisky rolled like waves on the sea.

'I remember, Brother,' Bally shouted. 'Ma was angry. She cry, *"The three of you will be killed in a feud between the villages."* I miss Ma. Yeah, I miss home.' Bally blubbed a few unintelligible words, put his head on his arms, and promptly fell asleep.

'He's exhausted,' Malkeet said out loud. He was not nearly as drunk as his brothers, and sat watching Jeet who, having caught the sleep bug from Bally, opened his eyes wide and muttered, 'the papers. Brother, the papers.' As his head fell on the table, he slipped into a deep sleep.

Malkeet thought of how hard the two of them worked in the restaurant. They'd taken an evening off to be with him tonight. He'd drop off there tomorrow and tell them when he was leaving to start his new life. They were right, the curry trade was set to boom in Glasgow, they'd do well with their own restaurant. Perhaps the next time he'd meet up with them they would be wealthy; possibly millionaires.

He read the papers. *Yes, the restaurant lease seemed genuine.*

Then he saw them. *Ah, sponsorship papers, that's what this evening is about then. They couldn't keep awake to complete their plan to outwit me.* He chuckled.

A vision of them in the village, following him to school when they were four and three, came to his mind. They'd sit outside the gate, under the neem tree, playing five stones or chasing each other, until he came out again, carrying his hessian bag, looking important. Then, he'd march past them, they'd trail behind him, trying to catch his attention or giggling with each other. And so it had gone on, he in front, Jeet and Bally behind. Across the seas to Glasgow with Ma in the background giving orders, ruling their lives.

Malkeet chuckled as his brothers snored in unison. *The best thing for them is my meeting Brenda and leaving. Escaping, perhaps that is what I'm doing. Running from the responsibilities that Indian boys are brought up to. Duty to parents. Duty to siblings. Duty to wife and kids. I want to go my own way.*

He rose to open the cupboard, to retrieve the blue airmail letter.

Tears flowed down Malkeet's cheeks when he'd finished reading. Perhaps someday he'd write to Ma, apologise for ruining her dream. Let her know what falling in love with a woman, who was not chosen for you, was like. Ma knew all about control, that's all he wanted for himself.

I'll sign the papers and deal with any consequences. There shouldn't be any. Ma's daughter-in-law, a wife I hardly know, and the boys will settle in Glasgow. I'll be faraway by the time they arrive. Ma will be happy, and she might find it in her heart to forgive me. But I won't complicate my life with my past, a past engineered and manipulated by others.

He signed the papers, as Jeet and Bally had hoped he would, placing them on the table, with Ma's letter. The sleeping pair would find them in the morning.

'Good luck, boys. Thanks for caring about my sons,' he sniffed. 'Sorry, I can't help more than this. Time for me to go.' Malkeet spoke the words out loud, although his brothers couldn't hear him. He let himself out of the flat, closing the door quietly. Taking a deep breath on the stair landing, he walked down to a new life.

The Shop at St George's Cross

Palo Stickland

My mate, Haroun, went to Pakistan to visit his relatives and came back with a bride. I was surprised to hear he had fallen in love and married because Haroun had been the local stud, the bronze god of our neighbourhood, since we were twelve. He'd always attracted the prettiest, most available girls. I was too shy, too pale and not quite ready for it all. I watched and envied him.

On their return his mother had a party, a kind of reception for the bride and groom. Family were invited, as well as friends from the local Pakistani community, and a few of Haroun's friends. I'm in all three of those groups because of my Mum being friends with Aunty Ashi. They lived next door to each other when I was born; when Mum returned to work she left me with Aunty Ashi. Omar, her youngest, and I were firm friends as we toddled off to nursery, played football in primary school, and grew up to watch Haroun attract all the girls while we stood on the sidelines. And now, he had got married to the most beautiful girl I'd ever seen.

The community hall was full of people when Omar and I arrived. Haroun and his bride, both emulating royalty in gold and red bridal costumes, sat on chairs on a platform with a canopy above them. We walked over to congratulate them.

Haroun was all smiles, 'Hi Omar. Hi John. Good to see you. This is Aunty Ashi's son,' he told his bride.

I felt a push as Aunty Ashi, panting as if she'd run right across the hall, addressed the bride, 'Layla, my child! I tell you about them. They friends from when they babies. This one. Omar, he is my son, born after five girls, and this John, my younger son, sent by Allah, to complete my family. You see, I deserved two boys after five girls, such terrors of daughters they were, bossy rebels, not like me, taking after their father. Now Omar and John, they good boys, no trouble. John, his mother pass away, and he only sixteen, but I tell him, keep the house, we are family, we help you, and he still there, in house next door. Layla, you come for a meal. We chat more.'

Then, Aunty Ashi turned to us, we jumped in unison. 'You boys, come eat now!' Layla gave me a little smile, which didn't reach her eyes, she dropped her gaze to her feet. I nodded and sensed that she must feel alone, Haroun was busy greeting his friends. We followed Aunty Ashi.

I didn't know my father; it was mum and me and Aunty Ashi until mum got cancer; was gone within the year. I left school and became a plumber's apprentice to mum's brother. Aunty Ashi's door was always open, her ears listening at the times she knew I'd be coming in from work. We were on the top floor of the tenement, it was safe. As soon as I'd put the key in my lock, I'd hear, 'John is that you, my son? Come through after you've had a wash. I make egg curry special for you.' Or it might be some other of my favourites, but I did love egg curry best.

One day I sat Aunty Ashi down to have a talk and began, 'I'm your adopted son and earning good money now. I'm going to give you a share of my wages as a good son should.' I'd rehearsed it so she wouldn't say no; I was as assertive as I could be. She burst into tears and all my bravado fell away.

'I too proud,' she sobbed. 'Your — your mum — she be proud too, in heaven. Now you need good girl to marry. You be settled and mum's spirit be at peace. And I be happy.'

'Aunty Ashi,' I stammered, 'this is a bit sudden for me. Let me wait until my apprenticeship is done.'

That was seven years ago. My business is doing well. I had a relationship, with a girl I met at college, but it's over now.

On the night of Aunty Ashe's party for Haroun and Layla, I sit at her kitchen table tucking into egg curry, while she converses in Urdu with one of the ladies. I think even Aunty Ashi doesn't know how much I understand, but I can pick up the general idea.

'What happened to that girl next door who was with your boy?'

'Oh, she only wanted a place to stay while she finished uni. Uni, that's short for university. He was besotted with her, though I knew she didn't feel the same, but I told myself, Ashi, you keep quiet. See what happens. Then, after she's lived with my boy, used his house and eaten his food, *namak haraam*, no gratitude. She says she wants a gap! What's this gappy-shappy year? I'm asking? A time to do nothing, I say. Off she goes to Australia, and surprise, surprise, she finds another boy over there. And that's it. She writes to my boy, *throw out my stuff but you can keep my cat*. I was so angry about it all. My boy took it well though. The cat likes him anyway.'

'He's got no woman then? Why don't you find him a nice girl from Pakistan, Ashi? Won't he listen to you?'

'Of course he listens to me. I asked him. He said, why not Aunty Ashi, but let's wait until my business is established. Plenty time.'

I can hardly keep my face straight as I bend over my bowl of egg curry. Omar comes to the kitchen door, 'What you doin' in here, John? Bring your food into the living room, watch the wedding video, might be one of us next. We need to know how it's done. C'mon.'

That was last year, Omar and the family have gone to Pakistan, I've been told to have my passport ready in case he finds a suitable girl, and I'm sitting in the pub with a pint and who should come along but Haroun with — no surprise really — a tipsy blonde attached to his arm. An image of the beautiful Layla shoots across my vision and I feel real sorry for her. *Haroun, you're a bastard*, I want to say, but, 'Hi Haroun,' are the words that come from my lips. *You're a coward, John*, the critical side of me says, but I grin at the pair of them anyway.

'Hey, John. I was hoping to bump into you. I need a favour, mate.' They sit in front of me, she cuddles in to him.

I nod, gulping a mouthful of beer. He continues, 'You know my mum has a shop on St George's Road, at the Cross?'

'Sells Indian materials, yeah.'

'That's right. Says 'Bollywood Fashions' above the door There's a leak in the toilet, at the base. She's been on at me to do something about it. You got a minute to have a look?'

'Okay. I'm passing that way tomorrow. I'll drop in.'

'Tell her you'll have to fit a new one, even though she'll ask for a repair. Time she upgraded that shop. It's a goldmine for her. We should go now. There's a new play at the King's that Linda wants to see.' He nods at the girl, shakes my hand and they hurry away.

Next day, Haroun's mum is behind the counter, cutting material for a customer. She smiles. 'Hello John. Must be quiet around your place with Ashi away.'

'My cat sits at her door, wondering why it's closed,' I answer.

'Layla! It's the plumber.' She shouts towards the back-shop. 'Show him to the toilet.'

And that's how I meet the most beautiful woman in the world properly. She's wearing a Pakistani salwar kameez ensemble, parrot green with gold strands at the wrists, tight at the waist, it shows off her figure. I lay out my tools, hoping she won't be called away.

She speaks English with a slight accent, 'It always leaked, but recently it is worse. And it smells.'

'Right. I'll have a look.'

'My mother-in-law says I must watch you work. That is how we do it in Pakistan. Otherwise the workers do a bad job.'

'Oh, I see. It's nice to have company,' and I think, *I can talk to her. Hurray.*

'Right.' As I investigate the problem, slowly, I ask Layla, 'How are you? I mean, it must be difficult settling into a new country?'

She shrugs, gives a wry smile, and turns away before I can see the expression in her eyes.

'Are you here, at the shop, every day?' I continue.

'Yes. I want to go to college, but she needs me here.'

'That's a shame. Perhaps you could go for a day, now and then. You know, a workshop or a conference. There's always something going on at the college.'

'I will find out but...' her voice trails off, she turns away again and now, I've finished inspecting the toilet. I stand up, she looks expectantly up at me.

'There's a crack at the back. It'll be a new toilet. And the wash hand basin could be renewed to match the new one.

'She won't spend so much money. But you tell her yourself.'

We're having a few warm days, which will be our Glasgow summer this year, so when I bring the new toilet and wash basin I decide to have my lunch across the road under the statue of St George and the Dragon.

'Don't want to waste the sunshine, we get so little,' I joke to Layla who is watching me again.

'I feel like I am in your way, standing in this small space. The workmen in Pakistan expect to be watched but it is different here,' she says. 'My mother-in-law has told me to watch you. I am sorry.'

'You shouldn't apologise. I quite like you... being here... I mean... to talk to,' I stammer, my hands shake and I think *what's wrong with you, man?*

'And the workmen always have tea,' she says.

'That's a good tradition,' I grin.

She smiles making me feel braver. I say, 'Haroun's mother reminds me of the statue across the road. The dragon.'

Layla giggles. I am emboldened. 'Why don't you come outside with your lunch? I'm going to sit in the sun.'

'I couldn't.' She shakes her head to emphasise her words.

'Why?' I'm unpacking the wash basin.

'Well. She wouldn't like it. The customers would talk.'

'You can sit on the other bench. There are three others around the statue. Every day you're in this shop, the sun would do you good.'

She looks over her shoulder, then turns to me, 'I might.'

And at that moment, my hand slips, the wash basin cracks, which means I'll have to buy another one. Another day on this job. *Oh good!* But I say, 'Oh no. I must be hungry. Better stop for lunch now.'

I tidy my tools away from the toilet, the part of the job which is finished, and it's then that I hear a woman's voice in the shop say, in Urdu, 'There's no baby yet? Why is that?'

Haroun's mother's voice answers, quieter. 'How can they have a baby? They don't speak. It was a mistake that I took him to Pakistan. He is with a white girl and it's all my fault. I don't know how to tell her parents.'

'Oh, poor Layla!'

I lift my bag and turn to see Layla's eyes, moist and gazing at the floor, her arms tight around her waist as she leans on the door jamb. I want to hug her. When she looks up she can see the anger on my face, my lips clamped tight. She intakes a quick breath, her eyes wide as she realises I understand Urdu. Turning away from the door, she lets me pass.

I report back to Haroun's mother in the front of the shop, 'The wash hand basin has a crack in it. I'll need to take it back for an exchange. I'll be here tomorrow, if that's okay.'

'I am not surprised. You've got to check everything at the warehouse these days. Alright, John. Do you want a cup of tea?' Haroun's mother and the customers look at me, I'm glad Layla told me about offering tea to workmen.

'That would be really kind of you. I was going to sit in the sun across the road. Could you bring it out or I could come back in to... '

The ladies nod their approval of my knowledge. 'Of course, that's alright. You go and sit in the sun.'

'I'll not have Ashi tell me I was inhospitable to her boy,' this she says to her customers in Urdu as I close the door.

I'm munching my sandwiches in the sun when Layla comes out with a mug of tea.

'The dragon actually sent you out!' I smile in surprise.

She grins and shrugs.

'I could get used to this.' I'm wishing she'd sit down. 'I mean, used to *you* making tea for *me*.'

She nods gently as if she understands completely and knows there's more to say. Much more.

She leaves me on my own, sitting under St George killing his Dragon, but as I load up the van, I see her walking across the road with a brown paper bag, her lunch. *Ah! Progress.* I think. *Good girl.*

The next day, I arrive at midday, to work on the wash basin in the afternoon. Parking the van, I walk towards the benches with my lunch. Layla is sitting in the sun, so I choose the other bench because I don't want her to have a problem with the dragon mother-in-law. As she rises, she pushes the brown bag towards me and walks across the road to the shop. I try not to stare after her.

I reach over to pull the bag towards me, inside there is a plastic container and a note which I open first. Four words, *Enjoy your favourite dish.*

Ah, she's been talking to Aunty Ashi.

I place the container in my lunch bag, feeling like I've something to hide, I open it and take a look at the egg curry. It smells delicious, looks great. *That's my evening meal sorted.* I finish my sandwiches hoping I'm not wrong about Layla, even having a daydream in which she's walking, no, running towards me, into my arms. Please, God, let that happen. Never thought I would ever pray for a woman.

I finish the job in the afternoon, the shop is full of customers all chattering away in Urdu and Punjabi. Layla is at the counter. The dragon tries to haggle on my charge for the work, but I stand firm, and she pays me.

'Great weather, we're having. I've got used to having lunch across by the statue. It'll probably rain tomorrow.' I glance towards Layla, hoping she takes the hint. She's busy talking to the women, the material spread over the counter between them. As I open the door, she says, 'Bye.' Turning, I see her nod and I'm positive someone up in heaven is on my side. I close the door, look up at the sky and mutter, 'Thanks, Mum. First prayer answered. Just one more?'

The next day is sunny again, I prepare my lunch, seeing the benches under the statue in my mind. Then in the brown bag that Layla gave me I put a note which I've spent all evening composing.

Hi Layla, This might be very forward of me, if so put the note into the bin right now, then I will understand. I think about you all the time. Please let me make life better for you. I'm going away next weekend. Any chance you'd come with me? And live with me? I know it's difficult for you but I'd like an answer before I go crazy dreaming about it, even if the answer is no.'

I'm working about three miles away but it's no bother to drive to St George's Cross at midday.

She's sitting on the bench that's shaded by the hawthorn bush, eating her lunch. I park about four cars away from the shop and cross the road. I walk round the statue, there are four benches surrounding it, two are taken up by others. A mum with a baby in a pushchair in one and an elderly couple in the other. As I walk towards the little park, I look up at St George on his horse, sword raised, and think. *'People pray to saints, my granny used to, so, hey, St George, I need a little help here, mate. Got a dragon to vanquish and a fair maid to rescue. There she is.'*

I'm at the other seat now and she has seen me. I look over at the shop, no one looking out. I take out the brown bag and while pretending I'm going to the waste bin, I place the bag near her, then sit on a bench, as if my stomach wasn't churning, as if my heart wasn't beating out of my chest. I take a drink from my water bottle and act as if I'm enjoying a rest in the sun. I can hardly sit still as I see out of the corner of my eye that she's opening the note, though it's still in the bag. She takes a long time reading, re-reading, I'm sweating, my T-shirt is damp on my back, I want to run away. She gazes around and up at the sky, then at me. I'm staring at the ground but I know when her eyes are on me, and I glance towards her. Her gaze moves to the bag in her lap, fingers move, she's folding the letter. Then, I'm thinking she's going to move to the bin, but she takes my letter and pushes it into the top of her dress, over her left breast and holds her hand there. I want to rush over to her, she takes a pen out of her pocket, writes on the brown paper bag, turns the bag so I can see the numbers, folds it, leaves it in the slats on the bench. She walks, with all the grace of a goddess, across the road to the dragon's shop. *How can she keep so calm?* Me, I'm drenched in sweat now.

The message on the brown bag says, *Yes. Text me. Be careful.* It's followed by a mobile number. I grab the paper bag, put it into my lunch bag and wait five minutes. I cross the road to the van, raising my arm in salute to St George.

Two months, many texts and secret phone calls later, I arrive at the shop at eleven on a Friday morning, the time agreed with Layla. There are two customers who turn to stare at me when I open the door.

Haroun's mother looks surprised, 'Hello John. What can I do for you this morning?' Layla is folding material at the counter, which she drops as she smiles, 'Hi, I'm ready.' Three pairs of eyes stare at her when she wheels her bag from behind the counter. In Urdu, she tells the dragon, 'I'm going now. I won't be back.'

I nod at the ladies, holding the door open, as the most beautiful woman in the world, looking happier than I've ever seen her, walks out of the shop with me.

Star Party

Julia Chalkley

Dusk was fading into full night, the trees and tents around her blurring at their edges and disappearing softly into the darkness. Sarah felt again for the torch tied to her belt and touched the edge of the big saucepan. It wobbled a little on the tiny Gaz hob and settled.

Osman struggled out of his tent and fumbled with his torch. Dim red light shone out over the camp table, then the beam flicked over Sarah's face and on towards his telescope in the field beyond.

'Food smells nice,' he said. 'Do we get to eat it this year?'

Sarah was grateful for the darkness that hid her face. 'Sure,' she said, as steadily as she could manage.

'What is it?'

'Spaghetti bolognese,' she said, then realised what he was really asking. 'Vegetarian version,' she added. 'Peppers, onions, garlic, mushrooms, tomato and tarragon sauce. No meat.'

'Cool,' Osman said. 'Don't trip over it this year, eh, Splosh? I'm looking forward to it.'

He shambled away to his telescope before her pretence of good humour could break up.

Sarah checked the red filter on her own torch and clicked it on. The bolognese sauce bubbled, popping wafts of tomato into the air. Sarah leaned over the pan and took a deep breath of the scent. Last year she'd left a disastrous first impression on the Bullmere Astronomy Club. This aromatic beauty was going to be her apology and her real introduction to her fellow astronomers.

The clouds had cleared in the west, and almost every telescope in the field had slewed around to take advantage of the view. Sarah glanced over to her own telescope, still hooded and north-aligned. No point in getting started. Any star in the western sky she asked it to track would have set before she dished up the meal. Anyway, the sky was due to clear completely by midnight and she was particularly keen on getting a good view of the Whirlpool Nebula — currently hiding in the thinning clouds overhead.

Grace crawled out of Marie's tent in instalments. Her top half emerged easily, then her boots tangled in the guy-lines and she struggled noisily before pulling her feet free with a series of loud twangs. Grace, Sarah thought. If only her parents could have seen her at twenty, they would never have given her such a cruel name.

'Can I help?' Grace asked. She stood up, collided with Marie's camp chair and disappeared from view as she fell out of the dim glow of Sarah's torchlight. Sarah reached out instinctively to catch her, clipped the edge of the saucepan and grabbed the saucepan handles instead, burning her hands in the process. Grace scrambled to her feet and walked more cautiously to the seat beside the cooking table.

'I'm fine,' Sarah said, 'You can keep me company if you like. Everyone else is off hunting stars. Do you have a telescope yourself?'

'No,' Grace said. 'I'm only here because Aunt Marie offered to run me back to uni after the party's over.' She sat in the camp chair, and disappeared again from the sphere of red light with a sound composed equally of clank and rip. Sarah grabbed the saucepan again in case the chaos escalated and asked 'Are you okay?'

'Yeah,' Grace said. 'Um. I think I bust someone's chair.'

'Mine,' Sarah said, 'Don't worry.'

Grace settled on Sarah's second chair, within crashing distance of the table.

'What are you studying at uni?' Sarah asked. She stirred the bolognese sauce with one hand and surreptitiously snagged a tea towel with the other, ready to rescue the saucepan in an emergency.

'Veterinary science?' Grace said.

Sarah threw her a look, lost in the darkness. 'Is that a question?'

'Um, no?' Grace replied. She shifted, and the chair cried a warning.

Sarah looked up, still stirring the sauce. A few strands of cloud coasted overhead, but the stars were hard and bright and clear beyond them. A meteor fizzed briefly through her view and the entire campsite cheered all around them.

'What are they cheering for?' Grace asked.

'Meteor,' Sarah said. 'Lyrid shower.'

'Oh, I saw a meteor in the Natural History Museum once,' Grace said.

'Not a meteor, a meteorite,' Sarah said. She almost added, 'of course,' in a sarcastic tone. Just in time she remembered her father patiently explaining the difference to her. She sighed. Be good, Sarah. 'Meteors are the light show when a piece of rock or dust or space junk burns through the atmosphere and meteorites are the physical parts that survive the fall and make it to Earth. Hold the light for me? I think this is nearly done.'

Grace stood up and the chair clanked to the grass behind her. She held Sarah's torch over the stewpot. 'There's a torch in our tent if you need it. I can't see properly in this red light.'

'White light destroys night vision,' Sarah said. 'We have red filters so that we can still see the stars. Try flashing a white light in your eyes and then looking up — you won't see anything till your eyes recover. If you switch on a white light here, you'll be shouted at to turn it off.'

'Okay,' Grace said, subdued. 'Thank you for telling me.'

The bolognese sauce smelled good, and Sarah took a taste — tomato, a burst of juice from a slice of sweet pepper, the aniseed tingle of tarragon and a sting of black pepper. The spaghetti was done and keeping warm in hot water over a low heat.

'OK, call them in. Dinner's ready.'

'Dinner?' Grace called softly.

The chatter continued around them without stopping.

'Bullmeres!' Sarah bellowed. 'Grub up!'

Within minutes the table was surrounded by astronomers. Sarah directed Grace to hand over plates and cutlery while she dished out a scoop of spaghetti and a ladle of bolognese sauce onto each offered plate.

'Prefer mince,' Marie said. 'Not a proper meal without a good chunk of meat in it.'

'Be grateful it isn't lentils,' Jon said.

'Oh peeeuw, not in a tent!'

'Vegetarian food is good for you,' Osman reprimanded. 'Good nosh, Sarah.'

'Thanks,' Sarah said.

'And on the plate this time,' Marie added, loudly. 'Not all over the grass like last year.'

Laughter. Sarah dug into her own food with vicious stabs of her fork. They were not going to forget the spilt curry. For as long as she remained a member of the Bullmere Astronomical Society, she would be known as Sarah the Splosh.

'Did you spill the food last year?' Grace asked her.

'Leave it, Grace' Sarah said fiercely. 'Just shut up, will you? Yes, I tripped over the cooking table in the dark and the pan fell off the stove and the evening meal ended up all over the grass. And I paid for the pizzas we had instead. So can everyone please get OVER it.'

The diners fell silent. Grace said 'Sorry,' very quietly.

Sarah made sure she was away from the table before everyone else had finished. She wanted to get her telescope aligned to the stars and ready when Ursa Major emerged from the clouds. More than that, she wanted to get away from clumsy Grace and her witless questions.

The night was still mild from the warmth of the day, though rapidly cooling under clear skies. Sarah concentrated on her camera and eyepiece, clicking off shots of the Whirlpool, the Pinwheel and the Andromeda galaxies. She avoided any contact with the others, moving away into the darkness if anyone approached.

Just after three in the morning, dark clouds stood up from the western horizon and ate the stars one by one.

Sarah threw the hood over her telescope. She headed for her tent, brushing past the obstacle of Grace and her stuttered words of apology with her hand up and a brief, 'Sorry, I'm bushed. See you tomorrow.'

As she settled into her sleeping bag, she considered whether to pack up her tent and clear off home before anyone else was awake tomorrow morning. When even the newest arrival understands that you're the joke of the club, it's probably time to quit.

The following morning Sarah spent a long time at the shower block. By the time she returned to the tents, most of the cars had gone. She remembered them saying something last night about a visit to Holt and lunch together. She hadn't been invited — didn't want to join them. She needed time alone to consider whether she stayed with the society or went back to stargazing alone from the peace of her garden. She'd miss the nights at the club observatory, but it wasn't worth being greeted by cries of 'Here comes Splosh!' every year.

Marie returned just after one o'clock and came to sit by Sarah.

'I've dropped Grace off at her digs,' she said.

Sarah nodded.

'She appreciated the meal last night, by the way,' Marie said 'She asked me to thank you. She wanted to say it last night, but she didn't get around to it for some reason. Funny kid, really. I blame my bloody sister, she doesn't shut up. Poor old Gracie doesn't get a word in edgewise at home, and I reckon she's lost the knack of speaking up when she needs to.'

'Oh — I'm glad she liked—'

'You know, she ought to speak up for herself more often.' Marie interrupted her. 'If she doesn't say what she thinks, she's going to be ignored all her life.'

'It's a bit difficult to—' Sarah began.

'Grace is a veggie as well, silly cow,' Marie went on. 'Do you know, she told me that last night's meal was the first good meal she'd had in ages. Seriously! Mind you, she's earning her living expenses by working in Burger King, and she must be stretching her budget by eating their leftovers. Enough to turn anyone vegetarian.' Marie reached for the wine bottle. 'D'you mind?'

Sarah shook her head and reached for her own wine glass. Just one. A small one. Then she'd pack up her tent and go before the others returned. Marie poured herself a full glass and set the bottle back on the table, leaving Sarah to serve herself.

'I hope you'll tell her I enjoyed her company,' Sarah ventured.

'Oh, I won't see her again for another year, I suspect,' Marie said. 'Glorious day. Heard tonight's forecast?'

Sarah didn't reply, and Marie set off on a long rambling story about her plans for the night's viewing and the problems she was having with her telescope and what Osman had said about her photographs of Jupiter. Sarah spent her time saying 'Hmm' and 'Really?' while she thought about the previous night. Grace trying to start a conversation. Grace listening to her short and dismissive explanation about meteors and meteorites. Grace trying to help and willing to keep her company. Grace wanting to apologise as Sarah returned to her tent. Sarah remembered the way she'd brushed her off like a mosquito and winced. That had been spiteful. Worse than the way the Bullmere club members had treated Sarah.

'Oh, and — you won't believe this...' Marie reached for the wine again.

'Yes?'

'Gracie said she'd like the recipe for your veggie bolognese. If you could spare the time.'

Sarah sat for just long enough for Marie to empty the bottle into her glass. Then she stood up, and her chair crashed to the grass as it had for Grace the night before.

'Don't need to do it right away,' Marie said. 'Stay and make the most of the sunshine.'

'Give me her address,' Sarah said, unzipping her tent. 'I'll send it to her tonight.'

Marie laughed as Sarah disappeared inside. 'Well,' she said. 'You're keen.'

Sarah came back with pen and notepad. 'Grace is the loveliest person I've spoken to this week,' she said. 'You could all take a lesson from her in how to make a new person feel welcome.'

'Honestly —' Marie said.

'You should be kind to Grace,' Sarah said, scrawling a spiral to get the ink moving. 'Sounds to me as if she needs a good friend.'

'I am kind!' Marie said, laughing. 'Really, do you think —'

'I think — I know — that you don't listen to her enough.' Sarah said. 'And that she deserves better. I'm going to send her my vegetarian curry recipe as well.'

'The one you —'

'Let *her* cook it for you, and see what you missed last year,' Sarah cut in. 'While you're eating it — don't say a word. Listen to her. Thank her if it's a good meal.'

Marie sat watching Sarah as she wrote. For once, she could find nothing at all to say.

The Recipes

Metric and Imperial Measures

These conversions are not exact, but they provide the same proportions for the recipes, and are close enough for all practical cooking purposes.

Weight
1oz = 25g
2oz = 50g
3oz = 75g
4oz = 100g
8oz = 200g
16oz/ 1lb = 500g
2lb = 1000g / 1kg

Liquid Measure
¼pt = 125ml
½pt = 250ml
1pt = 500ml
2pts = 1lt

Temperature Equivalents
Very Cool = 225°F = 110°C = Gas ¼
Cool = 250°F = 130°C = Gas ½
Cool = 275°F = 140°C = Gas 1
Cool = 300°F = 150°C = Gas 2
Moderate = 325°F = 170°C = Gas 3
Moderate = 350°F = 180°C = Gas 4
Moderately Hot = 375°F = 190°C = Gas 5
Moderately Hot = 400°F = 200°C =Gas 6
Hot = 425°F = 220°C = Gas 7
Hot = 450°F = 230°C = Gas 8

If your oven is a fan model, lower these temperatures in accordance with the manufacturer's instruction booklet.

Baccala (cod) Roman style

Ingredients:
1kg of baccala
200 grams of flour
Water
Vegetable oil
Black pepper

Preparation method
1. Soak the baccala in water for at least 24-48 hr, changing the water at least twice during this time.
2. Clean and wash the baccala; then cut it into rectangular pieces (1 kg should give you about 30-40 small fillets), leave it to dry (lose any excess water).
3. The batter: mix flour with water in order to get a smooth mixture (not too runny or too thick).
4. Add vegetable oil into a frying pan and heat it.
5. Take each small fillet and dip it into the batter, turning it on one side and then the other at least twice.
6. Put the fillet into the frying pan. Fry for about 8-10 minutes, turning it at least twice (until golden).
7. Place the filled on paper (to soak up excess oil); then place on a serving dish, sprinkle with black pepper, garnish with parsley and serve hot.

Beef stew with dumplings

Ingredients
Beef stew:
2 tbsp olive oil
25g butter
750g beef stewing steak, chopped into bite-sized pieces
2 tbsp plain flour
2 garlic cloves, crushed
175g baby onions, peeled
150g celery, cut into large chunks
150g carrots, cut into large chunks
2 leeks, roughly chopped
200g swede, cut into large chunks
150ml red wine
500ml beef stock
2 fresh bay leaves
3 tbsp fresh thyme leaves
3 tbsp chopped fresh flat leaf parsley
Worcestershire sauce, to taste
1 tbsp balsamic vinegar, or to taste
Salt and freshly ground black pepper

For the dumplings:
125g plain flour, plus extra for dusting
1 tsp baking powder
Pinch of salt
60g suet
Water, to make a dough

To serve:
Mashed potato
1 tbsp chopped flat leaf parsley

Preparation method
1. Pre-heat the oven to 180°C.
2. Beef stew:
3. Heat the oil and butter in an ovenproof casserole and fry the beef until browned on all sides.
4. Sprinkle over the flour and cook for a further 2-3 minutes.
5. Add the garlic and the vegetables and fry for 1-2 minutes.
6. Stir in the wine, stock and herbs, add the Worcestershire sauce and balsamic vinegar, to taste. Season with salt and freshly ground black pepper.
7. Cover with a lid, transfer to the oven and cook for about two hours, or until the meat is tender.
8. Dumplings:
9. Sift the flour, baking powder and salt into a bowl.
10. Add the suet and enough water to form a thick dough.
11. With floured hands, roll the dough into small balls.
12. After two hours, remove the lid from the stew and place the balls on top of the stew. Cover, return to the oven and cook for a further 20 minutes, or until the dumplings have swollen and are tender.
13. To serve, place a spoonful of mashed potato onto each of four serving plates and top with the stew and dumplings. Sprinkle with chopped parsley.

Black Forest Gateau
(Gluten free)

Ingredients
For the sponge:
6 large eggs
140g light brown sugar
60g cocoa powder
Pinch of salt
For the filling:
Tin of Morello cherries
3 tablespoons Kirsch
For the cream:
500ml double cream
50g icing sugar
½ teaspoon vanilla extract
Morello jam
25g dark chocolate to garnish

Preparation method
1. Set the oven to 180°C.
2. To make the sponge:
3. Separate the eggs.
4. Whisk the yolks and sugar in a large bowl until it starts to thicken.
5. Sieve in the cocoa.
6. Add a pinch of salt and fold in.
7. Whisk the egg whites until stiff (not dry).
8. Fold it all into the yolk mixture carefully, slowly.
9. Fill a deep cake tin, even off the top.
10. Bake for 35 to 40 minutes.

11. Leave it to cool in the tin. Don't be disappointed it will sink a little.
    (Or, you could always buy 3 chocolate sponge layers.)
12. Separate the syrup from the cherries and mix with 100ml kirsch.
13. Whip the cream, sift in the sugar then add vanilla and whisk to increase the volume.
14. Assemble the Gateau by cutting the cake into three horizontal slices. Put each one on its own plate and drip or brush the syrup onto the sponge. Do not put too much on or it will be impossible to build the cake. You can put what is left in a jug and offer it as a drizzle.
15. Layer the cake: spread jam on the sponge, spread on some cream, add cherries then sponge again etc.
16. Spread cream on top, add a few cherries and grate the chocolate.

Brown and Black Urid Dal

Ingredients
1 cup brown and black urid (check for stones and wash)
4 times water
1 teaspoon turmeric
1 teaspoon salt (or to taste)

For Turka:
I small onion finely chopped
2 tablespoons oil
Half teaspoon chillies
One teaspoon tomato paste
Half teaspoon garam masala
1 sprig coriander (chop leaves)

Knob butter

Preparation method
1. Boil water in a large pan.
2. Add pulses, salt and turmeric.
3. Boil for two hours, pressure cook for 10 minutes or slow cook for 4 hours.
4. When pulses are well cooked prepare the turka.
5. Put enough oil to cover onions in a pan (big enough to take the pulses).
6. Fry onions until dark brown, add chillies and tomato paste plus a little water to mix tomato paste with onions.
7. Raise heat and add pulses. Stir and leave to boil (should be a thick, creamy consistency).

8. Take off heat. Transfer to casserole if desired. Sprinkle garam masala and fresh coriander leaves over the dal.
9. When serving, stir before transferring to individual bowls. Add knob of butter.
10. Serve with chapattis, meat and vegetable dishes as desired.

Serves 4 as part of an Indian meal.

Chapattis

Ingredients
1 cup atta flour
Pinch salt
Water
1 tspn oil

Preparation method
1. Mix the flour and salt in a bowl. Add sufficient water to bring the flour to a soft dough.
2. Knead the dough for about 10 minutes.
3. Place the dough back in the bowl, brush with oil and cover with a cloth for at least 15 minutes.
4. Divide the dough into 5 equal pieces and roll each piece into a ball.
5. Using plenty of flour to avoid sticking, roll the balls into thin rounds.
6. Using a hot, heavy frying pan or flat griddle, lightly greased, cook one chapatti at a time, turning when brown spots appear underneath and the top is getting small bubbles. When both sides have been cooked this way, turn over a second time and press over the edges of the chapatti with a balled tea towel to encourage the chapatti to puff up.
7. Transfer to a warm plate, covered with a tea towel, and continue until all five are done.

Cheese scones

Ingredients
150g self-raising flour
40g butter
75g strong grated cheddar cheese (minimum)
1 egg
120ml milk
Mustard
Salt
Cayenne pepper

Preparation method
1. Pre-heat the oven to 220°C.
2. Cut the butter into small pieces and add to the flour then rub it in until the mixture looks like breadcrumbs.
3. Add most of the grated cheese to the mixture, together with a pinch each of salt, mustard and cayenne pepper, and mix them till the mixture becomes homogenous.
4. Mix the egg and milk and add those to the mixture, working it until a soft dough is obtained.
5. Roll it out to a thickness of about 20 millimetres (if you use metric measurement) or an inch (if you don't).
6. Choose your cutter and cut the dough into scone shaped portions, repeating until there is only enough dough left to form a single scone, which should be done by hand.
7. Put the scones on a baking sheet and blast them in the oven for about 12 minutes.

8. Allow them to cool, but they are best when fresh and warm and spread thickly with butter (not spread).
9. Eat them as soon as you can, before anyone else can get into the kitchen to steal them.

Serves 1, unless you're either prepared, or forced, to share.

Chicken Caesar Sandwich

Ingredients
Leftover chicken breasts or boneless thighs
Mayonnaise
Freshly chopped parsley
Lemon juice
Mustard
Black pepper
Tabasco sauce (if you like it hot)
One sliced tomato
One sliced red onion
Freshly chopped lettuce
Two slices of Italian bread (or one pitta bread)

Preparation method
1. Cut the leftover chicken (breasts or boneless thighs) into wedges and place it in a bowl.
2. Add black pepper (salt if necessary) and 1 teaspoon of freshly squeezed lemon juice.
3. Add 1 tablespoon of mayonnaise (for every chicken breast, adjusting amount to your preferred taste).
4. Add 1/2 teaspoon of mustard (for every 2 tablespoons of mayonnaise).
5. If you like it hot, add 1 teaspoon of Tabasco sauce (adjust to preferred taste).
6. Add the freshly chopped parsley and mix thoroughly.
7. Place the mix on the slice of Italian bread (or pitta bread).
8. Top it with slices of red onion, tomatoes, and freshly chopped lettuce.

9. Cover with the second slice of bread.

Chilli Oil

Ingredients
Extra virgin oil
Garlic
Crushed red chilli

Preparation method
Add 5 or 6 table spoons of crushed red chilli to 2 cups of extra virgin oil and at least 2 to 3 cloves of garlic, fry the lot for a few minutes (3 to 4 minutes), let it cool, than decant into a airtight bottle (if you prefer—you can remove the garlic).

Cider

Ingredients

Apples, 18 kg for every gallon you intend to make. A few rules;

Ripe as possible.

Bruised is fine; but if it's rotten or mouldy, discard the whole apple.

Either all cooking apples or no cooking apples.

A mixture of at least six different varieties if you can.

No more than a tenth of the weight to be crab apples.

They don't have to be cider apples; ordinary apples make a fair cider.

The following materials can be obtained from any decent brewing supplies shops;

Campden tablet

Powdered sodium metabisulphite

Powdered citric acid.

1 sachet of Young's cider yeast or EC-1118, or 1 teaspoon of dried bread yeast.

1 demijohn, 1 cork with a hole in it and 1 airlock.

Preparation method

1. Prepare a sterilising solution; mix half a teaspoon of sodium metabisulphite into half a pint of water, and mix a teaspoon of citric acid into another, separate half pint of water. Pour one half pint into the other and DO NOT SNIFF IT! Amazingly powerful stench. It will kill your sense of smell for hours. But it does a good job of sterilising.
2. Clean all of the equipment you are to use, and then sterilise it well by rinsing the sterilising solution

around it. Rinse thoroughly in clean water. Dirty equipment brews sour alcohol; sterilising solution left on equipment affects the taste of the cider.

3. Wash the apples; discard any mouldy or rotten ones, cut out any twigs, remove all leaves and dirt. My parents made wine with apples left over from the local fruit market and gathered from hedgerow trees. About half the apples were badly bruised, and as my parents grew more confident they stopped inspecting all fruit minutely for maggots. It tasted just as good as the first, severely inspected batches. Set your own standards, as long as you do not tolerate any dirt, rot or mould. I discard any fruit with maggots in, but that's a vegetarian's choice.

4. Destroy the apples. Smash them into a mush of fragments about 2 — 10 mm across. You can do this by chopping them finely by hand with a knife or corer/cutter, or with a scratter. Scratters are devices with rotary cutting blades — fitted to a drill, or the commercial mechanism of a rotating cutter crown within a protected hopper, all designed to chop an apple finely with the minimum of effort.

5. Leave the mush for 24 hours in an airtight container to remove excess tannin. It will go brown; there will be no harm as long as you have carefully excluded all dirt and vinegar flies. These are tiny black flies that are instantly attracted to fruit. They're called vinegar flies for good reason. Keep them out of your mush.

6. After 24 hours, press the apple mush to extract the juice. You can use a fruit press, available at any shop selling brewing supplies, or you can make your own — there are some good ideas for these designs on the Internet. If you don't want to spend money, use a kitchen juicer. The aim is to get as much juice as possible from the mash.
7. As the juice is pressed out, put it into a sterilised demijohn (a glass bottle with a one gallon capacity, available through brewing supplies stores, junk shops or relatives who used to brew their own wine). Seal after each addition to exclude flies.
8. When you've finished pressing, add a crushed Campden tablet for every three gallons of juice to kill off the wild yeast, seal against flies and dirt and leave for 24 hours.
9. After 24 hours, mix up a yeast solution;
10. Heat half a pint of water to 41°C /104°F
11. Add a sachet of cider yeast, E-1118 yeast or 1 teaspoon of bread yeast
12. Stir well. Leave until the mixture is within 10°C of the temperature of the sterilised apple juice, then add it to the juice and stir.
13. Seal the demijohn with the cork with a hole in it, with the hole plugged by an airlock filled with water. The air bubbled out by the fermented juice will bubble through the water, but no flies or bacteria can get in.
14. Instead of steps 8 and 9 you could leave the wild yeasts to create alcohol, still with the airlock to protect the brew. It works well, although it is

slower than commercial yeasts and produces a vile brown froth. Hold your nerve. It produces a cider that is milder to the taste than commercial yeast, and some of our relatives prefer our natural ciders to our commercial yeast ones.

15. Leave the jar of juice in a room where the temperature is between 15° and 20°C most of the time until it has stopped bubbling (about six to eight weeks). Keep checking every day that the fermenting fruit hasn't bubbled up through the airlock and contaminated the water in the airlock — then bacteria has a route in to affect your cider in its demijohn.

16. Rack off the cider — carefully transfer the juice to another, cleaned and sterilised, demijohn. Leave the lees behind. The lees are the creamy sludge at the bottom of a fermented bottle of alcohol, the remains of dead yeast cells and the particulate matter swept in during the juicing process. It does no harm, but you're aiming for a clear, golden liquid at the end of the process. Make sure there is minimal airspace at the top of the demijohn, top up with water if necessary. Add the airlock and leave to settle for another four to six weeks.

17. Keep checking the cider as it ferments. If it smells off, tastes sour or vinegary, or shows signs of developing a 'jellified' appearance — discard it. Try again next year.

18. Three months after the start — bottle it. Drink it. Enjoy it. Be amazed that cider can taste of apples.

Courgette (Zucchini) and Onion Frittata

Ingredients
(serves 2-4)
Two medium-sized courgettes (zucchini)
Olive oil
Four eggs
Milk
Grated parmesan
Black pepper
Curry powder
One onion

Preparation method
1. Slice thinly the two courgettes and half an onion and fry them in olive oil until golden.
2. Beat four eggs, add 1 tablespoon of milk, grated parmesan, black pepper, and a touch of curry powder, mix well.
3. Pour the mix over the courgette and onion and cook medium flame 4 to 5 minutes per side until the frittata is solid.

Cranachan

Ingredients
60g of porridge oats
150g raspberries
4 tablespoons malt whisky
4 tablespoons runny honey
600ml double cream

Preparation method
1. Scatter oatmeal onto a baking tray and toast in a low oven or under the grill until golden brown.
2. Blend 100g of raspberries until smooth.
3. Whip the double cream until stiff.
4. Mix the honey and whisky into the cream.
5. Fold in 50g of porridge and the puréed raspberries until a rippled (but not mixed) effect is achieved.
6. Spoon into tall, clear serving dishes.
7. Sprinkle remaining porridge and raspberries on the top of each serving.

Cup Cakes
Makes 8

Ingredients
75g self-raising flour
50g butter
50g caster sugar
1 egg
½ teaspoon vanilla essence
1 tablespoon warm water
Butter icing coloured to suit children. Can be topped with sweets.

Preparation method
1. Oven on at 180°C.
2. Sift the flour onto a plate. Cream the butter and the sugar. Gradually add the egg. Add a little flour to prevent it curdling. Beat until creamy then fold in the rest of the flour, vanilla essence and water.
3. Spoon into 8 paper cases.
4. Bake for 15 to 20 minutes. (Springy to touch)
5. Allow to cool.
6. Cover with coloured icing.
7. Enjoy.

Favourite Soup

Ingredients
1 onion, chopped roughly
300g carrots, peeled and sliced
1 tablespoon oil
100g red lentils, washed
1 teaspoon each ground cumin and coriander
1 litre vegetable stock
squeeze of fresh lemon juice to taste
chopped parsley, to taste

Preparation method
1. In a large covered pan, sweat the onion and carrot in the oil for about 10 minutes. Stir occasionally to avoid burning.
2. Add the cumin and coriander and stir for about 1 minute.
3. Add the lentils and stir again.
4. Add the stock, bring to a boil, cover and reduce heat to simmer gently for 40 minutes.
5. Allow the soup to cool gently then liquidise.
6. Add lemon juice and parsley to taste and reheat.

Serves 4.

Fish and chips

Ingredients
A piece of cod, haddock, or some suitable alternative
Flour and egg mixture
Chipped potatoes
Yesterday's newspaper

Preparation method
1. In fish shop, ask for fish and chips.
2. Pay for them.
3. Eat them, taking care to avoid gulls.

Serves 1.

Filled Parathas

Ingredients
200g chapatti or whole meal flour
200ml water
10 medium potatoes
1 small cup frozen peas
Half cup fresh herbs chopped fine
Half teaspoon thyme or cumin
Half teaspoon garam masala
Fresh lemon/lemon juice or pickle

Preparation method
1. Assemble griddle, two small containers for water and oil, and a tablespoon.
2. Cut potatoes into quarters and boil.
3. Place the flour in a wide bowl, add small amounts of water until it is mixed to a firm dough. Knead well. Cover and leave aside.
4. Skin potatoes and mash. Heat peas and mash with potatoes adding spices and herbs. Divide into six portions.
5. Divide the dough into 12 equal pieces, roll each piece into a ball and flatten ready to roll into small chapattis.
6. Prepare one paratha at a time. Roll out two small chapattis flouring as required. Moisten edges with water using your fingers. Place one ball of potato mix into the centre and flatten to the shape of one of the chapattis. Cover with the other chapatti, press edges firmly and roll out into about a 12cm round.

7. Lift the filled paratha onto the heated griddle. Turn when the colour changes slightly. Turn again until second side is cooked (light brown). Spread oil over second side with tablespoon. Press to aid cooking. Turn and spread oil on first side. Cook until the paratha is brown, especially the edges. Place in bowl or basket lined with kitchen paper.
8. Continue until all parathas are cooked.
9. Before eating, squeeze lemon juice on top. Enjoy with plain yogurt and/or lemon pickle.

Serves 3 with two parathas each.

French Onion Soup

Ingredients
1 tablespoon of oil
1 kg onions
2 cloves of garlic
Dark soy sauce
Lemon juice (optional)
1.7 litres of stock
Freshly ground black pepper

Preparation method
1. Heat the oil in a saucepan gently until a piece of onion dropped into it sizzles but doesn't smoke. Peel and dice the onions and garlic, then fry them until they are softened and golden (about ten minutes).
2. Add the stock, bring to the boil and let the soup simmer gently for about twenty minutes. Add a few drops of lemon juice and/or soy sauce and/or black pepper to taste.
3. Pour into warmed bowls. Sprinkle a few flakes of grated cheese on top and put the bowls under a grill on medium heat for a minute to melt and crisp the cheese before serving.
4. Serve with inch thick chunks of baguette.

Grandpa's Special Toast

Ingredients
Sliced bread
4 teaspoons of butter
2 tablespoons of granulated sugar
4 teaspoons of cinnamon

Preparation method
1. Beat the butter to soften it.
2. Add the sugar to the butter.
3. Toast the bread on one side.
4. Spread butter and sugar onto untoasted side and dust with cinnamon to taste.
5. Toast that side until crisp.
6. Enjoy.

(You can add the cinnamon to the butter and sugar mix. Then it is not so messy.)

(You can cut the bread into fun shapes before toasting.)

Iced Coffee

Ingredients
Ground coffee
Water
Caramel syrup — 2 desert spoons per cup
Sugar — half a teaspoon per cup.
Single cream — 3 tablespoons per cup
Ice cubes

Preparation method
1.   Cold press coffee grounds in a jug of cold water overnight. Stir a few times. Quantities are the same as for a hot coffee drink. Strain and keep the jug of cold coffee in the fridge until needed.
2.   Add syrup, sugar, cream and ice cubes to a jug. Allow a serving for each cup that is to be served. Add to the coffee and mix.
3.   Pour into glasses and serve with more ice.

Alternatives are: try different flavours of syrup, top with whipped cream, add a measure of alcohol, make ice cubes of cold coffee to enhance the flavour, try the drink as black coffee with only ice added.

Janet's Vegan Pie

Janet used lamb chops as her meat-eaters' side-dish, but anything goes! A leafy green vegetable goes well with it, too. She has also cooked everything separately for speed – this is the take-it-easy version.

Ingredients
50g green lentils
50g red lentils
50g pearl barley
1 large leek, sliced thinly
2 large onions, finely chopped
150g potato, sliced thinly
150g celeriac, sliced thinly (optional)
150g carrots, sliced thinly
150g mushrooms, sliced thinly (you don't need a lot, so go mad – any kind of mushroom will add taste and texture)
1 tin red kidney beans
Oatmeal
500ml vegetable stock, hot.

Preparation method
1. Put the lentils and barley in bowls of hot water to soak; do this a couple of hours beforehand.
2. Slice the leeks, and fry in butter or oil – I use a mix of butter and rapeseed or walnut oil.
3. Chop the onions, and allow to caramelise gently in a pan with just enough oil/butter to stop them sticking.
4. Layer the various ingredients in a pie dish: green lentils, then onions, then red lentils, mushrooms, barley, kidney beans – you get the picture; just try

to alternate white ingredients with coloured ones. Finish with a layer of sliced potato.
5. Pour the vegetable stock over.
6. Cover with foil, and bake at 180°C / Gas mark 4 for 1 hour, or until a skewer pierces the sliced vegetables easily.
7. Uncover, sprinkle with oatmeal (not porridge oats!), and place under a hot grill until lightly browned and crunchy.

Lamb Stew with Parsley Dumplings

Ingredients
about 500g stewing lamb or mutton, on the bone (eg scrag end or neck)
1 large onion, chopped
2 leeks washed and sliced
1 potato, peeled and diced
1/2-1 tablespoon pearl barley
a few sprigs of thyme
1 tablespoon flour
hot water
salt and pepper to taste.
For the dumplings:
55g SR flour
25g shredded suet
1/2 tablespoon chopped parsley
salt and pepper

Preparation method
1. Brown the meat in a little oil in a pan and set aside.
2. Add a little more oil if needed and soften the onions and then the leeks.
3. Put the onions and leeks in the pot of a slow cooker.
4. Sprinkle the pearl barley on top and lay the meat on top of that.
5. Sprinkle the flour into the frying pan and stir to mix with any remaining juices. Add the hot water and blend until smooth.

6. Pour the liquid on top of the lamb and vegetables making sure that the lamb is just covered. Add more hot water if needed.
7. Add a few sprigs of thyme and some seasoning.
8. Set your slow cooker to low for up to 8 hours or fast for around four hours.
9. When the meat is tender, remove it from the stew and keep warm (you can remove the bones if you wish at this point).
10. Turn the setting to high.
11. Mix all the dumpling ingredients together and bind with a little cold water.
12. Divide the mixture into small balls, somewhere between a walnut and a golf ball. Roll lightly between your hands until they are smooth and round then drop into the stew liquid and cook for half an hour or so. They should have plumped up and can no longer be indented with a finger.
13. Add back the lamb and serve.

Serves 2.

Melting Moments

Ingredients
200g butter
150g caster sugar
250g self-raising flour
1 egg
A few drops of vanilla essence
Bowl of cornflakes

Preparation method
1. Pre-heat the oven to 180°C.
2. Cream the sugar and butter until pale.
3. Add the flour, egg and vanilla essence.
4. Form the mixture into 3cm balls.
5. Roll in the cornflakes.
6. Place on a non-stick baking tray allowing plenty of space for them to spread.
7. Bake for 15 – 20 minutes.

Allow to cool.

Obatzda

The restaurant is based on a real place, *Maria & Josef*, beside Lichterfelde West station in Berlin. I often take Obatzda when I'm hillwalking (dunking bread into it beats soggy sandwiches any day!), but it's also good for nibbles with drinks, or a party dip.

Ingredients
300g Brie
180g soft cheese or Quark
50g butter
A good pinch of paprika (not the hot Hungarian variety, unless you like it spicy!)
Salt and pepper to taste.

Preparation method
1. Chop the Brie into small pieces.
2. Blend the soft cheese and butter together until smooth. If it seems stiff, add a little sour cream – it should not be runny, but soft enough to scoop onto a bit of bread.
3. Stir in the seasonings and the chopped Brie
4. Serve with crusty rolls, bread sticks or pretzels

Serves 4

October Casserole (Sailing Stew)

Ingredients
1 leek
1 medium onion
2 carrots (about 200g)
2 large / 4 small potatoes (about 200g)
1 parsnip, swede or turnip
(Or any variety of vegetables up to a total of about 500g)
3 tablespoons of olive oil
400g can of chopped tomatoes
300ml vegetable stock
Worcestershire sauce or red wine
Ground black pepper, thyme or basil

Preparation method
1. Chop the leek and onion finely and heat the oil gently until a fragment of onion sizzles but doesn't smoke when it's dropped into the pan. Fry the leek and onion until soft (about five minutes).
2. Pour the vegetable stock into the pan and stir well. Add the tomatoes and bring back to simmering point.
3. Peel and chop the root vegetables. For a stew to be served through the first days of a long sailing passage I leave all of them a substantial size as they will be cooking for a considerable time — about half an inch to an inch cubes (1 to 2.5 cm), with new potatoes left whole. If you chop it any smaller, you're drinking untextured soup by the end of the first day. Better to have something substantial to chew on.

4. Put the root vegetables into the stew. Add cracked black pepper and herbs to taste, plus a generous splash of either Worcestershire sauce or red wine, and simmer for thirty minutes.
5. Add any leafy vegetables (torn kale, shredded spinach etc.) about five minutes before serving.
6. To add a bit of variety, add any of the following;
7. Dumplings; 100g vegetarian suet to 200g plain flour with enough cold water to make a stiff paste — roll into small balls and roll in flour to cover before dropping into the simmering stew. Cover and simmer gently for 20 minutes.
8. Croutons; sprinkled onto individual serving bowls
9. Slices of crusty baguette served separately
10. For a long running stew, heat it up thoroughly before serving each time, and limit the number of times you reheat it. Keep the lid on the pan to reduce loss of liquid from condensation. Better to eat the lot within a day and run up fresh batches of porridge to feed the crew until the weather (and stomachs) settle in for the rest of the voyage.
11. The most important thing on sailing trips is to make sure the crew drinks fresh water at regular intervals. Nag them if you have to. Dehydration dulls the judgement, causes severe headaches and is dangerous to health in the long run. To that aim, I have not added salt to this recipe. There's enough salt water being thrown over you while you're sailing without drinking it as well.

Pasta with Roasted Peppers

Ingredients
Two red peppers
Two yellow peppers
One red onion
Garlic
Chilli sauce (on the side)
Extra virgin olive oil
Freshly chopped parsley or basil leaves
Parmesan
Salt
Vinegar (white or balsamic)
Spaghetti or rigatoni or penne (300g serves two people)

Preparation method
1. Roast the peppers on an oven or barbecue grill until cooked and the skin can easily be peeled, then leave it aside to cool.
2. Slice the onion and roast it on the grill until golden (alternatively chop the onion finely and add it to a pan with some chopped garlic and olive oil, fry until golden).
3. Chop the parsley (or the basil leaves).
4. Start boiling water for the pasta, add the pasta.
5. Peel the peppers, cut them in half and remove the white bits.
6. Cut the pepper in thin stripes, add the onion, salt, drizzle with extra virgin oil, and one or two tablespoon of vinegar, mix well.
7. Add the freshly chopped basil or parsley.

8. Drain the pasta, add to the pasta the mix of roasted peppers and onion, toss it well, sprinkle with scales of parmesan and serve. If you like it hot, add dry hot chilli or chilli oil.

Chilli sauce on the side

If you like your pasta well spiced and hot, cut down on the extra virgin oil and substitute that with the chilli oil sauce.

Special Lamb Curry

Ingredients
400g lamb chunks
3 tablespoons olive oil
50g butter
4 medium onions
1 teaspoon salt
1 teaspoon turmeric
Garam Masala spices (whole): 1 teaspoon cumin seeds, 5 black peppercorns, 5 cloves, seeds of 2 large cardamom and 5 green cardamom, 1 cm cinnamon stick, 2 bay leaves.
1 teaspoon chilli powder or 2 chopped fresh chillies (add near end of frying)
1 cup water (approx.)

Preparation method
1. Grind whole spices in pestle and mortar or electric grinder.
2. Melt olive oil and butter in pot (enough to coat and fry onions).
3. Add chopped or grated onions.
4. Brown onions, stirring occasionally.
5. Add spices, salt, turmeric and chillies, stir continuously until sizzling.
6. Add meat and enough water to avoid mix sticking to the bottom of the pot.
7. Cover and simmer until meat is tender.
8. Add wine (optional).
9. Add water for a more liquid sauce if desired.
10. Cook for about two minutes.

11. Serve with chapattis and natural yogurt, dal and vegetables.

Serves 4 as part of an Indian meal.

Spicy Eggs

Ingredients
6 eggs
4 medium red onions
1 tablespoon olive oil
50g butter
1 teaspoon salt
Half teaspoon turmeric
Half teaspoon ground black pepper
Half teaspoon chillies (ground, crushed or fresh. If fresh use 2 chillies finely chopped or to taste)
Optional: 6 tablespoons grated Parmesan cheese or 1 cup frozen peas (heated)

Preparation method
1. Break eggs into a bowl and mix with a fork.
2. Melt olive oil and butter in pot.
3. Add finely chopped onions.
4. Brown onions, stirring occasionally. If you prefer the onions crunchy then cook for about two minutes on a lower heat.
5. Add spices, salt, and chillies, stirring continuously until sizzling.
6. Pour in eggs. Stir quickly with a wooden spoon, keeping the eggs from sticking to the bottom and sides, until they resemble fine scrambled eggs.
7. Add cheese or peas. Stir and heat.
8. Serve with chapattis or square parathas and/or natural yogurt.

9. Square parathas are prepared as chapattis but at the rolled out stage, spread butter or oil over the chapatti and fold over to make a square and re-roll. Oil as for Filled Parathas.

Serves 4.

Vegetarian Spaghetti Bolognese

Ingredients
Olive oil
2 sweet (bell) peppers
1 large courgette
1 large onion
Clove of garlic
150g mushrooms
400g can of chopped tomatoes
Freshly ground black pepper
Tarragon
150g spaghetti
Enough grated cheese to sprinkle a little on top

Preparation method
1. Boil enough water to cover the spaghetti. When it reaches boiling point, add a splash of oil, put the spaghetti in and stir. Keep the water at simmering point for about fifteen minutes, stirring occasionally. Which gives you enough time to cook the sauce.
2. Peel and dice the onion and garlic finely. Pour the oil into a pan and heat gently. When a fragment of garlic or onion sizzles (but doesn't smoke) in the oil, it's hot enough. Don't overheat it, it will have a sour flavour. Put the onion and garlic in and fry for five minutes, until soft and light brown.
3. Wipe the mushrooms and slice them thinly. Fry with the onions for five minutes.
4. Wash the peppers, remove the membranes and seeds and slice into short strips. Fry with the onion

and mushroom mix for a few minutes. Not for too long; you can eat sweet peppers raw, and the real pleasure is the fresh, juicy taste of raw pepper which will be lost if you fry them for too long.
5. Wash, trim and chop the courgette into half inch thick cubes and add to the pan.
6. Add the tomatoes to the mixture and bring to a simmer. Cook for ten minutes, adding pepper and tarragon to taste. Add a splash of red wine if you want it to be more liquid; cook for longer if you need to reduce the liquidity.
7. Drain the spaghetti and put onto warmed plates. Ladle out the bolognese sauce onto the spaghetti. Sprinkle with cheese and serve.

Biographies

Annis Farnell...
lives with a husband and assortment of wildlife in a B-listed wreck with half an acre of garden. Has a degree in Earth Sciences and a Diploma in Creative Writing from the Open University, and has had a wide variety of jobs, including time at sea and working as a labourer on a building site. Interests are getting back to peak fitness, German and Scottish folk music, and classical and military history. Collects Biggles books. Has written three novels and had articles published in the local press as well as a recipe in a magazine.

Enza Vynn-Cara...
loves to travel and to learn languages by direct immersion into the local culture. Spanish is her next project and Spain is in her sight. She has been there four times, and plans a few more trips come next year. A self-learner whose passion for writing has become a full-time event, she aims to complete a BA in English Literature and Creative Writing within the year. She has written one novel (now in the revision phase) and has a second one in progress. She's also an enthusiast of writing short stories and flash-fiction.

Julia Chalkley...
grew up in the East End of London. She gained a degree in Earth Sciences from the Open University as an antidote to her career as an accountant, and went on to take a Diploma in Creative Writing with the OU for fun.

Currently lives in Essex with a husband, four cats, eight motorcycles and a lot of cider apple trees.

Elves...

has degrees in Chemistry and in Literature, despite literature being his worst subject at school. He can't write poetry and he can't cook, but he does enjoy writing and now has four novels complete, almost complete or under construction.

Mairibeth MacMillan...

taught for more than ten years before deciding that she had repaid any outstanding debt to society and opted for a career change. Writing allows her to spend more time with family and not having to brave the Scottish weather to get to work is an added advantage. She writes about whatever subject appeals most at that particular moment and is easily distracted by both research and shiny new ideas.

Mairibeth can be found on Facebook as Mairibeth MacMillan, Pinterest as mairibeth and Twitter as @MairibethM.

Palo Stickland...

is the author of a family saga called *Finding Takri* published by Dahlia Publishing in 2013. She has had short stories and poems published in several anthologies. Her aim is to begin a novel on 1st January every year. However, due to travel and grandchildren commitments, she is a wee bit behind schedule. Palo has a blog at palostickland.com and is on Facebook as Gurpal Devsi Stickland.

R Cohen...
is a Brit abroad. Having swapped the Thames for the Rhine, she has left London behind and now lives with her husband and son in Basel, Switzerland. She can often be found with a pen in one hand and a cup of Darjeeling in the other.
Meet up with Rebecca at
 rebeccacohenwrites.wordpress.com

Russet J Ashby...
 studied education in Edinburgh and with the OU. She worked in both secondary and primary schools on developing the learning environment for all. Now she writes from a garret somewhere in Scotland where her time, this year, has been spent trying to appreciate the art of short story writing. The trials of both poetry and novel writing continue to fascinate her too and the ultimate goal of finishing a novel that appeals to a publisher survives.

Sue Cook...
 Aspires to be the next Ian Rankin and earn enough for her accountant to take her seriously. She has been successful with stories for the women's fiction market.
You can see Sue's blog at optimisticscribe.wordpress.com
Sue is on Pinterest at ukpinterest.com/cook3230

Printed in Great Britain
by Amazon